MORE THAN A PROMISE

More Than a Promise

RUTH LOGAN HERNE

Franciscan
MEDIA
Cincinnati, Ohio

Scripture passages have been taken from *New Revised Standard Version Bible*, copyright ©1989 by the Division of Christian Education of the National Council of the Churches of Christ in the U.S.A., and used by permission. All rights reserved.

This is a work of fiction. Names, characters, corporations, institutions, organizations, events, or locales in this novel are either the product of the author's imagination or, if real, used fictitiously. The resemblance of any character to actual persons (living or dead) is entirely coincidental.

Cover design by Candle Light Studios
Book design by Mark Sullivan

LIBRARY OF CONGRESS CATALOGING-IN-PUBLICATION DATA
Names: Herne, Ruth Logan, author.
Title: More than a promise / Ruth Logan Herne.
Description: Cincinnati, Ohio : Franciscan Media, [2016]
Identifiers: LCCN 2015049798 | ISBN 9781632530851 (softcover : acid-free paper)
Subjects: LCSH: Single fathers—Fiction. | Man-woman relationships—Fiction. | GSAFD: Love stories. | Christian fiction.
Classification: LCC PS3608.E76875 M67 2016 | DDC 813/.6—dc23
LC record available at http://lccn.loc.gov/2015049798

Published by Franciscan Media
28 W. Liberty St.
Cincinnati, OH 45202
www.FranciscanMedia.org

Printed in the United States of America.
Printed on acid-free paper.
16 17 18 19 20 5 4 3 2 1

This book is dedicated to my oldest son, Matthew Blodgett, a wonderful man, a wonderful father, and a really good husband whose sense of humor helps smooth the crazy waters of raising three delightful children with his beloved wife, Karen. Matt, you've made me see the laughter in so many things, and you've been a strong shoulder in others. I love you!

acknowledgments

I sing in a choir called The Song Prayers. We're located at the front of the church, facing the congregation, and one Sunday a somewhat frazzled father walked in during the Liturgy of the Word. And not early in the liturgy...we were almost to the Gospel, finishing up a delightful New Testament reading. Trailing after him were three little boys who didn't look all that thrilled to be there: *#instantstoryidea!*

They tried to be quiet as they slipped around the back of the church and into a pew on the far side, where the boys acted like boys...and from that glimpse into this harried father's life, *More Than a Promise* was born.

Being a single parent is never easy. I know many single parents, I see the struggles, and I also recognize that the parents who embrace a commitment to faith seem to have an easier time with the commitment to parenting. Choosing a stepparent has to be so much more than a one-on-one marriage, because there are other hearts at stake. Little hearts. Hearts that have already withstood so much whether through death, divorce, or abandonment. Matt Wilmot's mental, emotional, and physical struggles are all too real for many young families today.

Elle was inspired by a mix of Thomas Kinkade's rise to fame and acclaim...and the sadness of his broken marriage. But I modeled her after women like my Aunt Isabelle, a woman who always took charge and moved forward. A woman like Sarah in *Sarah, Plain and Tall*. I wanted a woman wounded by life, but strong enough to cling to faith, hope, and love and find her true path, the road God charted for her long ago!

Thank you to Ericka McIntyre for her marvelous help in polishing this story, to Natasha Kern for her well-thought advice, and to Candle Light Studios, Mark Sullivan, and the Franciscan Media art team for the beautiful and thought-provoking cover. You guys are amazing! And thanking God for the gift of little boys and little girls, the tiny miracles that form our future.

—*Ruthy*

A capable wife who can find?
She is far more precious than jewels.
The heart of her husband trusts in her,
and he will have no lack of gain.
—Proverbs 31:10–11

chapter one

"Good morning, Jenny." Elle Drake opened the car door for her seven-year-old niece, waved to her pregnant sister, and then settled back into the driver's seat and backed out of Kate's driveway on the sun-soaked April morning. "Thanks for going to church with me, kiddo."

"You're welcome!" Jenny fastened her belt and threw her hands in the air in excitement. "Spring break is over, but next stop: summer vacation!"

Elle wanted that enthusiasm. She wanted that passion. She wanted what she couldn't have, would never have...

Her sister's life. Married to a great guy. Two kids and a baby on the way. No matter how famous her art had become, or how much money she accrued, she'd hand it all away to trade lives with her sister.

Foolish, she knew.

God provided. God was good. She'd been blessed in so many ways, but as Jenny chattered about her dreams and imaginings, Elle saw her personal hopes wither like old leaves, dry and brittle.

"Don't you just love spring, Aunt Elle? Like so much?"

She lied smoothly. "I do."

"Everything gets born in the spring," Jenny went on, each word a tiny arrow to Elle's heart. "Baby animals, baby birds, baby plants, baby leaves. And then we'll have our baby in the beginning of summer, and that's not far away! Mom and Dad are so excited! So is Grandma! Us too!"

A long time ago Elle had read a book about sisters, a beautiful story by Katherine Paterson. Two sisters, fraternal twins, so different.

She and Kate weren't twins, but the rest held true. And she couldn't even hate her sister for holding so much of what Elle wanted, because

Kate was nice and kind and good. The whole thing was ridiculously maddening.

Would her marriage have succeeded if she'd been able to conceive? She'd never know.

Would Alex have strayed if they'd had a family?

Yes popped into her brain, and she sighed because she was probably right. She'd married a rising dot-com businessman whose tracking software transformed the Internet into an interactive advertising experience, and made them crazy rich. When Alex Caulder had been a plain old nerd and she had been a struggling artist, they had seemed to be on the same page. He encouraged her, she encouraged him, and neither one saw how the future would unfold when two highly successful careers careened in opposite directions.

She'd loved him. And silly her, she had thought he shared her dreams, her goals, but then he ended up in the arms of a supermodel, so what did she know? She and Alex had been two prodigies, bound for wealth and fame along separate paths. If he'd cared enough—enough to stay true to his vows—would they have made it?

Probably not, because once he didn't need her, he'd wandered, dissatisfied. Shouldn't love, true love, be more than need?

Yes.

Her father had dumped his family early on, leaving Aggie Drake to run the ship, and run it she did. But from the time Elle was little, Elle knew what she wanted. Her dream was to have a husband, home, and family and make pretty pictures. She'd been close…so close. And now?

No husband. No kids. No hope of having a kid, and all of this hit hard today, her thirty-eighth birthday, tipping her dangerously close to a wrinkle-producing landmark age.

"Oh, Aunt Elle! Happy birthday! I almost forgot!"

"Darling, at my age, forgetting isn't a bad thing. We conveniently forget birthdays at this point in our lives."

"Well, don't forget mine," Jenny reminded her as she slipped out of her seat belt once they parked the car. "August fourth. Eight years old, ready for third grade and pierced ears!"

"Elle." Father Murphy waved as they walked toward the rose-bricked Catholic church. "I was hoping to see you. I'm looking for help on the restoration committee. Not to do the actual work, but I want an artist's overview."

The church had started a refurbishing pledge drive before she'd come back to Cedar Mills last year. Tough economic times had brought money in slowly but steadily. "It's an honor to be asked, Father."

"But?" His eyes twinkled like a movie-friendly Santa, sweet and cheerful, always looking for the good in others.

"Can I call you later? Chat about it?" She directed a look down to Jenny, and the priest nodded.

"Of course. I'm out after Masses today—we've got a youth service at the cathedral to launch our Teen Action Committee and Conference, but I'm in this evening and the rest of the week."

"Perfect. I'll call you either tonight or tomorrow."

"And we'll have our chat," noted the priest before he went on to greet the next arrival.

"Does that mean you get to help pick out things for the church?" Jenny wondered, and she sounded impressed. "Because you're famous?"

Fame and fortune, gilded in life, not love.

Knock it off, Negative NElle. What's gotten into you? All this over a meaningless birthday? You're being absurd.

"Maybe. We'll have to see," she finally replied to Jenny. She'd hesitated purposely in order to see who else was on the committee. Yes, it was a cowardly act, but Elle had some serious history with a few local gossips, and if screening her contact time made her life in Cedar Mills easier, she'd do it gladly. It had been bad enough to endure it all as an awkward teen. Now that her imploded marriage had gotten a respite from the tabloid news covers, she'd just as soon put it all behind her.

"Elle, I love that dress!" Janey Sue Martin met them on the church steps. "That had to be a Boston find because no one around here sells crepe like that."

"In the harbor," Elle told her.

"Do you miss it?" Janey asked the question quickly, then just as quickly backtracked. "Wait, I'm sorry, that was beyond dumb. Of course you don't miss it. I meant the shopping, Elle, not—"

"I know what you mean, and no." Elle shrugged off Janey's apologies. "With online shopping, it's no big deal, Janey. I miss the harbor. The water. Visiting the sea." She glanced around the bare-branched neighborhood streets stretching out in multiple directions. "There were always seeds of inspiration in the vastness of the water."

"In the beauty of the lilies Christ was born across the sea," Janey quoted the old line of music with grace and reverence. "I can see that. We're more Grandma Moses here. Or Wysocki."

"A different charm, yes."

"Has Father asked you to advise the committee, yet?"

"He just did, and I expect I have you to thank for that since you know about it."

Janey whispered as they stepped into the church. "I wanted company on the committee, yes, and another young vote. I'll be totally indebted to you if you say yes, Elle." She smiled and moved to the left.

Elle and Jenny went to the right and slipped into the fourth pew from the back, an old habit of tucking herself away, out of sight.

Another young vote...

God bless Janey Martin. Her choice of words shouldn't mean a thing, but they did. Elle's fault for letting a simple day take on major importance. As the choir began a soul-stirring prelude, she decided to let peace, hope, and love rule the day.

Her prayerful goal lasted all of ten minutes.

* * *

Sunday morning church was an unreasonable waste of time, and Matt Wilmot wouldn't give St. Casimir's the time of day if he weren't under threat of legal action. That reality made him downright ornery.

He'd managed to get his three motherless boys ready for nine o'clock Mass.

But not by his choice. Given options, carting the boys to church wouldn't make the list, but his former mother-in-law's minions would rat him out if he didn't show, all because of a promise he had made ten long years before. He'd gone to the required pre-Cana meetings ready to do lip service, and the nice priest had asked if he'd raise any children God sent him as Catholics.

His fiancée was Catholic, she wanted to be married in the church, and he wasn't about to mess up the wedding. So he promised.

Now here he was, dragging three naughty, not-quite-clean boys to a church he'd never attended, and all because their maternal grandmother threatened legal action. Grandma—Judge Gloria D'Amico—was mean enough to do exactly what she threatened.

The dashboard clock mocked him.

Despite his firm pressure on the gas pedal, they were already late and still a good three minutes from the church. Make it two minutes more to get the boys out of the car and into a pew…

You're toast, dude.

He turned left quickly. How noticeable would they be? Maybe everyone would be singing. They could slip through the side door and find an empty pew in the back. That should do it.

"I hafta go to the bathroom."

Seven-year-old Randy was trying to play the oldest trick in the book. Not gonna happen. Matt met Randy's gaze through the rearview mirror. "I told you to take care of that back at the house, Randy. We're on our way to church, and we're already late."

"But I hafta," Randy whined. He writhed for effect, probably hoping to get Amos riled up, too. When Randy cranked up the volume, four-year-old Amos was sure to follow. But he didn't have time for anything like that now as the digital dashboard clock turned to 9:03. "You need to wait."

"I can't." His pitch rose significantly.

"You can."

"I'll pee."

Matt blew out an exasperated breath. When pushed, Randy might do just that. One of these days... "All right. I'll take you when we get to the church."

"Me too," Todd added quickly.

"You'll go into church and hold our pew," Matt told him as he hunted for a parking spot. There were none.

"Alone?" Todd's voice pitched up to match his brother's.

"Um, yes." Matt did a quick left to right scan at the next little intersection. No spots. "It's church. Why not?"

"Mommy wouldn't have let me go in alone. She always held my hand."

Matt's tone had been short; the boy's was querulous. Eyeing the parking situation, Matt rounded the Park Street curve, circling the gazebo built long ago as a tribute to fallen heroes in a town square filled with statuary. It was a custom in Cedar Mills, Ohio, to erect a statue to any fallen soldier who'd lived there more than twenty years. The reality was, if you could live in Cedar Mills for more than twenty years, you deserved a statue. Taming his negative thoughts, Matt keyed in to the desperation in Todd's voice.

"You were littler then, but all right. I'll go into church with you. Then I'll take Randy to the bathroom." He shot a glance to his oldest boy, a sensitive child who reminded him so much of his late wife. Dark hair, dark eyes, a winsome smile and a tender heart.

He shut down the memory. This day needed pragmatism, not sentiment. "Can you watch Amos for me?"

Todd nodded. Matt knew the older boy would actually draw support from having his younger brother around, not vice versa. What he didn't know was what to do about it. He spotted an open space, parked, then jumped out and rounded the car. The boys tumbled out the door like a bunch of pups fresh from a kennel. "Stop that. You'll get messed up."

"I don't like stupid church clothes anyway," said Randy. "Can't we just go play on the playground and *say* we went to church?"

New guilt hit Matt because he'd been thinking the very same thing.

"No. Church is important." It was a bold-faced lie—church wasn't important. Not to him, and not to his sons. He was here because of a foolish promise made in courtship, a promise his former mother-in-law now held around his neck like a tightening noose with a millstone attached. He was here, yes.

But it was the last place on earth he wanted to be.

"Which way is it?" asked Todd, spinning in a half circle.

"This way." Matt picked up Amos and hurried around the corner at a fast clip. The two older boys dashed alongside, loving the chance to race down the sidewalk, neck and neck.

Carrie used to handle all this stuff. Running to preschool, helping with events, getting the older boys to church.

She'd been good at it. On top of that, she liked it. Hustling here, bustling there. True, her kitchen skills weren't all that great, and she hated yard work, but she could drive his Caterpillars and dump trucks with the best of them and never thought twice about it. If they settled for slapdash dinners frequently, it wasn't that much of a hardship. He would have gladly traded a seven-course meal for the chance to have his wife back again. Just for a day.

"I hafta go bad." Randy's voice rose. He ran for the church, clutching the front of his pants, over the top like always.

"All right, all right. We're here, Randy. Cool your jets."

He'd hoped to slip in quietly, but the massive interior door was hung on the noisiest hinges he'd ever heard, exponentially magnified by a moment of prayerful quiet within the church.

It wasn't just any squeak. Long and loud, it started high, then slid low like a badly tuned viola, followed by a deep, discordant *thunk* as the door clapped shut. Eyes turned their way while the middle-aged priest offered praise and thanksgiving for the glorious morning.

Matt ushered the boys into a pew. He arranged Amos with Todd, then slipped back out again, Randy's hand clutched in his. "I'll be right back," he whispered as he left the pew. He tried to ignore the look of fear Todd sent him and the quiver of Amos's lower lip. He'd no more than turned his back and taken a step when Amos cried out, "I want to come."

Todd tried to shush him in typical big brother fashion. Loud. "You can't. You stay here with me."

"No." Amos stuck a stubborn lip out and slipped off the pew, his eyes darting from Todd to his father. "I'm going with Daddy."

Matt leaned in. "Stay with Todd, Amos," he whispered. "I need to take Randy to the bathroom." He tried to ignore the curious glances and downright stares that were coming his way from multiple directions.

"No."

"Amos."

Amos's scowl intensified. He stamped his foot, indignant. "I don't want to go to stupid old church. I want to go home."

A few gasps and a sprinkling of snickers indicated mixed reactions to Amos's declaration.

"Amos. Shush. You need to be quiet." Matt placed a finger of warning to his mouth in a noiseless plea for silence.

Amos's round face darkened as Matt felt Randy tug more firmly on his arm.

He knew what that meant. If he didn't hurry, there'd be a puddle on the floor. "I'll be right back," he said firmly to Amos.

Turning again, he headed for the door, only to hear the sound of little footsteps pounding behind him. Not knowing what else to do, he scooped up the preschooler and toted him along. At the door, he glanced back.

Todd looked scared to death. Since his mother's death, the eight-year-old had grown timid and reclusive, one more in the list of things he didn't know how to handle. He did know he couldn't ignore the fear. With a nod, he indicated to his oldest son to come along.

Todd scurried, his movements awkward, his gaze cast down, avoiding the people around him, secreted in his own private world of loss and anxiety.

They trooped out en masse, the door offering its excited squeal as they pushed it open. Once downstairs in the bathroom, all three had to go. Why had he expected anything else?

Matt scratched his head.

By the time hands were washed and zippers closed, long minutes had passed. Matt rubbed a tired hand across his brow. How on earth had Carrie done this every week? Even with just two little boys, it had to be exhausting.

Starting back up the stairs, he mulled the idea of leaving, trying again on the following Sunday. But that would be the chicken's way out, and Matt was not about to model that behavior for the boys. They had enough on their plates as it was. Wilmot men stuck to their guns.

Hoping to allay the inevitable noise, Matt eased the big cherry door open. His strategy simply managed to draw out the peal of the groaning hinge with no noticeable decrease in volume.

Great.

Eyes down, he calmly ignored the fresh interest in their direction, letting the boys slide into the pew while he took the pole position.

He drew a deep, cleansing breath and optimistically picked up a book. He got about twenty, maybe twenty-five seconds of peace and quiet before havoc reigned.

He didn't know who started the current standoff. He'd been busily turning the pages of his book, trying to find the appropriate Scripture for the date, when Amos squealed. Matt turned quickly.

Big fat tears found their way down the youngest boy's cheeks, plopping onto his shirt.

When Amos cried, everything ran. Mouth, nose, eyes. His face was a spigot. Searching pockets, Matt came up with nothing resembling a tissue, and Amos's face was only getting sloppier. Sending a scolding look to both Randy and Todd, he picked the boy up. To his relief, the tall, angular woman behind them handed forth a wad of tissues. Nodding his thanks, he turned to use them, pulling the little boy forward in his arms. But before he could make headway with the tissues, Amos swiped his mucky face against Matt's shirt collar. Tears, snot, and saliva were now mixed and embedded in easy-knit cotton. It didn't get much better than that.

"Amos, shhh. I've got you, buddy." He swabbed the little guy's face as best he could while Randy and Todd began to squabble over squatter's rights in pseudo-whispers.

"I want to be on the end."

"No, I do. Get off, Randy."

"It's my turn."

"No, it's not. Get off. Dad!"

"Stop." He hoped his low tone sounded as murderous as he felt. He swabbed the bulk of tissues across Amos's face once more and snuggled the littlest Wilmot against him. He started to stuff the wad into his pocket, but paused to dab at the slick moistness of his collar, refusing to think about what he was wiping away, or, more likely, just spreading around. What was the good reverend saying?

"Be still, and know that I am God! I will be exalted among the nations, I am exalted in the earth."

It was a psalm. He remembered that much from his childhood. Which one, he had no idea. His mother liked going to church; his father had been too busy building a seven-figure business to take Sunday mornings off, so by the time Matt was big enough to help out, he'd partnered with his dad on weekends. Leafing through the book once more, he got to the right page just as someone passed gas.

There was no way of telling who it was. Giggling and holding their noses, Todd and Randy wriggled in boyish glee, fanning their hands to their faces. Noxious fumes wafted out along the pew, drifting back to the innocent people behind them. People who, Matt was certain, had just wanted to come and pray. Not have front-row tickets to a circus sideshow.

He grabbed Randy's arm and propelled him up and across the kneeler, planting him firmly on his right. Todd was now alone on his left. They couldn't monkey around if they weren't together. Standing for the Lord's Prayer, he adjusted Amos's body along his hip, holding the boy solidly, despite his size. They'd no more than gotten into the fifth line of the old prayer when Todd grabbed his arm. "Randy's making faces at me."

"Ignore him." Then to Randy, "Stop. Now."

A few seconds passed. "He's still doing it." Todd's voice was whiny, but that had become more normal than not.

"Randy. I said stop." He directed a firm look at his middle son, named for Tim Allen's fictional devil-may-care boy on *Home Improvement*. He and Carrie had loved to watch reruns of that show. What had they been thinking?

Randy frowned, placed his hands along the seat in front of them, and started to do presses. Up. Down. Up. Down. Then he sighed, loud and long, trying to draw attention away from the altar. Unfortunately, he succeeded. "I wanna go home."

"You need to sit and be quiet. Or stand and be quiet. *Just be quiet.*" Matt's tone deepened with indignation. "People are praying."

His collar grew tight around his neck. Or maybe his neck was swelling, filling the folded-down, snot-encrusted cotton blend. He wasn't sure. At the moment, he didn't care. Randy's face grew darker. His lower lip puffed out in classic warning. "I wanna go home, *now.*"

"Hush. When church is over, we'll go, and not a minute sooner. Get a prayer book."

"Don't want a prayer book. Wanna go home."

His lips quivered in anger. His eyes shadowed. Tears were sure to follow. The woman behind Matt reached between them and tapped Randy's shoulder. The boy turned, looking stormy, ready to erupt.

"Would you like to look at this?" she asked quietly. She handed forth a brightly colored children's book. *The Story of Jonah.* Randy eyed it, curious, then looked from the woman to the child beside her and then back up.

His expression changed from obstinate to downright fearful, but he got quiet real quick, so Matt didn't really care why.

The tall woman sent Matt a commiserative look. Matt inclined his head in thanks yet again, palming Randy's buzzed head.

Peace. At last.

For about ten seconds. Todd tugged his arm. "I hafta go to the bathroom."

"We just went." Matt didn't try to hide the exasperation in his tone.

"Number two."

Well, that explained the gas. Matt bit back a sigh. It wouldn't do any good, anyway. He leaned back, allowing Todd room. "Go ahead."

"Alone?"

Matt nodded, refusing to look down. "Yup. You know where it is, and you're almost nine years old. Go take care of your business."

Todd's face crumpled into abject misery. "I'll hold it," he whispered bravely. From his rigid stance, that's just what he was doing.

Matt leaned down, balancing Amos. "Go to the bathroom now. It's not good to hold it."

"I can't go alone."

"Yes, you can."

"I can't. Mommy never let us go into a strange bathroom alone. She said it wasn't safe."

"This isn't a strange bathroom. It's church. Now go." Pushing back, he helped his oldest across the kneeler, toward the aisle that led to the squeaky door. How long did services usually last, anyway?

Randy stuck his foot out at the last minute, successfully tripping his brother. Todd went down in a heap, slapping his mouth against the pew in front of them, putting a top tooth through his bottom lip. Quickly setting Amos down, Matt grabbed the older boy, who was now crying hysterically, examined the lip, saw the injury was minor, and quickly held the wad of used tissues against it to stanch the flow of blood. The people in front of him turned, their looks less than friendly, and who could blame them? Shaking their heads, they turned back.

Todd pulled away, staring at the tissues, horror-struck. "That's got boogers on it, Dad. And you put it in my mouth." He wailed the words like Lucy in a *Peanuts* cartoon after she'd been kissed by a dog.

Looking smug, Randy innocently perused the renderings of Jonah in the whale's belly, while Amos tore a page out of the prayer book that

Matt had handed to Todd minutes before.

The priest raised his hands. "The Lord be with you."

The congregation answered in one voice. "And with your spirit."

"The Mass is ended. Go in peace, to love and serve the Lord, our God."

"Thanks be to God!"

Thanks, indeed.

Matt was exhausted. It was 10:02, and he was literally wiped out. Todd was carrying on like he'd suffered a mortal chest wound while Amos cheerfully pulled out a second page of prayer, crumpled it, then lobbed the paper ball at the unsympathetic couple in front of them. Matt dropped his head to Todd's for long seconds and just breathed.

Eventually the church grew quiet as people filed out. Matt felt the looks but kept his face down, his eyes averted.

He didn't want sympathy or understanding. Least of all, conversation. He'd just committed two hours to this dog and pony show, between prep time and church time, which could have been spent grading the Dillman house for its final landscaping, or backfilling the garage at the Asuki home in the new development on Glendale, preparing it for the concrete floor to be poured day after tomorrow.

But, no. He'd come to church with his boys, doing the duty Gloria D'Amico thought was so all-fired important. It wasn't. It was a travesty. If there was a God, some overseeing supremacy credited with universal creation, the guy sucked at his job. If Matt mucked up people's infrastructure the way God mucked up lives, he'd be out of work.

But there was nothing casual about his mother-in-law's custody threats, which meant he had to conform somewhat. At least make an effort. He and the boys had messed up too often of late. He didn't like that Gloria was right, that he needed to change things up, and he resented her interference, but the boys' behavior in church underscored the problem. His kids were brats, plain and simple.

After long moments, he raised his head, his nose twitching in recognition. "Todd. Stop your crying and get downstairs to the bathroom. Hurry."

Sniffling, the boy finally did as he was told, one hand firmly on his bottom as he hurried through the squeaky door that was now propped open.

Of course.

Reaching over, Matt scolded Amos for the pulled-out pages. He realigned them as best he could, his big hands awkward. Picking up his youngest, he turned to Randy, who was still holding the woman's book about Jonah. Matt glanced around, looking for her, feeling guilty that she'd left them with the book. Then again, she probably figured the book was a small price to pay for getting out of church alive. Randy leaned back and gave his father an angelic smile. "Can we come again next week?"

Over my dead body. That's what Matt wanted to say, regarding the mischievous boy who was more adept at starting trouble than the other two combined. "Sure," he replied, Gloria's threat echoing in his head. "If you're good."

Randy's smile only deepened. "Oh, I'll be good, Daddy."

Matt eyed the boy. The kid had been good all of six days in his life, and each of them had been a Christmas Eve.

It was April fourth. *Doomed.*

Matt sighed once more as Todd returned to them, a telltale bit of toilet paper clinging to the boy's left shoe.

Sure, they'd come again, and the boys would be good. *Right.* Three winsome faces looked up at him, their expressions the epitome of innocence and trust.

Matt didn't stand a chance.

chapter two

"Have you ever seen such commotion at Mass in your life?" Orrie Wimple spoke loudly as small throngs of people moved toward their cars. "What a bunch of uncouth, uncivilized little demons those Wilmot boys are. I hear their teachers are fit to be tied, and after that little demonstration, I can see why."

Muriel Brownley was quick to agree. "My Angie works in the middle boy's class, and she says he's always messing with something or other, starting a fuss, raising a ruckus. I know Gloria wants them in church, but honest to Pete, I can't imagine what good she thinks it will do at this late date."

"Probably figures something is better than nothing," said a third woman Elle didn't recognize. "Not worrying a bit about those around them, or what kind of disturbance they make. But of course, Wilmots have money, and they're the only game in town when it comes to big equipment, so who's going to take that on?"

"Such a good point." Orrie had the audacity to look self-righteous, despite the fact that she'd just come out of church and was raking a fellow parishioner over the coals. "Someone should take those boys in hand. Teach them a thing or two."

"If *that* was Matt Wilmot's plan, he should have put it in place a few years back, before those little heathens got so out of control. Those boys could use a mother with a strong backhand, that's what!"

Nowhere in Muriel's scolding tone or timeline was there room for a bereaved young husband and father to grieve. Their lack of compassion ignited a curl of sympathy within Elle. She'd been the object of town gossip growing up, and more recently, no doubt. She knew the fallout and hardships firsthand. But her quaint farmhouse and studio were within sight of the Wilmot place, and she'd seen her share of their interesting behaviors now that the weather was getting soft, so she couldn't deny that the women had a point.

"No one in their right mind would take on that crew now," Muriel finished. "No matter how good-looking the father is, or how much money lines the bank accounts. It's a travesty, I tell you! Bye, gals. See you next week!"

"Lord willing!"

"Have a good day!"

The women split into various directions as if their words of condemnation weren't any big thing.

Elle knew better. She followed more slowly, holding her niece's hand as they strolled down the concrete walk. Points of green poked through winter-faded mulch, offering hope of spring. Yellow daffodils and pale jonquils waved in the cool morning breeze, a welcome sight after a long, cold, lonely winter.

"Aunt Elle, I forgot my book!" Jenny stopped mid-step. "That naughty boy has it!"

Jenny was right. They'd left the book with the middle Wilmot boy when they slipped out of church, but she was pretty sure the overwhelmed father could use a little time alone right now. But if she *didn't* go back and get Jenny' ook now, she'd later have to cross the field that separated their homes and get it from the Wilmot house, and that wasn't about to happen. She'd picked her oversized house and barn setup deliberately, with enough space on either side to ensure privacy. Of course, she hadn't counted on three raucous boys who had no respect for boundaries or rules. She turned back toward the church, hesitated, then decided against it. "I've got the whole set of books at home, Jen. We'll get that one back another time, OK?"

"Why not now?" Jenny looked up, perplexed, and what could Elle tell her? That she wanted to keep her distance from her neighbors?

That would sound downright weird, but it was truth. She'd come home to Cedar Mills determined to quietly go her own way on her own terms. Stirring up the tempest living next door wasn't about to happen. "Let's give them time to regroup." She took Jenny's hand and resumed walking toward her SUV, when a voice stopped them.

"Ma'am?"

Elle turned. Matt Wilmot was coming her way, holding the littlest boy in his arms. The older boys trailed along behind, glancing left and right, plotting, no doubt. The thought of that almost made her smile because she'd plotted a few things in her time.

"Your book."

"Ah." She accepted the book and handed it to Jenny. "Thank you."

"I'm the grateful one, ma'am. The book was a help. I'll make sure to think of that next time."

"A long service is hard for little ones." Elle looked past him toward the boys. "And some not-so-little ones."

Her words irritated him. She saw it when his shoulders rose. So did his chin. "Where I come from, boys will be boys."

Elle had no trouble believing that. The older Wilmot boys, Matt and his brother Jason, were born leaders on the athletic fields and in school. Local papers had carried weekly updates on them, touting their gridiron abilities at the big Cedar Mills centralized high school. "Whereas I find manners a necessity regardless of gen' ?r."

His collar rose. He tightened his grip on the wet-nosed boy in his arms. "Well. Thanks so much for the book." He turned, called to the boys, and strode fast and hard in the other direction.

"He doesn't sound happy."

Out of the mouths of babes. Elle looked down at Jenny. "I don't expect he is. But you've got your book, and that's good. Now let's get you back home to your parents. Auntie's got work to do back home, but I'm sure glad you took the time to go to church with me today."

"I like being with you." Jenny gripped her hand more snugly, then ruined the sweet moment by adding, "Mommy says you're lonely and sad, and I thought if we could go to church together, maybe you wouldn't be lonely and sad anymore."

Elle's heart bunched in her chest.

She wasn't lonely or sad. She was…alone. Big difference. And mostly she liked being alone; she'd gotten used to it these past two years. Maybe this was her destiny, her calling: to live alone, creating beautiful art with the talent God gave her and being a doting aunt to her two nieces and Kate's upcoming baby. After failing miserably at marriage, the lack of challenge in her current choices seemed downright therapeutic.

She dropped Jenny off, gently refused her younger sister's invitation to dinner, and drove back to Randolph Road. She pulled in and parked the car as a chill rain started to fall. It began as a light, steady shower, but by the time she'd changed into work clothes, the storm had intensified. The roof shed water into the gutters, except for the back entrance to the house. At the very spot she needed to pass through, water poured through a gap in the gutters, but what would it matter? Running to the barn would soak her anyway.

She slipped into her muck boots and a slicker, then dashed for the converted barn. She stepped inside, hit the lights, and sighed.

Home.

Here in this hand-designed haven of creative flow, she could be alone with her work, her prayers, and her thoughts. She didn't need anyone, no matter what her sister Kate thought. She was fine on her own. Better, actually, than so many others, pretending at love.

She closed the door behind her, set the music to play, and studied her schedule. The *Lilies* project called to her, a design she'd tried to mentally engage for her upcoming East Coast tour, but she didn't dare dive into that randomly. When the inspiration was right, she wanted the project done once, and done well, but the image in her head wasn't quite right. She knew better than to force the flow.

She moved to the painting room and pulled on a smock. Her mother had made her a stack of new smocks, done in silly patterns to make her smile. She pulled up her stool, got herself comfortable, and arranged her array of stamps, brushes, and paints.

Eyes closed, she let the music and the moment blend their inspirations. Little boys, adrift, undirected. Old women, critical and sharp. A small girl's hand, wanting to ease the loneliness she sensed. All buffered by the deep loss in Matt Wilmot's harried, gray gaze.

She reached for bold tones, but then the image of his smoky eyes came back to her. Shadowed. Worn. And the littlest boy's eyes, a clear blue. The middle boy, hazel with impish lights. And the oldest boy, with the big, dark eyes, so needy and whiny she longed to scold him herself.

She lined up the palette of colors in front of her, then reached beyond and drew out a duckling yellow. She mixed in a stronger yellow, just enough to brighten the hue. She set the yellow among the eye-shaded colors and sat back, pleased.

The yellow brought joy to the mix of somber and soft. A splash of warmth to a cool collection.

She arranged her stamps, set the bowl on the turner, and began her pattern, bottom first. As she touched the stamps to the bisque, a testimony to the Wilmot family sprang to life beneath her fingers. A family diverse, torn, saddened…and then blessed with a splash of joy.

She took her time, but the work moved quickly in her experienced hands. And when she was done, the unfired bowl offered a more in-depth look at the troubled family just down the road.

Sympathy welled within her. She'd been the object of cruel talk when she was a teenage misfit, a girl who cared nothing for dresses and dancing, and everything for art and sports and solitude. So different from her popular, cheerleader younger sister.

And here she was, back in Cedar Mills. Kate was married to a doctor and had her teaching degree and two perfect little girls, Becca and Jenny. In a couple of months, she'd add a son to the mix. The ideal life by so many standards.

Elle straightened her shoulders and surveyed her beautiful studio.

She had her art. She had the talent God had given her and a resilient spirit.

No husband any longer. And no children to soften the blow. Not one person to call her own, and all of that had been played out for the world to see because that's what happens when you're married to one of the richest men in America and he goes rogue.

She breathed deep and scolded herself.

Saints had been content with far less. She would be grateful for what she had and not rue what Alex wrenched from her when he walked off with another woman, a woman able to conceive his child. She hadn't been able to make him happy. She'd tried and failed, and he'd left, a simple scenario.

And now he was remarried and expecting a baby. Bitterness put a chokehold on her. She'd been stupid once and publicly embarrassed by her husband's caught-on-video escapades with another woman.

Never again.

And why was she dwelling on it? Because of a wretched birthday, another reminder that her biological clock was winding down.

Let it go...accept God's grace and blessing as given.

A good reminder. She shrugged off the negativity and kept right on painting, losing herself in the movement of the turntable and the paint-tipped sponges. No matter what harm was done by mean-spirited hearts, in this room—in this potter's shed—she could fix anything that came her way. And that would be enough.

It had to be enough.

chapter three

The first shriek of terror stopped Elle's heart three days later.

The second scream pumped enough adrenaline into her system to start it up again. She raced for the scruffy field separating her property from the Wilmots', ready to save someone's life, but then the middle boy shrieked back as he wielded something in the air. A branch? A sword? An antique scythe guaranteed to cut anything the size of a small limb, including a boy's leg?

She stopped when she realized they were playing a game, and she'd been set to race across the field to save their sorry lives.

Another shriek made her cringe. With all their shrieks and screams, what would happen if something actually went wrong? Who would run to help them? No one, she supposed as she moved back toward her small barn. No one would believe a real danger cry, because once spring had come, that's pretty much all the boys did when they were home. What on earth would summer be like, when the three little hooligans were home all day?

Elle had no idea, but she was smart enough to dread it.

She sidestepped chicken droppings as she crossed the yard. Her mistake for thinking the idea of free-range chickens made sense. She would have an enclosure built soon. Nothing too fancy, just solid. She was tired of chicken poop. The rainstorm two days before had encouraged the hens to roost on her side porch, huddled along the top step like birds on a wire. And what calling cards they'd left behind then. No, sir, a chicken run would be built and functional in a timely fashion.

Distracted from her return to the barn, she stopped to feel for eggs under the sitting hens. Three were lined up, like women for the bathroom, vying for a single nest of straw, ignoring the other nesting spots. "You're not over-bright," she scolded, "but you lay nice eggs. Eight this morning. Thank you, ladies." As if they understood the accolade, two preened their feathers, fluffing and arching their necks at the praise. She grinned.

Right until she heard the gunshot. The proximity of it sent shivers down her spine. Racing from the hens' nests beside the barn, she turned to the Wilmot house, her heart thudding.

She heard the babysitter screaming, then saw her, hands in the air, storming about the yard, yelling an interesting assortment of things unsuitable for little ears. But then, the little darlings *had* shot at her. She had every right to be upset.

* * *

"Cherry bombs," her sister, Kate, reported later. "Those insufferable little boys got hold of some cherry bombs and set one off. They scared Andrea Perkins to death. Matt said he had them left over from a Fourth of July picnic four years ago. The sheriff was not pleased."

"I expect not." Matt's words came back to her, his "boys will be boys" line. She didn't disagree, but living to adulthood would be a plus, wouldn't it? At this rate, she was pretty sure the trio of miscreants next door didn't stand a chance. "Of course, most of us survive childhood, Kate, even with occasional mishaps." She tossed Matt's line out to gauge Kate's reaction. "Boys will be boys."

"Head cases," retorted Kate. "Every one of them. Why, Angie Godfrey says—"

"Angie Godfrey talks out of turn," cut in Elle. "She should know better. Being a teacher's aide gives her access to confidential information. *Confidential* being the key word." She sent Kate a knowing glance.

Kate flushed. "You're right. She does talk too much. But these boys are off the charts, the older two anyway. No one knows too much about the younger one. And she really cares about what happens to them."

"Hmph." Elle's tone said Angie Godfrey's time would be better spent helping the boys instead of running them down.

"Of course, if Matt ends up marrying Kim Sedgewick, the boys would have a mother again."

Kim Sedgewick? The former Miss Dairy Queen who spent more time on makeup and nails than her job? Elle couldn't have heard right. "You think Kimberly Sedgewick is maternal?"

"Well, no." Even super-nice Kate couldn't pull that one off. "Not really. All right, not even slightly. But it must have some appeal for her, or why would she chase him so openly?"

Elle shook her head. Personally, she didn't see the cute and curvy Kim as being farsighted enough to realize that winning Matt Wilmot's heart would also win her the honor of motherhood to three rambunctious boys. But it wasn't her concern. Other than that maybe the noise level would wind down a bit.

Kate changed the subject. "The first spring family social is at the church on Saturday. Come with us, OK?"

Elle kept her tone brisk. "No can do. The title says it all."

Kate looked blank.

"Family?" Elle glanced around as she snapped and folded the newly dried sheets. "Do you see one?"

"Elle."

"Seriously, Kate. What on earth would I do at a church social filled with young families? That many kids in one area would probably turn the rest of my hair gray in one night. L'Oréal and I have a tough enough time chasing roots as it is."

"Your hair's beautiful."

Elle grinned at her. "I already told you to take the eggs. Buttering me up is completely unnecessary. But always welcome."

"If you change your mind…"

"I won't."

"Still." Seven months pregnant, her younger sister got up awkwardly. Elle reached out a hand to help her, and Kate huffed a breath once she was back on her feet. "If you do, come with Mom and Jeff and me. The girls love having Aunt Elle around."

That was true. She loved her time with Jenny and Becca. She spurred them to things their mother would have never considered as a kid, but Elle had no such qualms. The higher they climbed, the farther they threw, the faster they ran brought praise from Aunt Elle, along with quiet nods of satisfaction from their father. He was proud of his two tomboys, and when the girls showed interest in dissecting fish and frogs to better understand the workings therein, Jeff saw the beginnings of two promising medical careers. Both he and Kate acknowledged that Elle was an invaluable resource.

But being the tagalong at a family social underscored the spinster twist of her current lifestyle. She'd stay home this Saturday and work on the chicken coop, finding greater satisfaction in fewer droppings on her walk.

* * *

Matt studied the layout for an upcoming project as he estimated the number of good-weather days required to do the initial groundwork. His phone buzzed a text. He glanced down and then went right back to his work.

Another text followed the first—Gloria, asking to take the older boys for the weekend.

When he didn't answer instantly, she texted him again, short and terse.

He could imagine her outcry if the tables were turned, if he treated her the same way, texting repeatedly during a court session. And he wasn't letting her take the boys again, not with her adverse attitude. Life was tough enough lately. He didn't need her to feed negativity into his sons or ply them for information she'd use against him at some time. Enough was enough.

He picked up the phone and called his mother. "How's Dad doing?" he asked when she answered.

"Better," she told him. Her cheerful voice said Dad was probably nearby. "He's grumpy that his recovery from a quadruple bypass isn't moving at breakneck speed like he would prefer, but he wakes up breathing, so that's a plus."

Matt knew that wasn't the only thing making his father grumpy. Daniel Wilmot had taken a big risk eighteen months before. He'd signed for a major loan to fund new equipment, and then a year of almost constant rain had slowed or paused several projects. They'd scraped through winter, barely making payments. With a new season just beginning and his father's unexpected surgery, Matt knew they had to make every moment count to push Wilmot Excavating back into the black. "Put him on, will you? I bet I can cheer him up." He waited while his mother passed off the phone, and when his father answered, Matt said, "We nailed the subdivision project in Glendale. That puts us at maximum hourly capacity through fall. Pretty sweet, right?"

"It'll be sweeter when I can get back to work," his father replied. He sounded grumpy because he was grumpy. And worried. And plenty sore, post-surgery. "Some might be meant to sit around and watch the world go by. I'm not one of them."

"Are you giving Mom a hard time?"

Dan Wilmot was silent for drawn-out seconds. "Possibly."

"Well, stop," Matt told him. "We've got all crews on board, Jason's overseeing his team, everything's moving according to schedule for the moment—"

"One big rain can mess that up. Or equipment breakdowns."

It could, but Matt didn't have the luxury of anticipating trouble. He knew his father's nature. Dan would chomp at the bit, wishing he was more active, while driving Matt's mother crazy, and all because of the massive balloon payment looming in eleven months. Defaulting on that payment meant losing equipment and credit standing, not something a business could take lightly. "Nothing we haven't dealt with before," Matt told him. "You heal up and get better."

"Mom wants to know how the boys are doing. She misses them."

Matt had taken the boys for a brief—*very brief*—visit when his father needed emergency surgery after collapsing on the job. No one with a healing heart needed three busy boys racing around. Not for a while, anyway. "They're into everything, driving sitters crazy. Were we that bad?"

"Yes, of course."

Matt wasn't sure that was true, but then for all that he and Jase had done, they had known their mother was no pushover. If they messed up, Mary Lou Wilmot hadn't been afraid to go a little crazy on them, and they'd turned out all right.

There was no loving mother to raise the expectations for his boys. Would they be better behaved if there was?

Maybe. At least they'd be double-teamed. "Dad, tell Mom I love her, and we'll see you guys once we've given you a little more R & R time, OK?"

"I'll tell her. And good job on nailing that contract, Matt. I know you're burning the candle at both ends for me. I appreciate it."

"It's all right, Dad."

It wasn't all right. Jason should be doing more, stepping up to the plate, but Jase didn't stretch well. Never had. He liked things laid out, methodical, one job done, another job waiting in the wings.

That was great as long as Matt took lead overseeing multiple spinning plates, plus putting himself in the driver's seat of rigs daily. With Dad out for weeks, that extra pair of hands, eyes, and feet was sorely missed, but if Matt pushed Jase too hard, he'd drag his feet purposely.

Kind of like Randy.

Matt closed his laptop, said goodbye to Susan, the office manager, and headed for his pickup. Jase had one daughter and a stay-at-home wife.

Matt had three sons, no wife, and his middle son was a constant in-your-face challenge, much like his Uncle Jase.

He loved his boys, but if equitability was formed by ratio, his balance fell way short in the scheme of things. He took on more work and ended up with more work. How was that fair?

But then, burying a twenty-nine-year-old wife wasn't fair either.

As he turned out of the driveway, a shaggy, neon-orange spotted animal loped down the side of the road, heading in the opposite direction.

Neon orange. The very shade of paint we use to mark dig lines. And you have cans of it in the garage.

He had to meet the town building inspector from Glendale, but Matt was pretty sure he'd be hearing from the dog's owner eventually, because generally speaking, neon-orange dogs weren't indigenous to Cedar Mills, Ohio.

chapter four

If the Wilmots were a hashtag, they'd rock the "trending now" list daily. Their ongoing antics still fed the gossip flow when Elle stopped by the old-fashioned general store to pick up kitchen supplies on Friday afternoon.

"Why anyone would bring three little hooligans into the Lord's home is what I'd like to know." Orrie Wimple looked down her hawk nose at the three women gathered before her. With matching grim expressions, they huddled in a clutch near the counter of Wimple's Mercantile. "Not a hint of manners among them, and just look at the deals they've pulled. The Stillers' dog, oh that poor thing, as if he wasn't an ugly-enough mongrel anyway. What is Matt thinking? He should keep them right there at home until they've got manners enough to behave around respectable people."

Elle should have kept quiet.

But of course she didn't. "I expect Matt Wilmot thought he'd be surrounded by goodness and mercy in the house of the Lord." She came up behind the group purposely, unafraid to speak her piece. She sat a small basket of items on the checkout counter and looked at each woman as she spoke. "Unfortunately, it appears he was mistaken on that. I think he deserves credit for trying. Not too many young fathers would attempt to bring their boys to church without a mother along. Matt Wilmot has lost that option. So…"

Orrie broke right in with a typical response in no-nonsense fashion. "A firm swat on the behind would go a long way in that family, if you ask me. They're undisciplined and disrespectful. Scaring Andrea like that with a cherry bomb. Spray-painting a neighborhood dog! And raising a ruckus in school. Why, I heard the middle one told the Glogowski boy to 'bite' him." When the group of women gasped, she nodded, smug. "And all over a little teasing. What little boy doesn't tease and torment?"

"Well-behaved ones?" Elle kept her tone bright, her expression candid.

Orrie pressed her lips into a thin line as she totaled Elle's order. "It might seem that simple to someone who's had no children."

Her words stung, but Elle would never let the old woman know it. She buried the jabs, deep and low, to be examined at some time when she was alone. Certainly not under the watchful eyes of some of the sharpest tongues in Cedar Mills. She grasped her paper sack and held Orrie's gaze. "I've got no cows either, but I know how to get the milk. And wasn't there a whole segment on tolerance and understanding in the Sunday homily? For those that were listening, of course." She rested her attention on the small group long enough to see them squirm. "Good day, ladies."

She could only imagine the buzz that would follow her retreating footsteps.

Bugger them, anyway. Snotty old gossips, without a nice thing to say. How anyone could pick on a sad, young widower, with three mischievous little boys—

Her sympathy ground to an abrupt halt when she turned into her driveway ten minutes later.

Chaos reigned. On one side, two little boys stood watching, eyes wide, their hands clasped tight against their mouths while a Bobcat earthmover tore through her yard and her perennial flowerbed with a terrified young boy at its wheel.

She screeched to a halt, slammed the car into park, and jumped out the door. "Turn it off," she yelled as she raced across the yard to the small dozer-like machine. "Turn it off!"

The boy, the oldest one, was too scared to understand. Terrorized, he kept turning the wheel, as if that small vestige of control would somehow help him out of a very dangerous situation. The small, powerful machine reacted to every quick turn with amazing speed. Heading straight for her porch, he turned abruptly at the last possible moment, steering directly for the old, wide-trunked oak at a pretty fast clip. Terror froze his movements, his eyes trained on the tree and the tree alone as it loomed in front of him.

Elle didn't think, she reacted. Racing to his left, she grabbed hold of the front-end casing as the wheels came close enough to her toes to send a whoosh of air across her ankles. Pulling herself up and in, she grabbed the wheel, turned it sharply right, and missed the aged oak by inches, but couldn't recover in time to save her quaint wooden wishing well, a gift from her parents when she bought the house the previous year.

Turning the key, she shut the ignition down. The noisy engine ground to a halt, but not before they heard the sound of splintering wood beneath the thick-treaded rubber runners.

For a moment, they sat in silence, woman and boy. She thought she might have wet her pants. She was sure he did. Finally, finding her breath and ignoring her racing pulse, she faced the frightened boy at her side. "Well. That was fun."

Her voice said it was anything but. The boy gulped as big tears welled in his eyes. She hardened her own in return. "Are you OK?"

He nodded. Then he eyed his wet pants and grimaced.

Commotion moved their way in the form of an overwrought father. The onslaught cut their conversation short. "Are you all right? Todd! Are you all right? Dear God in heaven, what were you thinking, boy?"

Matt hauled the boy out of the driver's seat and hugged him. Short moments later he held him away. "What's the matter with you? Haven't I told you that you must never go near my equipment? I mean, look at it, Todd." He turned the boy, his arm waving at the assorted apparatuses kept behind the house. Inside several large Morton buildings stood enormous equipment used to facilitate the wide-ranging family excavation business. Dump trucks, shovels, cranes, bulldozers, Cats.

It was a little boy's dream: full-size Tonka-style construction vehicles everywhere you looked. "Every one of those is a lethal weapon in the wrong hands. You could have been killed. Or killed Mrs…" He looked at her blankly, his forehead furrowed.

"Elle Drake, Mr. Wilmot. I moved in last summer." She stuck out a hand.

"You were in church with us."

"Yes. Behind you."

"I'm sorry." He reached out a hand to clasp hers. "So very sorry. And I can't thank you enough for climbing up there, saving him. I don't want to think of what could have happened." He turned as the shock wore off and fatherhood set in. "What were you thinking, Todd? Don't you ever, ever pull a stupid and dangerous stunt like that again. Do you hear me?"

At the boy's frightened nod, he pulled him back into his chest. The boy clung.

"Ahem."

They both turned. Elle directed her gaze to the splintered wood-pile that used to be a nice little wishing well with a natural finish surrounded by a lush shade garden. Matt spoke right up. "I'll pay for that, of course."

She leveled him a look, then shifted her gaze to the boy before bringing it back to the father. She arched a brow. "You didn't do it."

He nodded. "Of course not. But my boy did, and I take responsibility for his actions."

Gaze steady, she eyed the boy with a look she had learned as a summer-camp counselor at Glen St. Mary's, a specialty camp run by a Rhode Island church staff. The church brought city kids out of the hood and gave them two weeks of abiding in nature…with rules…and lots of good food. Elle had run their arts and crafts unit for three years while she attended the Rhode Island Institute of Design. She'd worked with some tough kids in her time, and one thing they'd learned quickly about the young art director: She didn't back down. The oldest Wilmot boy was figuring that out right about now. He squirmed. "Better he take responsibility for his own actions. We'll clean this up today, and then I'll expect him at five thirty tomorrow."

"Because?" Matt looked puzzled.

She inclined her head slightly. "To work off the damage, of course."

The boy blanched. Matt looked as if a new and amazing thought had come his way. "Him work it off?" He eyed the boy with greater interest. "What a good idea."

Todd shook his head in mute appeal. Matt stuck out his hand again. "Five thirty it is. And I wanted to thank you for your help in church the other day. I didn't know we were neighbors. With work and the boys, I honestly haven't been looking much to the left or right these days."

She knew that. Half the town knew that. He scrubbed his hand through his hair, and the movement made him look crazy attractive and maybe also just crazy, but raising a brood of kids alone might have that effect.

She'd wanted a family. She'd tried, oh, she'd tried. Tests, timing, shots, calendars, more shots, and more tests.

Nothing worked. And when she started wrapping her head around the idea of adoption, Alex was wrapping himself around Miss Swimsuit Edition. She pushed that aside as Matt bent toward his son. "You need to apologize to Mrs. Drake."

She swallowed a sigh, then corrected him. "It's Miss Drake, actually. Elle."

"Kate's sister?"

Of course he'd remember Kate. Any red-blooded male would. "Yes. And once he gets cleaned up at home, send him back over. We'll take care of this mess in the yard and my perennial bed. Tomorrow we'll start working on the well."

The boy stuck his lower lip out a country mile, but Matt ignored him. "I'll send him back straightaway."

Climbing into the seat of the Bobcat, the father suddenly paused, his forehead creased in wonder. Then, arching a hip slightly, he looked at the seat below him. The puddle that used to be there had wicked into the backside of his jeans. Until then, he hadn't noticed the obvious wet spot trailing from his son's pants.

He didn't sigh. She gave him extra points on that. With a direct look to the boy, he said firmly, "I'll meet you at home. Unless you'd like to drive?"

The boy missed the wry note entirely. Eyes wide, he stepped back, his hands coming forward to try and mask the wetness of his pants. "I'll walk."

"See that you do, then." Matt put the Bobcat into gear and drove away while the boy walked across the overgrown field between the houses. Elle stood, watching him go, studying the mixed dynamics.

The oldest boy was soft. That was obvious. And starved for attention, although his father's affection was plain to see. Then, along the back property line, where lilac bushes grew in nine-foot wonder with just an occasional break in the greenery, she spotted a buzzed blond head sporting a devilish smile as the middle boy peaked back around the corner of the pink-toned lilac bush.

This was the height-challenged monster-child who thought she might be a witch because she wore funny dresses and had a big oven in her back shed. She'd heard his chatter from Kate's girls, and she'd noted the look he'd given her in church.

He had *ringleader* written all over his impish face. Elle regarded him from a distance, mulling the situation.

One way or another, little brother was going to meet his match.

chapter five

Elle was on her knees in the perennial bed a little later when a small shadow fell across what was left of the newly erupted shoots. She rocked back on her heels and met the boy's gaze. "You're here."

The boy scrubbed the dirt with the toe of a well-worn sneaker. "Yeah."

"Good." Voice crisp, she handed him a garden fork and a trowel. "We need to smooth and soften the soil wherever there are tire marks. Otherwise, the ground will get hard, and the flowers and plants won't be able to push through."

His brow furrowed. "Those did." He pointed to some thin sprouts of iris, bravely poking narrow points up and out of the ground.

"Japanese Iris," Elle told him. "They're pretty hearty. But the others are more fragile. What's your name?" She stayed matter-of-fact on purpose because driving big, motorized machinery in your neighbor's yard wasn't exactly a minor offense.

He kept his face averted. "Todd."

"Good name. Well, Todd," she waved a hand of direction. "You scooch down over there and watch me. Then do the same thing."

He followed directions, eyeing her as she worked the fork gently into the compacted soil and then smoothed the looser surface with both hand and trowel. He bent low, examining fuzzy points of green just breaking ground, and brushed a hand over one.

"Hosta," she told him, seeing the motion. His look followed hers. "They grow well on that side of the garden because the tree shades them. Over here, they'd have a harder time. Too much sun."

"My teacher says plants like the sun. Maybe you should talk to her. She knows a lot."

"Most do," Elle agreed. "But some plants like a lot of sun, others just a little. Hostas are like that."

"But how do they know?"

"Hmm?"

He cleared his throat as he made gentle swipes between the furry points of the hosta root. "How do they know they don't like the sun?"

"I've no idea. Maybe we can look that up later on my laptop. Would you like that?"

His eyes widened. He darted a glance to the door, then back to her, as if wondering if her oven were big enough to roast little boys. "Dad won't let me go in strange people's houses."

She accepted that, still working. "Dad's smart. We'll check with him. Maybe another time."

Still uncertain, he half-nodded. A commotion across the empty field drew her attention. Two pairs of badly hidden eyes regarded her. She pretended not to see.

They worked side by side until the garden bed looked reasonably undisturbed. The boy didn't complain or whine. She gave him silent merit for that. From what she overheard on a regular basis, whining was what he did best.

"Well." She stood, surveying their handiwork. "That looks better. I'll get us a glass of lemonade, and then we'll clean up the front yard."

The boy's eyes widened in appreciation at the mention of the drink. When she returned with the pitcher and two tumblers, he downed his rapidly. "More?" She held the pitcher out in invitation.

He nodded, and she filled his glass halfway this time, studying him. He was tall and lean for his age, with dark hair and eyes. His skin had a touch of olive to it, a tribute to his mother's side, but his hair, perfectly straight, stuck out at odd angles as if he'd slept crooked. Eyelashes that should have been illegal swept his cheeks, and a timid, thin mouth hid teeth that would need an orthodontist's care. He lacked confidence, and she wondered if it were situational or chronic. She hoped for the former but suspected the latter.

"All right, young man. I haven't got all day. Let's clean up my wishing well." Hoisting the wheelbarrow, she angled it up and away, pushing it to the front yard, the boy trailing behind. "Mind the nails, now."

It didn't take long to do the cleanup. Half of the well was intact, which meant they'd only have to reconstruct the splintered half. Once done picking up the pieces, she directed her attention to the youngster before her. "You work hard."

He acknowledged the comment with a thrust of his shoe into the dirt.

"I'll get the wood tomorrow. We can start rebuilding when you come over."

He nodded. "Can I go now?"

"You may."

He was off like a shot, racing through the weedy lot. When he came upon his two younger brothers spying on him, he dropped to their level. She couldn't hear what they were saying, but she read their expressions. Todd looked relieved, the middle boy looked skeptical, and the little guy seemed to hang on their every word.

Elle was pretty sure the younger ones had thought big brother would be today's dinner. That he'd survived a trip into the crazy lady's yard was a feat of some magnitude. Seeing them compare notes, eyes wide, made her wonder at all they missed. No mother to laugh at their silly jokes, read them stories, scrub behind their ears, or snuggle them to sleep. How much different would their lives and attitudes be with a woman's guiding touch?

The middle one saw her watching. Maybe he thought she was too far away to see, or maybe he just didn't care, but he put his thumbs in his ears, made a nasty face, and waggled all eight of his fingers.

And then he laughed, pleased with himself, which made Elle wonder how brave the little monster would be if he was within reach.

She shoved her shoulders back and put a firm lid on whatever sympathy she thought she felt. Those three weren't just imps. They were barbarians. Ruffians. Brats.

Boys.

* * *

"Does she have all her teeth?"

Todd shrugged while he scrubbed the toe of his shoe into the soil. "I guess."

"Whaddya mean, you guess?" Randy demanded. "You were standing right next to her, you musta seen 'em."

"I guess she does." Todd thought hard before he decided. "Yeah, she's got all her teeth."

"Are they yellow?"

Todd scrunched his brow and looked at his younger brother. "I don't think."

Randy clapped a hand to his head, as though Todd were a lost cause. "Didn't you look?"

"Kinda."

"Then were they? I think all witches have yellow teeth."

"That's baby stuff. Besides, *you* saw her in church. She reached right over and handed you a book. You should have noticed. And maybe she isn't even a witch, Randy. Did you think of that?"

Randy snorted. "We saw her go into that barn dressed all weird. That's where she's got that big oven, like super big. And jars of stuff. Lots of 'em."

"You don't know for sure. You were too chicken to go over there yourself," Todd reminded him.

"Amelia is friends with Jenny, and 'Melia said she's got an oven big enough to roast us in and hotter than anything," Randy insisted. "When it's cold out, you see smoke. Smoke doesn't just appear!"

Todd shrugged. "Maybe."

Randy groaned. "Amos and I were ready to shoot her with our lasers if she tried anything."

Todd was pretty sure fixing a garden wasn't worth shooting someone with a laser. Or a ray gun or a lightsaber. "We just fixed the garden," he explained. Then a thought struck. "But…she did want to show me stuff on her computer."

Randy's eyes went round. "In the house?" His voice almost croaked.

"Yeah."

"Did you run?"

"No. I told her I couldn't go in strange houses."

"She might have cooked you in there." Randy clapped a hand to his head again. He looked really silly when he did that, like the Three Stooges guys that Dad used to watch. Back before Mom was gone.

"'Melia said the big oven is out back." Todd waved a hand toward Miss Drake's fancy barn with all the windows. "She asked me in the *house*."

"Well, maybe she's got more than one oven! I bet most witches do. You should tell Dad."

"No way."

"What if she eats you tomorrow?"

Todd thought hard, eyes downcast. Then he lifted them to meet those of his little brother. "If anything happens to me, you gotta take good care of Amos."

Randy swallowed hard.

So did Todd. Then he stalked off to bed, wondering if it might be his last night to sleep there…ever.

* * *

No way in the world could Matt fall asleep that night.

Dire possibilities raced through his mind as he replayed the evening's events.

I could have lost my son.

What if Todd had run straight into that big, old oak? What if he'd driven into the road? Thoughts of what could have been tormented Matt.

He stole into the boys' rooms once they were asleep. Most nights he collapsed in a heap on the couch after the boys had gone down. Falling asleep in the living room, then dragging himself down the hall to the bedroom in a comatose state was still better than facing his big, empty bed alone.

He reached down and touched Amos's curls. The little guy needed a haircut—they all needed haircuts, but no one else was willing to take them to the shop in town, and Matt knew it wasn't a quick walk-in, buzz 'em kind of deal. So he put it off, and they looked like a bunch of shaggy, unkempt puppies.

Randy...

So innocent in sleep and such an instigator when awake. With Randy he had to be on his toes twenty-four hours a day, seven days a week, because if the kid sensed weakness, he seized the opportunity. Blond and hazel-eyed, Randy looked and acted like his Uncle Jason in a lot of ways. Jason was a pain-in-the-neck kind of kid all the while they were growing up.

So was Randy.

He turned toward Todd's bed. Todd looked worried, even asleep. His brow knit, and his chin quivered, as if peace evaded his oldest boy, and Matt didn't have a clue what to do about it. Matt had always been self-confident, so the thought of teaching that quality seemed impossible. You either were, or you weren't, right? So how did that bode for his oldest son, so unsure and uncertain?

His boys. Motherless children. And he'd almost lost one of them today because he was too busy working, and he'd pretty much run through any capable and available babysitters in Cedar Mills.

He needed help, and with construction season upon them, he needed it quickly, but Matt knew his options were limited. He'd called a nanny service.

They'd laughed at him.

Then he'd called the high school, looking for an older teen, maybe a boy, to help.

No one called him back, which meant their reputation preceded them.

He stared at the boys. A weird part of him was tempted to pray for them as they slept, but why would he do that when there was no point? And why did seemingly intelligent humans feel the need to turn to some pie-in-the-sky allegiance as something bigger and better? Couldn't they just accept that out of the billions of planets formed in the big bang, theirs got lucky?

As he started to pull the door shut, Amos yawned, rolled over, and rubbed his eyes. He peered toward the light, spotted Matt, and sat straight up, arms out. "Daddy."

Matt walked back into the room, reached down, and brought his littlest boy to his chest. He smelled wet, which meant they couldn't get rid of nighttime diapers yet, but his hair smelled like waffle syrup.

Matt didn't care about either. He cuddled the boy close and brought him into his bed. Amos quickly grabbed a corner of the blanket, curled up, and went back to sleep. So sweet. So young. So very innocent. And with no memory of the woman who died giving him life.

Anger welled inside him, old anger beside new angst. His mother-in-law was angry with him, Todd had almost suffered a grievous injury—or death, he admitted, which added a thick layer of reason to his mother-in-law's concerns—and no one in their right mind wanted to watch his children.

Doomed by his own ineptitude.

As he pulled off his shirt, a light turned on across the unkempt field separating his house from his neighbor. The barn door opened at the back of the yard, and Elle Drake emerged.

She turned, closed the barn, locked it, and moved toward the gracious oversized farmhouse.

He'd thought she'd go off on him after Todd's motorized fiasco in her yard, and she would've been well within her rights.

But she hadn't. She'd faced him and the boy and laid out a path of redemption. Todd had done the damage. Todd would fix his mistakes.

Such a simple concept. Why hadn't he thought of that?

He watched her climb the back steps. She opened the screen door, crossed the service porch, and walked into the house.

She'd left both doors to the house unlocked.

A thread of concern wound within him. Cedar Mills was a peaceful town except for some razor-sharp tongues, but there'd been a rash of burglaries on the outskirts of town the last few months. No one had been hurt, but the thought of his neighbor possibly walking in on strangers bothered him.

Her light blinked out, and Amos yawned. So did Matt. Calmer now, he finally crawled into bed and fell asleep next to his beloved little boy, even if he didn't smell all that good.

chapter six

Matt spotted Gloria's number in the office phone display the next morning. He wanted to send her straight to voice mail like he'd been doing the past several days, but eventually he'd have to talk to her.

The D'Amicos used to live in Cedar Mills. They'd moved to the other side of the county after losing Carrie, but they had plenty of local friends. They were regularly updated about the boys' antics, from the disastrous church trip to the cherry bomb incident. And no doubt they'd heard about the Stillers' dog and his partial neon-orange makeover. Matt had fronted a cool hundred dollars for the dog to be shaved down.

He hesitated, then grabbed up the phone because putting it off wouldn't make it go away. "Hello."

"Well, at least you answered this time." Gloria D'Amico used her scolding voice, the one she employed in court. The voice that said that nothing intimidated her. Ever. And she was always right, one of those traits where a little went a long way.

"Gloria, you know how busy life is right now," Matt explained again. "It's construction season, we're dodging rainstorms as best we're able, my father is recovering from heart surgery, and I've got three sons hell-bent on destruction. I would appreciate a little more understanding and a lot less flack. Could we at least agree on that, please?" Susan was sitting about six feet away in the small office space they shared in the foremost Morton building. She glanced up, met his gaze, and winced in sympathy.

"Here's what we can agree on." The clipped tone of Gloria's voice said she wasn't sparing sympathy for him, and she never hesitated to let everyone know why. "My grandsons need a strong role model in their lives, but more than that, they need someone who cares enough about them to put them first. Someone willing to put money aside and focus on them. *Their* needs, *their* skills, *their* safety, Matt. And you're not doing it."

"So last week you reamed me out about church, and now it's safety."

"Both are important in the real world." She clipped her tone purposely. "A reasonable adult would know that."

"Gloria," he paused because they'd been tap-dancing around this for the past year, and Matt was tired of it. Maybe he was just plain tired, but piling on Gloria's drama was more than he could deal with right now. "I haven't been able to do anything right since Carrie died, and frankly, it's getting old." He'd never spoken up to her in the past. He'd hemmed and hawed and tried to gloss things over, but right now all he wanted was for people to leave him alone. "You know my father's been sick, you know he had surgery, you know how busy this time of year is, and you know no court is going to give you my children—*my sons*—and yet you won't stop.

"Do you want me to cut off visitation with the boys?" he asked point-blank. "Because you're leaving me little recourse," he continued, ignoring her sputters on the other end of the call. "When they come home from seeing you, they're filled with stories about everything I'm doing wrong, and how their mother would have done this and that and the other thing. You're conflicting them, Gloria, and you're doing it on purpose. That's not fair."

"Not fair? I'm unfair?" Her voice rose exponentially. He'd never called her on her behavior before. He'd thought it would get better, but the opposite was true. She mourned the loss of her daughter. So did Big Al, her husband, Carrie's father.

Well, get in line, Matt thought, because he'd lost his fair share that day, too.

"I'll tell you what's unfair, Matthew Wilmot!"

Now he'd done it. He'd stood up for himself and opened the floodgates.

"It's unfair to bury a twenty-nine-year-old daughter. It's unfair to expect a wife to work, raise a family, and have so many children. A good man would understand the drain of pregnancy on a woman's system and exercise restraint, but not you! No, you had to have a third child."

She was complaining about Amos. Sweet, beloved, tender-hearted little Amos, the child who never knew a mother's touch. A baby who never nursed at Carrie's breast, who never gazed up into his mother's eyes. A perfect, beautiful little boy, already denied so much.

"Carrie would have been perfectly happy with two children, but she jumped through hoops to make you happy, Matt, and it was never enough." She clipped out the final words as if giving a closing statement to a jury. "Don't you dare talk to me about justice. Justice would be celebrating my beloved daughter's birthday in person next month. Ordering her favorite cake. Sending her flowers instead of planting them in the ground at Cedar Mills Cemetery.

"Be warned, Matthew," she continued. "People are keeping their eyes and ears open. I'll know exactly what's going on, even though I'm an hour away. I've helped prosecute a lot of people in my time. If I have to protect those boys by taking you to court, I won't hesitate to do so. You just think about that while you leave those sweet boys untended or with inept childcare providers. Their safety should be worth at least a little of your time. Don't you think?" She cut the connection, which saved him from saying things he shouldn't.

She'd never been a big fan of him as a son-in-law. He and Carrie used to laugh about it, because it was kind of funny.

It wasn't the least bit funny now. Her threats and anger cast a pall over everything, and Matt didn't doubt that she had folks reporting back about everything he and the boys did.

She never offered help, but why did she feel the need to be a hindrance? Did she really blame him for Carrie's death?

Well, he blamed himself—so they were on the same page there—because he'd liked the idea of a big family. So had Carrie. The thought of losing her with something as normal as pregnancy never occurred to either of them. And then she was simply…gone.

"I'm so sorry, Matt." Sympathy softened Susan's tone. She'd worked for Wilmot Excavating for over a decade, and there wasn't much Susan didn't know about the Wilmots or their business. On top of being a trusted employee, she was a solid friend. "That's a rock and a hard place if ever there was one."

"It sure is." And there was no end in sight. He was a man out of balance, and there was no time to figure out how to restructure things, because they hadn't been right in years. He walked out the door and got in the big rig to head for a posh neighborhood where three households had ordered new inground pools and wide-scalloped patios to surround the pools. Fairly quick, easy money compared to some other jobs they had lined up. Thinking that brought Gloria's words back to mind.

Did he think about money too much?

Looking around his house you wouldn't think so, but Matt knew the truth. The company was worth a great deal, but that expansion loan cinched the account strings mighty tight after last year's rain debacle. They drew good salaries, and the business was well-run, but there was no way they could afford a second bad year on top of his father's absence, in light of the money coming due. A solid season this year would make all the difference.

Movement to his left caught his attention. His neighbor was outside wearing some kind of long skirt or dress or…he had no idea what it was, but the way she moved in it, as if free, made him smile.

She was an odd duck. His mother used that expression, and he'd always thought it was a weird turn of speech, but it fit his neighbor. Tall and structured with short, kind-of-fun hair, she reminded him of those women who played a part in every chick flick, the cute heroine's neighbor or bestie, just plain enough so the heroine looked that much better.

She looked his way as the big rig rumbled down the wide drive his father had created on the off-side of the house.

He waved. He wasn't sure why he did it, because she had every reason to rue the day she bought the property close to his, but when she raised her arm and flashed him a smile, something softened up inside him.

He'd been dodging neighbors for over a year. If one wasn't complaining about the noise of the rigs pulling in and out, the other was complaining about dust, and of course the boys' nonsense had raised more than a few eyebrows.

Chin tucked, eyes down, he'd kept to himself on purpose until Elle Drake literally saved Todd's life.

He pulled onto the road and turned right. The weight of the rig sent dust into the air, successfully screening her, but for some reason, the everyday normality of waving to his neighbor made him feel a little better.

* * *

Matt Wilmot waved to her.

Elle felt like a gawky eighth grader when the most popular boy in class pauses in front of everyone to chat.

The whole thing was ridiculous. Elle knew it. She blamed it on being single for over two years and spending too much time alone. Maybe her mother was right. Maybe she should get out more if a neighbor's wave stirred up that much internal energy. In any case, the guy looked amazingly good in the cab of a monster-sized truck pulling a mammoth trailer and some kind of crazy-big shovel. The rumble of the rig only added to the moment.

The large grassy field between their properties offered enough space to keep her pottery safe from harm, but the size and stature of huge equipment had its own appeal to a former tomboy like Elle.

Elle had been headed for the potter's shed when the wave interrupted her before she resumed her path.

Familiar smells rose up to meet her as she opened the door. Clay and earth, fire and ice. Molten smells, hard smells, chemical smells. The light bounced from overhead, filling the viewing gallery and the workshop, chasing the shadows. Shapes of every kind leapt out at her. Curves and angles, at once warm and cool, beckoned. She grabbed a ball of clay and placed it on the bat, palms resting lightly, fingers dancing, letting her mind float free until her leg rocked forward and the wheel began to spin.

Her artist's hands splayed and molded, collapsed and shaped, until the beginning of a pot emerged beneath her fingers. Adjusting the speed of the wheel with her foot pedal, she alternately slowed and hastened, feeling the clay come alive against her skin. Head back, eyes closed, she didn't need to see this part of the ancient process. It was enough to feel, to let the work flow and mold beneath damp fingers.

She often sang while she threw. Hymns of old, songs of new. Or prayed silent prayers, her spoken voice more disconcerting than her singing one.

In the potter's shed, her tough façade made way for the warmth of woman. Her height and lankiness didn't seem out of place at the wheel. She was just right, the wheel proportioned to fit her stance perfectly. With the wheel and the clay she was on equal footing, not to be found lacking. By anyone.

She'd made a large batch of clay the previous week. Waiting now, calling to her, the various-sized clumps would be transformed into whatever shape, whatever size, whatever color her hands and the ensuing chemical changes wrought. Unlike her life, it was all up to her, to do as she pleased, totally under her control...

In the potter's shed.

chapter seven

"Well." Elle stood, stretched, and surveyed what she and Todd had gotten done that evening. Earlier in the day, she had cut the wooden slats to repair the rustic planter. When the boy stepped through the privet hedge along the front divide of properties, the slats were ready to be installed on what was left of her wishing well.

But watching the boy with a hammer had been almost painful. Not because he hit himself. He was far too slow for that. The tension in his face as he tried to do the job tugged at her heart.

She'd even rationalized buying a smaller hammer in town that afternoon, although at five foot nine she'd never had a problem wielding her full-weight Stanley.

"I'll get us a snack." Hoping he might be a little more confident if she wasn't nearby, she strode to the house for lemonade and cookies.

Covert action along the property line caught her attention as she glanced out the window. Two sets of round eyes peeked around the corner of the hedge, glances darting right and left. She saw the middle boy's mouth move. Then he cupped his hands around his mouth and called Todd's name. She couldn't hear the entire one-sided conversation, but she got the gist when she heard the word "cauldron."

Todd glanced at the house, fearful. Even from the window she saw the gulp. But then, God bless him, he turned back, stoic, and began hammering again.

The creak of the back porch door announced her arrival. When she turned the corner of the house, the two younger boys were nowhere to be seen. But something stirred the lower right section of the privet for a space of about three feet. She hid a grin as she set the cookies and lemonade on a level board.

"You deserve a break." She examined the latest nail. Not too bad. It wasn't yet flush, but he hadn't bent it this time. Definitely an improvement. She took a seat on the grass just outside the circular garden surrounding the wishing well. "So. How's school?"

He swallowed some lemonade and shrugged, eyes down.

"Do you have Miss Feldspar?"

He nodded.

She laughed. "She taught me when I was in school. Fourth grade, back then. She caught me drawing when I was supposed to be reading. Embarrassed me in front of the entire class. She warned me to get my priorities straight and then asked me what pleasure there would be in producing great works of art if I ended up illiterate. She then proceeded to take my drawing, roll it up, and put it away." That very drawing now hung, framed, in Miss Feldspar's third-grade room. Even back then her talent had been obvious to some. And Miss Feldspar had sponsored her to the tune of twelve hundred dollars a year when she went off to the art institute to pursue her dream. Her hands clenched, reflexively.

"Did you cry?"

She tucked her long legs Indian-style and leaned back. "Naw. I knew she was right. So I did my reading like I was supposed to, then practiced my drawing when I got home. Or at recess. I didn't have a lot of friends."

That fact garnered his attention. "None?"

"A couple. I was kind of different."

"Yeah." His glance around said she still might be considered that way, but he didn't seem nearly as intimidated. She nodded to his empty glass. "More?"

"Yeah."

She raised her eyebrows, holding the pitcher aloft, keeping her expression pointed.

"Yes, please," he amended and then watched as she filled the glass again.

"Have some more cookies, Todd," she encouraged. She kept her voice loud enough to carry to the rustling corner of the hedge. "You like chocolate chip, don't you?"

He nodded as he picked up a cookie. "They're my favorite."

"Well, good, then. Take all you want."

The bush almost danced. Little sounds that could never be mistaken for birds issued from it. Then, full tilt, the littlest Wilmot came running toward his big brother. He stopped by Todd, eyes wide, staring at the plate of freshly baked cookies. "Can I have one?"

"May I have one," she corrected.

He frowned in confusion.

"May I have one, please?" She repeated, giving him an expectant look.

"You already do." His face pinched in wonder. His gaze traveled from the cookie in her hand, then back to the plate where a pile still lay.

She couldn't check her smile completely. "What's your name?"

He worked his mouth, eyeing the cookies, then swallowed before he answered. "Amos."

She nodded. "Good, strong name. It means brave. Are you brave, Amos?"

He shook his head vigorously. She smiled. "Well, some names we have to grow into."

"What does my name mean?" Todd asked, his mouth half-full.

"Don't talk with your mouth full, Todd." She stretched out the name, thoughtfully. "Hmm. I may have to look that one up." She already had, but she wanted to string out the moment. "Oh, wait. Let me see. English. Meaning fox, wily and clever." She shifted her attention to the nearly completed lawn ornament. "Well, you've certainly been clever here."

"Really?" The quick flash of pride in the boy's eyes was reward enough for the exaggeration.

"Oh, yeah. We're almost done. With this phase, anyway."

He frowned once he deciphered her meaning. "This phase?"

She nodded as she watched Amos from the corner of her eye. He hadn't taken his eyes off the plate. His little-guy expression was almost spellbound. She decided to ease his pain. "You may have one when you ask politely."

Amos looked confused and surprised at the audacity of her expectation. But then his glance went back to the tray. "Please?"

She shook her head. "May I have a cookie, please?"

The ridge between his eyes grew deeper. "I said please."

"You need to use a whole sentence. You're a big boy."

"He's a baby." Todd gave his brother an exasperated look.

"Am not."

"Are too."

"Am…"

"Enough!" She eyed the two of them. "You." She looked at Todd full face. "Stop picking on your brother. You're older. And, you." She swiveled in the grass, redirecting her attention. "Are certainly old enough to talk in complete sentences. If you want a cookie, you need to ask the way I told you."

His expression darkened. She saw him weigh up the distance between her and the cookies. In a deliberate motion, she moved the plate closer to her side.

He thought a moment. A long moment. Then, tucking his lower lip back into his mouth, he muttered, "May I have a cookie, please?"

"Absolutely." She held out the plate. "Do you want to sit with me while Todd finishes up?"

A rattle from the telltale bush drew his attention. But the cookies and the sight of the fresh lemonade had him sinking down into the grass. The day was cool, typical for April. But the sun hinted warmth, and the hedge blocked the northeast wind, always a chiller in spring. She cocked her head to the littlest boy. "Would you like some lemonade, Amos?"

He nodded eagerly. She made a show of standing up. "I'll get a glass." Ignoring the bushes completely, she walked back to the house. No sooner had she rounded the corner of the porch than Randy darted from his hiding place, raced to the plate, grabbed two cookies from the top, and ran back to the anonymity of his bush.

She smiled to herself at his daring. When she returned with the glass, she studied the cookie plate in mock surprise. Todd watched her nervously. His eyes darted from her to the plate to the bush. Amos was oblivious, his eyes trained on the lemonade she was pouring.

"Oh, boys, I forgot to tell you. The two cookies that were in the middle of the plate? The biggest, chocolatiest ones of all?" She made a face of exaggerated regret. "I have to apologize because they may have inadvertently been poisoned."

Todd's movements came to an immediate stop. "What?"

She pointed to the plate for emphasis. "Yours were fine, Todd. And yours too, Amos. But I had set two cookies right there on top that may have come in contact with a rare, anticoagulant virus that affects little boys especially hard. You didn't eat them, did you?"

Todd gulped. Amos looked from the plate to the bush as if finally getting it. Kind of. Then they both shook their heads. "Good." She nodded briskly. "I thought I put them right there on top, but I could have been mistaken. I meant to throw them away, then got busy with something else. Such a hurry, you know." She beamed an angelic smile at the pair while they looked from each other to the bush multiple times. A bush that was now surprisingly still.

Gotcha.

chapter eight

"What's wrong?" Matt hurried to the bedroom where the sound of Randy's mewling and retching pierced the spring night air.

"He's sick, Dad." Todd looked worried. Very worried. And while that wasn't unusual, his distress seemed genuine.

"I see that. Here, lie down, son. Let me check you over." He lifted the boy onto the lower bunk, his hands gently palpating. After a moment, he shook his head. "No fever, no stiffness. What hurts, Randy?"

"Everything. But mostly my belly." He elongated the word belly into multiple syllables. "I think I've been poisoned."

"Poisoned?" With all that had been happening lately, adding poison to the list of potentially fatal catastrophes didn't seem improbable. Matt's stomach dropped to the vicinity of his feet. His throat constricted. "Did you get into the medicine cabinet? Or my chemicals?"

"Noooo…"

"What did you eat?" Matt's mind ran the gamut of possibilities. If not the medicine cabinet or the locked chemical cupboard of the business operation, what could it be? Cleaning supplies?

"Cookies." With the single word the boy groaned, his clasped hands grabbing his belly. "Poisoned cookies."

"What?" Matt looked from Todd to Randy and back again. Thank heavens Amos slept on, oblivious to the excitement of a poisoned older brother. "Who put poison on the cookies?" Saying it, he couldn't believe the idiocy of the question.

"The wiiiiiiitch." Randy drew the title out, his voice fading painfully at the end.

"What witch? There's no such thing as a witch, Randy. What are you talking about? Who put poison on the cookies?" His voice was spiking out of control, but nowhere near the panic level building within. He grabbed the boy by the shoulders, ready to shake answers out of him before he set about saving the kid's life. "What kind of poison was it?"

"A big name."

He turned at the sound of Todd's voice. "What? What big name?"

"Anti-something something. I've never heard of it before."

"Where did you get it?"

Todd shook his head vigorously. "I didn't get it, Dad. My cookies were fine. And really good, too."

Matt stopped. Took a breath. Then saw Randy writhe once more, his hands clasped tight to his little belly. "I mean where did he get the poison, Todd?"

"I told you, Dad. The wiiiiiiitch." Randy moaned the last a little too loud and long with exaggerated conviction.

His drama calmed Matt's adrenalin rush. He took a seat on the edge of Randy's bed. "So. Some witch gave you cookies. Just stopped by and started handing out goodies to all the little children, hmm?"

"No, Dad." Todd rolled his eyes because Matt wasn't getting it. "She brought out a plate of cookies to share when we were working on the wishing well."

"The witch was at Miss Drake's?"

"She issss Miss Draaaaaaaaake." The extended drama behind the mournful wail was Oscar-worthy.

"Oh." He nodded as if filled with newfound understanding. "I see. Miss Drake's a witch."

"Yes." Todd whispered the word, but looked kind of regretful, like maybe he hoped she wasn't a witch.

"I wasn't aware." Matt aimed sad, puppy-dog eyes to his younger son. "And she poisoned you, boy?"

"Yeeeeeessss," Randy moaned, his expression pained.

"Not on purpose." Todd leapt to the woman's defense, and it was kind of nice to see his shy son taking a stand. "She didn't know anyone was going to eat the poisoned cookies. Randy snuck 'em."

"You stole cookies from Miss Drake?" The shock in Matt's voice surprised Randy. He stopped clutching his belly. His gaze darted from Matt to Todd and back.

"I didn't steal 'em."

"Did too," Todd declared.

"Did not."

"Did…"

"Knock it off before I kill you both. You." He pointed a firm finger at Todd. "Go brush your teeth and get ready for bed. And you." He turned back to Randy, his voice firm. "Will write a note of apology to Miss Drake for stealing her cookies. Right now."

"But what if I die?" Randy wailed.

"Then we'll have a real nice funeral. Knock off the theatrics, get up, get to the kitchen, and start writing. There's paper on my desk."

Randy followed the directions as if insulted, his footfall pounding angrily across the tiles. Matt stood, his gaze drawn to the window overlooking the small field separating his home from that of his neighbor.

Her lights were on, the soft, gold glow burning steadily from the east side of the house. The back building was bright as well; the bank of windows stretching around the corner of the shed to the north face beyond were lit from within. The soft light cast a glow into the yard adjacent like one of those pretty paintings you see all over. He felt Todd creep to his side. He put an arm around the boy's thin shoulders.

"Randy says that's where she makes it."

He frowned and tilted his chin down. "Makes what?" The boy's eyes were trained on the lighted, barn-like shed well behind Miss Drake's house.

"The poisons." His tone said "duh."

"Really?" Matt pretended interest to draw Todd out.

"Yeah. She has an oven."

"So do we, Todd."

"No. Different from ours, I guess."

"Mm-hmm. Well, until you know for sure, I'd keep your opinions to yourself. There are no witches. There's no such thing."

Randy picked that moment to hurry back around the corner, his poisoning momentarily forgotten as he scurried to his bed. He offered a piece of paper to his father that read, *I'm sorry I took your poyzen cookies.*

Matt accepted his efforts. "This will do nicely. You may take it to her tomorrow."

Randy's face blanched. "Can't you?"

Matt lifted his shoulders. "I'm not the one she poisoned. Your brother has to do some chores for her to help work off the building materials for the wishing well. You can go over when he does."

"But…"

"Good night, Randy. Sweet dreams."

* * *

Randy looked like he was walking Stephen King's "green mile" the next afternoon. He trudged at Matt's side, head down, body quaking. The last was inflated in an unsuccessful quest to garner Matt's sympathy. Todd walked firmly, unfettered by guilt. It was a strange reversal of roles for the boys, to have the older one's confidence leading the way. Matt paused at his neighbor's drive and sent the boys on ahead as he watched.

He'd promised to walk Randy back home. He glanced at his watch, conflicted. He still had initial grading to finish in Sweet Hills. Junie Oliver had come over to babysit. Her mother ran the day care in town. She watched Amos and other children daily. He hired Junie, hoping she'd learned from her mother's example. She was watching Amos and would marshal Randy once he'd confessed his wrongdoing. Matt could only hope the boy made it quick so that he could make the most of the remaining daylight hours and finish the site he was working on.

He straightened as Elle came around the corner of her house, a long, funny dress swirling with the movement. He studied her, watching as she twirled in the sun. In the dress, she looked even taller and more angular than she normally did. But younger somehow. Carefree.

Her short bob of pale blonde hair moved in the east wind that kicked up its heels a little more fiercely today. She spotted the boys and strode forward, pausing in front of Randy.

He was too far away to see her eyes, but her stance indicated she was playing hardball with the little insurrectionist. And despite her stern demeanor, Todd seemed easy in her company, and Matt couldn't remember a time when Todd seemed comfortable around others.

He liked the change.

* * *

Elle hurried outside the following afternoon. Her potter's sack billowed in the wind. She laughed, spinning in careless abandon, the bright, country colors of the sack turning with her.

Then she saw the boys. "Oh. Hello." Standing still, she tilted her head, flashing a welcome smile to Todd and a look of interest to Randy.

"Go on." Todd elbowed his little brother. "Give it to her."

She waited patiently as the six-year-old considered. His chin was so low it almost met his toes, and his shoulders were hunched with fear. Or guilt. *Good.*

"Do you have something for me, young man?" She kept her voice firm.

Still Randy hesitated.

"Go on," Todd insisted, giving him a shove. "I have work to do."

Elle appreciated Todd's willingness to right a wrong, and the fact that he was standing up to his brother was a definite plus. She tilted her head, folded her arms, and cleared her throat. "If you have something for me, I need it now. Todd and I have to get to work."

The boy shook. She almost caved, but from the easy stance of the child's father, she figured the kid would probably live through the confrontation. Matt Wilmot looked calm but impatient as he glanced at his watch one more time. She stooped and reached out a hand. "Is this for me?" Her look indicated the folded piece of paper Randy held tightly in his left hand.

"Y-y-yes." The stammer was endearing, but a little too frantic for believability.

"May I have it?"

Silently he handed it over, his shoulders quivering as she read the confession. She fought the urge to laugh out loud. When she'd read the missive, she let him suffer in silence for long, slow beats of her watch. Then she spoke. "So. You took the cookies."

The shaking became more exaggerated. "Yeah."

"And how did you feel last night?" She bent lower so he could see her look of concern.

"My belly hurt." His little reply was barely a whisper.

"The poison wore off by this morning," offered Todd helpfully.

"Well, I'm glad of that." She straightened, eyeing the note. Then she turned a stern look to the middle Wilmot. "Look at me please, Randy."

He raised his head slowly, a boy on his way to the gallows. Elle met his gaze. "Usually when people steal, they get punished. But I think spending an evening with a little-known poison pulsing throughout your system was a high enough price. And you were very brave to come over here and confess to me. I admire bravery. And honesty. So does God." She nodded for emphasis, as if punctuating the thought. "Next time you want something, please ask."

His head bounced up and down. He lifted his gaze to her and stammered. "They were real good, 'cept for the poison."

"One of the best batches I've ever made," Elle agreed. "Guaranteed to put some meat on your bones."

Sudden fear widened Randy's eyes. He glanced from her to the potter's shed, then back. He took little steps backward, almost tripping, and his face looked pinched. Then he swiveled and ran across the drive to his waiting father. Matt lifted a hand in acknowledgment. She raised hers in return before dropping an easy hand on Todd's shoulder. "You ready to work, kid?"

He nodded. "Yeah."

She steered him toward a door in the corner of the small barn. "Ever take care of chickens?"

He shook his head. "Dad says pets are too much responsibility, and he doesn't have time to be responsible now."

She almost laughed, but caught herself in time. "Well, these girls aren't exactly pets. I use them for eggs."

"Huh?" Todd looked baffled.

"The hens lay eggs. Every day. I collect them in the morning and at night." Deftly reaching under a hen, she pulled out a coffee-colored egg. He stared.

"It's brown."

She nodded. "These are Rhode Island Reds. It's a kind of chicken," she added, seeing his puzzled look. "Just like there are different kinds of dogs, there are different kinds of chickens. These lay brown eggs."

"I don't like brown eggs." The boy's voice was absolute.

"You don't like them, Sam-I-Am?" She laughed at the bemused expression he angled toward her. "Sorry. Couldn't resist. Anyway, we're going to clean out the henhouse. First, we'll take this short broom and sweep out all the old nesting material. Then we'll rake it up, clean up the pecking yard, wheelbarrow it all over to the compost pile behind the barn, and spread new straw for the girls to nest in."

"It smells." He wrinkled his nose.

"Yes, it does."

By the time she had overseen that job and the feeding that came after it, she figured he'd had enough for one day. As they walked back from behind the barn, with Todd maneuvering the now-empty wheelbarrow, he pointed to a large puddle off the edge of the access path. "That's a lot of water."

She followed his gaze. "My gutters are leaking, and the septic system isn't leaching properly. I keep getting standing water there, and with all the rain we've had this spring, it just hasn't gone away."

"My dad could fix it."

"Could he?" She smiled at the obvious pride in the boy's voice.

"Oh, yeah. He knows all about septic systems and drainage. He teaches me all the time so I can help him when I'm bigger."

"That's great, Todd. But try to resist the urge to jump on one of those earthmovers and do the job yourself, OK?"

He ducked his chin while she laughed and smoothed a hand over his straight hair. "Want some cookies?" she asked as they paused by the back step.

"Yeah. I mean, yes, please."

"It's getting late. Is Junie babysitting at your place?" When he nodded, she continued, "I'll wrap a few up to send home for all of you. You share, OK?"

He nodded. "I will."

Stepping inside, she held the door and looked back at him. "Would you like to come in?"

He hesitated. Then, squaring his shoulders, he walked up the steps. "Yes, please." Stepping in, she saw him look around the room, eyeing her living space.

The open upper cupboards, a look she'd loved but now abhorred as too labor intensive. She'd gained a greater appreciation for doors with the daily dust generated by Wilmot Excavating trucks lumbering up and down the gravel drive. Staggered shelves displayed folk art of all kinds. Plaster, glass, metal, wood. She mixed mediums in a slapdash way, the result a hodgepodge of quaint and gritty. Her own work sat amongst the rest, little pieces she'd fired for her own enjoyment, her own use. The little sugar and creamer set she'd made in bright, whimsical tones, a band of vibrant pansies rimming the top. She couldn't begin to count how many of those she'd sold in the past fifteen years.

Funny. Her work decorated both the president's quarters and the Ohio governor's mansion, but one of her favorite pieces was a simple set of breakfastware.

"Here are the cookies." She handed him a bag with the top creased tightly. "No poisoned ones today."

His nod was sober. "Thank you, Miss Drake." He started for the door, head down. But then he brought it up and glanced around. "I like your house."

The spontaneity of his sweet words pleased her. "Thank you, Todd. I'll see you day after tomorrow."

He nodded, his hand on the door. "Right after school."

chapter nine

Three days later she came out of the pharmacy as Matt Wilmot left the post office next door, lugging two large boxes in capable hands. "Can I open the truck for you, Mr. Wilmot?"

"Matt, please. And yes, thanks. I'd appreciate it."

He set the two boxes in the back of the extended cab Dodge, then leaned against the door to look at her. His face was serious, but his gray eyes looked amused. His hair, dark and wavy and in need of a cut, moved in the spring breeze. The soft wind brought a sweet, spiced scent her way, the kind of fragrance that invited her closer. Therefore she purposely kept a firm distance. "Poisoned cookies, huh?"

She glanced away as she fought a smile. Then she shrugged lightly. "Mishaps occur despite our most strident precautions."

His face creased in a grin. "The precarious life of a thief is wrought with risk. He apologized in good form, I take it?"

"With a little extra shaking and quaking to convince me of his sincerity."

"Which is probably not nearly as sincere as it should be." Exasperation colored his tone. "Did Todd finish up with you all right?"

The wind shifted a sweep of hair across her cheek. Elle lifted a hand and brushed it back. "He did great. By the third day, he was quite comfortable working around the house and the yard. I was wondering if I could hire his services now that he's comfortable around me. I tend to get caught up in work and lose track of time. If Todd could do odd jobs around the place to keep me on an even keel, I'd be grateful. And he's good company."

* * *

Caught up in work, she said, like he should know what she did.

He didn't, and wouldn't Gloria love that? To find out he let Todd get a job with a stranger who happened to live next door. And who looked kind of sweet and quaint in long dresses and made really good cookies. But the threats hanging over him were real, and Matt wasn't stupid enough to risk giving Gloria more ammunition, so he stalled for time. "He's only eight. That's a little young, isn't it?"

"I think it would be a confidence builder for him. And it probably wouldn't hurt to separate him from his younger brother now and again. He's good with his hands and an avid worker."

Matt recognized the truth in that. Randy's aggressive personality took over Todd's meeker countenance too often. Still he hesitated.

"If I promise not to poison him?" Her voice was serious, but her eyes were teasing.

"Well, there's that." Matt thought a moment, then gave cautious agreement because lately, everything he'd said yes to went bad. "If he really wants to do it, I won't object."

"Now there's a ringing endorsement."

"No, I didn't mean it that way. It's just..."

She jumped to the defensive and didn't let him finish. "You don't have to explain, Mr. Wilmot."

"Matt," he said again.

Her tone went cool and decisive. "We don't really know each other, but if you ask around the town, you'll find the rumors of my eccentricities to be true. I do things my own way, and that sets some tongues wagging. But I'm good with kids, even undisciplined ones, and I think I can help Todd develop his self-confidence."

He zeroed in on one word. "Undisciplined? You think my boys are undisciplined?"

"You think they're not?" The surprise in her voice was enough to push him over the edge.

"Let me tell you something. My boys have dealt with more in their young lives than any kid should have to face. And I think, despite your no doubt well-informed although childless opinion, I'm doing an OK job."

Her expression said otherwise as she ticked off her fingers. "In the past three weeks, they've exploded cherry bombs, stolen my clothesline, painted a stray dog, attempted to hang their little brother playing Wild Wild West, and run amok with a piece of heavy machinery in my yard, successfully taking out both a perennial garden and a sizeable lawn ornament. Any two of those would offer tangible support to my assessment. Taken as a whole, I rest my case."

The list *did* sound undisciplined, possibly life-threatening, and long, but that didn't stanch Matt's anger. His stomach clenched, and his hands fisted at his sides. Didn't he try to do his best? It was next to impossible to find a babysitter adept enough to handle three adventurous growing boys. Hadn't Carrie always said a good imagination was a boy's best friend? He rounded the truck and climbed into the cab, not trusting himself with words. He slammed the door, shoved the truck into first, and roared away, leaving the woman staring after him.

He got half a block up the road before he realized his behavior wasn't much better than his boys'. When he got to the intersection, he glanced back. She stood perfectly still, looking after him. Then, with a slight shrug, she turned and walked away, her chin tucked in defeat.

He felt like a jerk. Hadn't Todd looked stronger, healthier going over there? Hadn't he stood up to Randy more than once this week, holding his ground? He made a decision, bit back a groan, then shoved the truck into reverse, glad there was little traffic this early in the day. He ground to a halt alongside her car. "Elle?"

He knew his voice was gruff. He didn't care.

She looked up, surprised.

"He'll start tomorrow if he's willing."

She blinked and said nothing, but he thought he saw a ghost of a smile touch her lips. Nodding, he pulled away with the odd feeling that he'd just taken a huge step forward. Toward what, he didn't know.

But it felt momentous.

chapter ten

The old dream haunted when Matt needed sleep the most. Was it worry that brought it on, because they'd had two major pieces of equipment break down this week, on top of short staff and boys harboring a death wish?

Psych 101 probably had a label for it. Matt didn't want a stupid label. He just wanted seven hours of unbroken sleep, something that hadn't happened much in four years.

He could handle the kids breaking into his sleep time. They were kids, after all. But not the recurring dream.

Why now, during such a crazy, busy time, with his father still out and his workload swelling? He needed sleep, but almost every night, just shy of four A.M., he relived the scene. Newborn Amos in his arms, eyes buttoned shut against the fluorescent light, and the doctor striding his way, pulling down his surgical mask.

In the dream, he anticipated the doctor's words and edged back, as if moving away from the obstetrician would change the outcome.

Reality had been quite different. He'd moved forward, holding his newborn son, waiting to be told he could go see his wife.

And then the doctor had him give the baby over to the nurse, ushered him into an alcove, and broke the news. Carrie had thrown a pulmonary embolism and died.

Just like that his life turned upside down. Joy became sorrow, and time became something to get through.

He crawled out of bed reluctantly, knowing the May sun would join him soon. The boys were still asleep, and he went through the morning motions as if everything were all right, as if any of this was normal.

It wasn't, but he did it anyway, burying himself in writing job proposals while drinking strong black coffee.

His phone rang with a call from his mother about the same time Amos dashed downstairs. He picked up the phone and the sleep-tousled preschooler, determined to sound normal. "Hey, Mom, how's everything? How's Dad doing?"

"Chomping at the bit," she told him. "Wishing he could be back on the job, and wondering how you're holding up. He's on edge and fret-ting over not being there, not doing his share. Tell me something that will settle him down a bit."

Of course he was on edge. Without seeking Matt's advice, his father had created the timeline they labored under now, but when did a father listen to a son? He sighed and lied smoothly. "Everything's good. We're swamped with work, but I've got Jason's crew overseeing the Wessington development, and I'm on Sweet Hills, and as soon as we're caught up there, I'm moving to do the scheduled excavation for the ice rink in the town square. Then on to the strip mall while Jason takes on the wing for the Veteran's Outreach. By that point, Dad should be back, and we'll reassess the schedule to see what can be done before the fall weather turns. Tell Dad I'll stop by tomorrow night and go over everything with him if he follows your directions. The contracts alone should be enough to calm him down."

They wouldn't, Matt knew, because the down payments on these jobs wouldn't meet the bank's requirement late winter. If they completed the jobs—barring inclement weather or catastrophe—they could still do it. But it would take nearly eight months of solid work, signed, sealed, and delivered.

"Well, calming your father down is an unlikely scenario," she answered, "and you know that, but he would like to be brought up to date. He hates being immobile, and if you fill him in, I won't have to strangle him. The choice is yours, darling."

Matt laughed because Mary Lou Wilmot was the gentlest creature alive. And she'd been available to help with the boys occasionally before his father's heart attack. A quadruple bypass later, she was full-time nurse and facilitator while Matt and Jase ran the business and Matt floundered for after-school care.

"Dad knows there couldn't have been a worse time to get sick," she went on. "Good weather and a jump on construction season is huge. And the pool contracts are a sweet deal, on top of the new subdivision. I'm impressed, Matt. So is your father."

The stronger economy was inspiring lots of folks to risk home-improvement loans, and inground pools had become a pricey current rage. Each one contracted would be like frosting on the cake once they were done. "Thank you. Flexing our wings is good for us, both of us." He didn't mention that he'd been picking up Jase's slack far too regularly. "We've been taught by the best, and we're making decisions that would please Dad, at least most of the time. It's OK to not mention that last part to Dad."

"Oh, I won't, because I am not a glutton for punishment! Matt, I'm sorry I'm not around to help with the boys more. You must be going half-crazy. Have you found help?" she asked. "Anyone who can handle them?"

He hadn't, but instead of saying no outright, his neighbor's image popped into his brain. Her no-nonsense manner, her eccentric humor, her quick assessments. "The boys are adept at driving sitters crazy, but my neighbor is helping out some. Todd's doing some work for her."

A long pause greeted his words, and then his mother asked, "Todd? Really?" in a voice that said successful Middle East peace talks would have been more expected than Matt letting Todd do something like this.

"Yeah." He didn't mention why Todd was working on those initial projects, or that the boy had almost killed himself. Some things were better left unmentioned to mothers. "She likes his work."

"Matt, that's wonderful!" She sounded really happy to hear this, which meant Matt had pleased two people with a decision concerning

his children, his neighbor and his mother. Lately, that was some kind
of record.

"It's good for him. He's really enjoying some independence."

"Sure he is. That's so important for kids! I'm really glad to hear this,
Matt."

Too glad, Matt decided, which meant she too thought he was messing
up in the child-raising department. "Boys are getting up. Gotta go,
Mom. Give my love to Dad."

"Will do, and tell Todd I'm proud of him. Never mind, I'll call him
later and tell him myself."

"Sounds good." He'd deliberately left the equipment breakdowns
out of the equation. His father didn't handle lost time well when he
was healthy. Getting him riled up about it now would do no good.
He'd shoulder the angst of that to protect his father's recovery. There'd
be plenty to do once Daniel was back at the helm. For the moment,
getting him strong and healthy was the focus. Right along with keeping
his boys alive and the company running smoothly.

* * *

"Elle, I love that you're back home, but you need to get out more,"
Aggie Drake breezed into Elle's kitchen that afternoon. "Out of this
house, out of the shed, out with people! You're young and beautiful..."

Elle controlled a quick comeback. Arguing her mother's broad defi-
nitions of youth and beauty would only frustrate them both.

"You're too secluded," Aggie finished. She opened her bag and posi-
tioned her laptop on the broad kitchen table before she tossed her chic
jacket onto the back of a chair and took a seat.

"I'm on a two-lane road, in full view of my neighbors and any passing
traffic." Elle pulled out a pitcher of unsweetened tea, one of the few
things they both liked. "No one in their right mind would call this
reclusive." Her mother's well-meaning concern mimicked Kate's, but
the pair of them, dainty and feminine, would never get it. They couldn't
get it by right of exclusion.

She'd been born the ugly duckling in a family of swans. Unlike the sweet fable, no metamorphosis turned her into anything other than a tall, angular, plain woman. She loved them both, but they were so much alike, a true mother-daughter duo, petite, blonde, curvy, and feminine.

Elle had always been set apart. She knew it. They knew it. Right now she just wanted everyone to leave her alone. Why was that such a difficult concept in her big Polish family? She poured tea, then finished placing a boxed oval platter in its nest of shipping peanuts while her mother brought up an Excel spreadsheet. "You had a call nearby?" Aggie was an insurance adjustor for a group of local agents.

"Next door."

The thought of something happening to the Wilmot boys brought Elle's chin up quickly. "At the Wilmots'? Are the boys OK?"

Aggie waved off her concern. "Not the Wilmots. The Kretzkes. They own the ranch house west of here. Some kind of electrical foul-up blew their circuit panel and damaged the basement wall. No biggie."

"Oh." She was relieved that it wasn't her troublemaking little neighbors to the east. Todd had been working for her for nearly two weeks. He'd done a wonderful job of taking over chores she shrugged off. The henhouse, now fully enclosed by chicken-wire fencing, was always neat and clean, its biweekly mucking just enough to keep it environment-friendly. He'd helped her move flowers and had actually done a pretty decent job of cleaning the kitchen one day when she'd lost herself in clay for long hours. She only had one broken glass to show for it, which he'd swept up very nicely.

"I see your puddle has grown," remarked her mother. "And gotten smEller. The clock's ticking, Elle. It's got to get fixed."

Elle flushed. "I know. I keep meaning to call someone to fix it, but the idea of strangers with big equipment tearing around so close to the pottery shed makes me quake."

Aggie stayed intent on the pale screen before her as her fingers moved swiftly across the keyboard. "You need to lighten up. It's not like they're going to run a bulldozer into the shed. They'll dig a hole, clear the old leach lines, put new ones in, and cover it all back up. Probably two days' work. Maybe three. You've got to get this done."

Once the box was sealed, Elle sat down opposite her mother. "I will. But I'm in the middle of next year's *Lily* collection, and I can't afford to break concentration to monkey around with huge earthmoving equipment outside the window."

"Well, you need to." Her mother's voice was absolute.

"I'll look into it," she promised as her mother sat back. She right-clicked with a decisive move and shut down her computer.

"Done." Aggie took a long swallow of the fresh, cold tea. "This is such a good blend, Elle. Better than anything I can buy."

Elle took the hint and crossed to the old-fashioned jelly cupboard. She pulled open the beadboard door and withdrew a sealed jar, then filled an envelope full of crushed tea leaves, blended with spices and peels. "I think it's the blend of ginger and citrus that makes this one so good."

"Whatever it is, it works," agreed her mother. She rose and hugged Elle. "You have an innate talent for knowing what goes well together, my girl. But an uncommon desire to be alone. I heard Will Michaels asked you out."

Elle did snort this time. Her mother winced at the sound. "Really, Elle."

"Will Michaels is about as pompous and stodgy as they come. You couldn't possibly think I'd consider dating him?"

"Or anyone," Aggie noted with a wry look.

Elle looped an arm around the older woman's shoulders. "The choices are somewhat limited in Cedar Mills. Of course there is old Mr. Thornton. He's been widowed nearly thirty years now. I'm expecting him to come calling any day."

"Elle." Her mother looked stressed. "Just because things didn't work out with Alex, doesn't mean they can't work out with someone."

The irony of her three-decades-long-single mother making the suggestion seemed lost on Aggie, and Elle wasn't about to dredge that up, but she'd moved beyond the age of dating advice a lot of years ago. "How many men do you know who want a nearly forty-year-old barren wife that got short-changed in the looks department?"

"You're absurd." Aggie waved off her objections. "You have this skewed self-image. I wish you could look in the mirror and see what we see. A beautiful, gracious, accomplished woman."

"Accomplished, yes. The rest is nice, but it's not like I need the sweet-talking, Mama." She leaned her head against her mother's. "I like who I am. I just—"

"Wanted a family."

"Desperately." She made a face of regret. "That was always my goal, a kid or two to dote on, just like you did with us, even though you did it all on your own. Kate and I couldn't have had a better mother. I wish it had been part of God's plan, but apparently not." She thought she'd moved beyond the bitterness of disappointment, but lately it weighed harder and heavier. She laid the blame on the stupid April birthday.

Aggie clasped Elle's hands and brought them up for her kiss. "From such hands and heart come much wonder," she murmured in a rare display of sentimentality. She turned toward the shed. "Show me the newest *Lily*."

The *Lilies* began six years before as a single project, inspired by life, lack, and love. In each project, there were always children, as if intrinsic to the scene. In the first edition, sold out long ago and with ridiculously high resale value now, were little children. Dressed in simple tunics, they played along a dusty road, a road that seemed to lead to nowhere in particular, with a bank of lilies offset. And there, beyond the flowers, a hint of Christ's welcome in spilled light, bringing hope into the world, a new world for those children and all to come.

And when the U.S. president's wife had ordered a copy, she set the tone. In less than a year, a facsimile had gone into mass production, opening a new venue for her personal designs through Hyland Manor, a well-respected manufacturer.

She thought she'd arrived—married to a software guru, financially blessed from multiple directions. Her beautiful creations garnered a huge following that had mushroomed over the years.

Many of her struggling artist friends had turned their backs on her. Was it jealousy or disdain? Elle didn't know, but art purists considered mass production a sellout, and as Elle's fame spiraled up, her friendships thinned along with her hopes for a child.

They'd tried everything.

But after years of tests, interventions, false hopes, and dashed dreams, there had been no baby and no hope for one other than adoption. Elle had been ready to make that leap.

Alex had had other ideas. He had kindly explained that he'd been seeing someone else for quite a while—although how he justified that when he had a perfectly good wife at home, she wasn't sure—and that he was filing for divorce so he could marry his gorgeous supermodel girlfriend.

Elle left Massachusetts six months after the divorce.

She hadn't wanted to come back to Cedar Mills and the small-town gossip atmosphere she loathed. But there was family here, and she loved them.

If she'd still been a struggling artist, she could have stayed in New England. The artist colonies welcomed those like themselves, but once she wasn't struggling for those sales and contracts, she wasn't nearly as welcome in their midst.

Her mother reached out a hand to the shed door, interrupting her thoughts.

Elle forestalled her with an arm. "Hang on, Mom. Close your eyes. This new one is different, and I want you to see it with the light just right." She opened the door and hit the switch. A bank of lights spotlit featured pieces or collections in the gallery. The newest *Lily* project sat front and center, bathed in light. She turned back to her mother. "OK. Now."

Aggie opened her eyes. She stood silent and still, then moved forward in little steps. "Oh, Elle."

"You like it."

A single tear tracked a path down Aggie's cheek. "I love it. It's intrinsically perfect, Elle."

"*The Beauty of the Lilies.*"

Her mother turned. "From 'The Battle Hymn of the Republic.'"

"And the Bible. And my heart."

She'd put her heart right there in the design of a blue-and-gold-trimmed plate rim surrounding an image of a mother and child in a field of lilies. The figures seemed almost transparent, but what shone through the image was the mother's complete love for the child she cherished against her breast.

"It's so completely different from what you've done before, Elle." Aggie stroked a finger across the beautiful scene. "How long did it take to create the imagery?"

"That's just it." Elle looked at the intricate images on the finished piece and sighed. "I didn't really create it, not in the usual sense. It's more like it flowed out of me one night as the music was playing and the moon was high. I could see her there, holding the baby as the moon shone down, the flowers blooming around her."

"You've brought transcendence to life in Mary's hope and faith."

"And longing." Elle studied the work of her hands. "Do you feel that, too? The longing in her to be the best mother she can be?"

"I do."

She smiled.

"Is this what Hyland Manor expected?"

"We'll find out soon. I've submitted the pictures and samples. We'll see if I've met their expectations. And if not?" She shrugged. "I met mine, and that's the most important part of all."

"Oh, honey." Aggie slipped her arm around Elle's waist. "Of course they'll love it. It's stunning."

Elle, too, wanted them to love the new work, but not because of the money or the increased following of her creations. She wanted them to

love the design so more people would see the shining love of a sacrificial mother for her infant child.

The *Lilies* series wasn't bold like her Asian floral series. It wasn't
romantic like some of her early gardens that had a more Kinkade-style
feeling.

Pure peace and contentment called from this design. A call to
worship. A song of praise. Aggie blessed herself, and Elle smiled to
see it.

"I'm glad you like it, Mom. I wanted you to."

"It's the best you've done."

Elle angled her head, considering. "So far."

chapter eleven

Elle spotted Matt and the boys in church that Sunday morning. His efforts to blend in fell short. Todd read to Amos in a slightly loud voice, which drew stares from the people around them. Randy made Amos cry, and Matt looked none too peaceful by the time Father Murphy blessed the congregation. Seeing Todd tug Matt's arm in her direction afterward, she paused.

They hadn't spoken since that day in the street when he'd taken offense at her remark. He'd allowed Todd to work, and she was grateful not only for the help but the trust that implied. "Morning, boys." She smiled down as they approached.

Randy's socks were unmatched, Amos clutched a bag of Cheerios like it was the last meal on the planet, and Todd's cowlicks made his hair look downright crazy.

"Miss Drake!" Todd hurried forward, excitement in his eyes. "I got ninety on my math test and moved into the Blue Group for reading."

She capped his head with her hand. "Blue Group, huh? That's some pretty good reading there, buddy. Keep up the good work." She smiled down at him, then raised her eyes to his father. "Good morning."

"Miss Drake." He used the formal name politely, his eyes cool.

She sighed inside. Was he really a grudge-holder? That was downright stupid. And right out of church, besides. The Holy Spirit had his work cut out with this guy.

"How are you, Randy?"

The boy shied away deliberately, which meant he wasn't one hundred percent sure she wouldn't roast him if she had the chance. "Good."

Amos stuck out his book. "Todd readed this to me."

She squatted to check out the slim volume and didn't minimize her appreciation. "Wow. *The Berenstain Bears and Too Much Birthday*. That sounds good."

He wriggled in agreement, his round face and big eyes shining. "It was weally, weally good. I wike Bwother Bear best."

"I like him, too." Elle smiled into the little guy's eyes, and when he smiled back, it was as if his joy blessed her heart.

"Daddy's taking us to breakfast," Todd told her. "Can you come, too?"

She and Matt demurred in unison.

"Oh, I'm sorry, honey, but…," she began.

"I'm sure Miss Drake has other things to do."

The way he said it meant he *wanted* her to have other things planned, and because Elle wasn't real fond of being told what to do, she directed her very best and brightest smile at Todd. "Actually, it turns out I have nothing pressing today after all." She ignored the inner voice reminding her of the deadline for the upcoming East Coast tour. "I'd love to go to breakfast with you gentlemen."

Matt didn't groan but looked like he wanted to. Todd whirled. "Did you hear that, Dad? Miss Drake is coming to breakfast with us!"

"I heard." The boy's enthusiasm didn't appear to be contagious, but right now, Elle didn't care. "We're going to The Sugar Maple on Thorne Road," Matt reluctantly told her.

"Wonderful. I keep meaning to get over there but haven't done it yet. This gives me the perfect opportunity." She bent low and handed Amos's book back to him. "Thank you for showing that to me, Amos." Then she directed her attention to Todd. "Want to ride with me?"

"Yayuh!" He looked eagerly at his dad. "Can I?"

Matt shrugged. "Sure."

She eyed the other boys. "Anybody else?"

Randy stepped closer to his father, and Amos just smiled. She jerked her thumb to the left. "I'm parked down there."

"OK." He moved to her side with a newly acquired air of confidence, then turned to his father. "See ya, Dad."

Matt couldn't look more chagrined if he'd been run over by one of his own bulldozers, but Elle was pretty sure he'd survive the ordeal. He squared his shoulders. "OK."

* * *

"Elle, I'm glad you finally got over here." Her mother's next-door neighbor grabbed menus and approached Elle and Todd when they walked into The Sugar Maple a few minutes later.

"Me, too." She set a hand on Todd's shoulder. "Sandy, this is one of my neighbors, Todd Wilmot. We need a table for five. His father and brothers will be joining us."

"I've got one in the back we're just clearing," Sandy told her. "Give us a minute?"

"Of course."

The all-day breakfast restaurant was a popular post-church gathering spot on Sunday mornings. Orrie Wimple noted them from a few booths away. She looked at Elle, then Todd, then lifted both brows in question. When she brought her gaze back to Elle, the little smirk said she found their neighborliness interesting.

It wasn't anything of the sort, but Elle had no intention of letting Orrie know that. Let her think what she would, the cantankerous old bat.

Ignoring her, Elle led the boy to the historic display built into the brick wall of the restaurant. Artifacts of early Hopewell Indians shared space with pioneer implements and historic letters. Todd pointed to a spear-like weapon. "What is that?"

"A hunting spear with a flint tip. The Hopewell mined flint and used it for weapons and art." She pointed to a small flower, swirled in black and red. "That's carved from flint." She heard Matt and the other boys step in behind them. "Has your dad ever taken you to the flint museum or the earthworks?"

Todd shook his head. "I don't think so. Have you, Dad?"

Matt looked down at Amos as if weighing options. "Amos and artifacts. No."

"I can't fault you there," Elle agreed easily. "These guys are a little young. Not you so much," she said to Todd. "But Randy and especially Amos could use a couple of years under their belts to appreciate it better."

Todd turned her way, excited. "Maybe you and I could go," he suggested. His eyes lit up at the prospect of exploring together.

Elle hesitated. She'd already horned in on their breakfast, simply because the boys' stubborn father hadn't wanted her along. It had been an obstinate and maybe foolish thing to do, based on the stern expression on Matt's face. Todd misunderstood the delay. "It's OK if you don't want to take me."

She refuted that as Sandy approached, menus in hand. "I'd love to, Todd. Let me and your dad talk about it. I love seeing the artwork displays, so you may find me a boring partner. But if we can work out a time, I'd enjoy a trip over there. Once school's out."

He groaned, and she cuffed his shoulder. "Knock it off, brat, or we go nowhere."

"OK." The boy grinned up at her and took her hand. "I'm having pancakes. I'm starved."

* * *

Matt pondered the unexpected morning all the way home. At what point had he started having fun? Somewhere between the bubble-blowing contest in the chocolate milk glasses and the spoon-on-the-nose antics, he'd relaxed and laughed until his belly hurt. He had watched as Elle bantered with his sons, holding even Randy's attention, which normally would have been focused on tormenting the other two.

But the kid hadn't stood a chance. She'd drawn him a maze on the back of his place mat, then challenged him to find ways through it.

When he finally did, breakfast had come, and the time for torture was long past.

Amazing.

"Dad? Can Miss Drake come with us again? I had fun."

Matt caught his oldest son's earnest look in the rearview mirror and surprised himself with a positive answer. "Me too. We'll have to check her schedule."

Todd sat back against the seat, satisfied. Randy rolled his eyes. "She wants us to eat," he asserted, insistent. "She wants to fatten us up, then roast us in her oven. Can't you guys see what's happening here?" He slumped down, dismayed by their lack of foresight.

"She didn't seem that hungry," Matt argued, hiding a grin. "For a woman who thrives on little boys, she's mighty thin." Too thin, he thought, remembering the angular curves in the loose-fitting dress she'd worn today. Even with the easy fit, he could see she was more than slender.

"Dad." Randy's tone was quite knowledgeable. "They eat little girls, too."

"Ah." Matt paused a moment. "You're sure of that, son?"

"Yeah. I saw it on TV."

"Then I'd better take away your TV. And stop calling Miss Drake a witch. You'll hurt her feelings."

"Who cares?"

Randy was in one of his obstinate moods. Matt shot him a look as they pulled into their drive. His next reply surprised him more than the boy. "I do."

When she pulled into her driveway a few seconds behind him, he crossed the grass field. "Elinora?"

She turned, disbelieving. "Really? My mother doesn't even call me that."

"Well, I've been trying to figure out what you prefer, but you're some-what stubborn...," he paused, thinking. "Or maybe I should say your Heisman nature," he struck the famous Heisman pose, one hand out, thwarting contact, "doesn't let people in easily. I was wondering when we could do breakfast again. Or lunch. Possibly dinner." He smiled at her, into her very pretty blue eyes, and held her gaze intently. "Maybe all three?"

* * *

Matt Wilmot was asking her out.

Matt Wilmot was flirting with her.

Matt Wilmot was certifiable.

Her heart caved. She fluttered her hands, surprised. And when his smile deepened, she knew she was in deep, deep trouble, even worse than the free-range chickens fiasco. "Just call me Elle."

"Like *Legally Blonde*. OK, Elle." Matt said her name as if testing it. "I like it. So, my boys and I would like to hang out with you again. If you'd like to, that is."

"I would."

He breathed as if relieved and seemed genuinely happy, while Elle was still trying to grasp the fact that he was asking her out. "So—"

"But I'm leaving to kick off an East Coast tour for my contracted work," she explained. "I start in Manhattan and end up in Philly. I'll be gone for two weeks."

He looked genuinely disappointed. "When do you leave?"

"Tomorrow."

"Two weeks? Really?" He looked and sounded frustrated.

"Yes." She couldn't believe this was happening. It had to be a joke, wasn't it? Like one of those cruel high school pranks where the to-die-for handsome guy asks the wallflower nerd out for a date so everyone can laugh at her when she gets excited.

"Who's going to watch the chickens?"

"My sister."

"The one who was in my high school class."

The beautiful, spunky cheerleader with great hair, eyes, and teeth. "Yes." She waited for him to mention the vast differences.

He didn't. Instead, he motioned toward the house.

"Do you have a security system on the house?"

She nodded. It was a necessity on the barn-like shed because so much of her work was housed there. "On the house and barn."

"Good. But I'll keep an eye on things anyway." He swept her house and yard a concerned look. "I'm not here during the day, but I'll let the office manager know too. We've had too many break-ins on country roads lately, and that's not something you want to come home to."

He seemed sincerely concerned. He seemed...honestly nice. And interested, which meant she'd have to spend the next two weeks wondering if this was, perhaps, a dream...or a setup...or—

"Then when you get back, will you have supper with us? The weather should be more dependable, and maybe we could cook out. With two of us watching, the boys shouldn't be able to get into too much trouble." He smiled and stepped back. "Unless we get distracted, of course."

"By?" She met his gaze head on, not daring to think he was serious, and yet he looked downright serious. And handsome.

He let his gaze drift to her mouth and linger there. Then he winked and headed across the field. "I'll see you in two weeks. OK?"

She breathed deep and nodded. "OK."

* * *

Longest two weeks ever.

Elle reviewed every aspect of that conversation at least twice a day, hunting for loopholes, and found none.

Matt had asked her out, and he'd done it in the charming, genuinely interested way men use when they're serious.

Unless she was wrong. She was out of practice. Heck, she'd been born out of practice, so what did she know of flirtations and teasing and all the stuff romance was made of? She and Alex had fit together, two talented loners that never went to a prom, like a *Big Bang* episode, only real.

She pushed herself to focus. Hyland Manor was paying her to entertain and capture the crowd's interest with her work, faith, and humor. And in between, she thought about Matt.

A lot.

She met with executives and buyers, she was wined and dined, she was shown around some of the best-known shops for collectible enthusiasts, and Hyland Manor set up three separate demonstration venues so that customers could come and see their favorite artist at work.

That was the part she liked best. The schmoozing was done by necessity. Successful entrepreneurs needed to network, but what she loved
most was meeting the people, hearing their stories, seeing their eyes.

Even that didn't get her mind off Matt Wilmot, which was outlandish.
Wasn't it?

As she drove west through the Pennsylvania mountains, she had to
slow herself down. He was probably messing with her. Or just being
friendly. Or, worse, being a straight-up flirt with no thought to her
feelings. But the closer she got to Ohio, the more anxious she was to
get home, just to see, because thinking about it was driving her stark
raving mad. In the best possible way.

chapter twelve

The serious-sounding voice mail might not be the last message any parent wants to get, but after a week of rain and mud-mucked brakes, one of the last things Matt wanted to do was sit in the hot seat in the principal's office because Randy couldn't behave.

But that's just where he found himself, and Mr. Atkins didn't look amused. "I appreciate you coming in on such short notice, Matt."

Matt stared at his seven-year-old son and settled into the seat next to him. "I'm real sorry I had to, Mr. Atkins."

Randy squirmed, chin down. *Good.*

"Randy, would you care to explain to your father why I called him in?"

"No, sir."

The principal sat straighter. "Then let me rephrase my words: Randy. Explain to your father why I had to make him leave work and come down here to school."

Randy huffed. "Because Mrs. Kominski doesn't like me."

The principal frowned. "I think what you mean is she doesn't like the choices you make."

Randy frowned right back at him. "I think I know when someone likes me or when they don't like me. Mrs. Hanna liked me a lot last year. Didn't she, Dad?" He turned honest attention toward Matt. "Remember how she said I was a good little monkey?"

"Those were her exact words," Matt replied. "But this is a different teacher and a different year, Randy. What did you do to make Mrs. Kominski upset?"

Randy shrugged. "Breathe, maybe."

It was a smart-aleck answer from a smart kid, but not what Mr. Atkins wanted to hear. "Randy, tell your father what happened, please, and why you're being suspended."

"Suspended?" Matt turned quickly and stared at the principal. "He's seven years old, Mr. Atkins. What does a seven-year-old do to get suspended?"

"Cheating and insubordination."

"Cheating?" Matt stared at Randy. "Randy, you're two grade levels up in math and four levels up in reading. Why would you cheat?"

Randy scowled, and Mr. Atkins cut in, "Not for himself. For one of his friends."

"You were cheating to help a friend?"

Randy drew his legs up and put his chin down, silent and stubborn.

"Randy, is that what happened?"

Still nothing.

Matt turned back to the principal. "Was Randy caught cheating?"

"He was. The other student was struggling with a test paper, and Randy was observed reading over his shoulder and talking to him. When Mrs. Kominski asked him to sit down, he continued whispering into the other student's ear, while keeping his gaze trained on the test paper. Mrs. Kominski repeated the command to take his seat, and Randy told her in no uncertain terms that he'd sit when he was done and not before."

Oh, Randy...

"Under the circumstances, I have no choice but to issue a two-day mandatory suspension and a warning in his permanent folder."

His permanent folder.

Those words used to strike fear in Matt's heart as a boy, the thought that any bad thing he'd done might be permanent... He remembered being in awe of that idea, awed enough to behave most of the time. Jason hadn't cowed nearly that easily, and neither did Randy. *Great.* "Shall I take him home with me now?"

"Please do." Mr. Atkins stood. So did Matt. "He can return to school on Thursday, with a letter of apology to the teacher, of course."

That would be his second letter of apology in a few weeks. If nothing else, the boy's writing skills were getting a workout. "We'll be here, properly prepared."

"I'm not writing a letter."

The principal paused, and his expression darkened.

"You will write the apology because that's the punishment, Randy. There are consequences to our actions, good and bad. We've talked about this countless times." Matt turned back to Mr. Atkins. "Again, we'll be here Thursday, with the note."

"I'll run away first!" Randy stared up at Matt, and this time it wasn't Randy's typical in-your-face snark Matt saw. It was anger, pure and simple. "Nobody can make me write a letter to that lady! Ever!" He turned and raced out of the office, then down the hall.

"He needs to think before he reacts to everything, Matt." The principal didn't look angry, he looked concerned, and Matt was grateful for that. "Mrs. Kominski's been with us for several years, and while it's understandable for kids to have the occasional personality conflict, Randy's reactions are beyond the norm."

"I'll handle it."

"I hope so, Matt." The principal's expression indicated Randy's antics had been building up. "With kids like Randy, you've got to say what you mean and mean what you say."

What could Matt say to that? He'd been trying to follow through on things with the boys, but every now and again he was downright tired of being the constant bad guy in their lives. He followed Randy's path to the parking lot.

He called Jason, filled him in, and asked him to stay late. When Jason began to argue, Matt cut in. "Jase, I'm not asking you to stay. I'm telling you to stay and oversee that job, because that's what partners do. Don't you dare hang me out to dry on this, and heaven help you if the shoe is ever on the other foot and you need me to cover."

Jason's tone sounded a lot like Mr. Atkins when he said, "That won't happen because when I tell my kid what to do, she does it."

Matt hung up the phone, not daring to say another word.

The ride home was silent and seemed longer than usual, and when he sent Randy to his room, Randy didn't do his normal stomping routine.

He went quietly, almost meekly, as if the whole thing weighed heavy on his narrow, little shoulders, and that made Matt feel like the worst father ever.

*　*　*

Gloria didn't text him her disapproval that night.

She showed up right at his door, and after the week Matt had had, a showdown with his former mother-in-law ranked low on his wish list, but when she appeared on his front steps, he had little recourse. "Gloria."

She came through the door, looked around, and cringed, but Matt refused to apologize for the mess. First, it wasn't that bad, mostly kid stuff strewn around after a busy day. And second, it wasn't her business.

"Where's Randy?" she demanded, as if being a judge gave her the right to interrogate the kid. It didn't.

"In bed," Matt replied. "Like his brothers. And while your information gathering is notable, this isn't your concern, and I'm too tired to argue tonight."

"Too tired to clean, too tired to mind your kids, too tired to set rules and follow through with them." She leveled a hard gaze at him. "We're not talking a minor offense here, Matthew. Cheating on tests at age seven is an egregious matter, and refusing to follow the teacher's simple direction is appalling. You may be able to turn a blind eye to the path Randy's taking, but I see kids in court for serious offenses all the time. The one thing most of them have in common is a trail that goes back to grade school, and no one cared enough to do anything about it. So I'm asking you." She folded her arms and braced her legs. "What are you going to do about this? Because I'd like to keep my grandson out of jail, if I can."

"Jumping from a second-grade mistake to life in prison seems like a huge leap." He moved to the door and motioned that she should use it.

"Go home, Gloria. They're my boys. I'll handle them."

"Except you don't."

He sighed and didn't try to hide it because the woman was beyond tiresome, even when she was right, which wasn't as often as she thought.

"You brush things off, you shrug your shoulders, you turn a blind eye—"

Matt wondered how many idioms she could put into a single sentence, then mentally congratulated himself for remembering they were called idioms.

"But this will all catch up with you. It always does. And when it does, I'll be there, ready to make my move."

"Good night, Gloria. And the next time you want to come by, call first." He held the door open.

She charged through, angry, but she'd been angry for so long that it just seemed normal now.

He went to close the door but stepped outside instead, gazing west to his neighbor's house. The laugh-filled Sunday morning seemed like a long time ago. Why hadn't he asked for her cell phone number? She wouldn't be home for days, and what he wanted and needed right now was a serving of Elle's common sense and humor. He stared hard west, then went back inside and looked up her mother's number, called it, and got Elle's number from her.

And when Aggie Drake wondered if everything was all right at Elle's house, he could honestly say yes...

But his own house felt totally out of order.

* * *

Elle almost ignored the call.

She didn't recognize the number, there was no name attached, and it had been a long, tiring day outside of Baltimore. On the third ring, she swept her finger to the screen. "Elle Drake."

"It's Matt."

Matt.

Her heart did a mini-dance. She'd been pacing the floor, planning a talk for the following day, but now she sank into the hotel room chair and curled her feet up. "Hey! What's up?"

"I'm not sure. I just needed to talk to you."

"Uh-oh." She heard the regret in his voice, and maybe something else. "Someone's in trouble."

"That's a given, isn't it?"

She laughed softly. "With three boys, I think it is. Who's in the hot seat now? Let me guess. Randy."

"The odds were in your favor."

"He's a tough little character. What did he do this time?"

"You got time? Because it's a little convoluted. Or do you want the abridged edition?"

"I've got time."

"Well then." Sounding frustrated, he went through the whole thing with Elle, step-by-step.

"Have you talked to the teacher?" Elle asked when he finished.

"No. Just the principal."

"Well, backtrack this and go to the source," she told him. "The accused always has the right to face his accuser, doesn't he?"

"I hadn't thought of that. I took the principal's rendition at face value. You think she might have a problem with him?"

Elle could remember some cool and cutting grown-ups from her time. For some adults, it didn't pay to be different. And Randy liked to push the envelope, and not all adults handled that kind of kid well. "I think Randy needs to know you don't assume he's guilty, and his reaction seems out of synch with his normal attitude. My gut says there's more to this story."

"Why didn't I think of that?"

"Because Randy's guilty ninety-nine percent of the time," she told him, laughing. "Don't beat yourself up too much, because the kid sets himself up by being naughty and kind of obnoxious. But I'd go to the source and figure this out from the beginning if it was me, Matt."

"I'll set up a talk with the teacher and Randy, but I'm embarrassed that I assumed guilt. My bad."

"It's not," Elle told him softly. "We trust the people in place to make good decisions, and they usually do. But when a kid's reaction goes out of the norm, that's a big red flag to me."

"How do you know so much about kids and red flags? And why didn't you and your loser ex-husband have a bunch of kids, Elle? Because you're great with them."

She kept her reply even, but it took effort. "We tried. It didn't work. Even with the wonders of modern science. In retrospect, maybe it was a good thing. Broken families are tough on kids."

"I'll share mine," Matt told her, and he didn't sound flippant or teasing. He sounded sincere. "You have a way of making me see things about them, of cutting to the chase. They respect you, Elle."

"They're afraid of the kiln," she told him, laughing, and it felt good to laugh with Matt over crazy kid stuff. "They're still not sure I won't cook them."

"Speaking of your kiln, your work is beautiful, Elle."

"You looked me up online."

"Well, yeah." He sounded as if that was a given, and that made her pulse dance a little faster. "The YouTube videos are amazing."

"I can't believe you watched those."

"I enjoyed them." Her heart beat harder still. "You had the audience enthralled. Me too."

"People like to see the process of pottery making, even in abbreviated form. Of course, each step takes a lot longer in the shed. I can't wait to come home."

"Yeah?" His voice went quieter. Deeper. "Because of the shed and your work? Or...," he drew the question out for long, slow seconds. "Our date?"

"Mostly...," she returned the favor, savoring the silence. "The date."

"Yeah?" He sounded relieved, which made her feel crazy good.

"Yeah."

He laughed then. "I'm glad you're coming back soon. I don't like seeing your place empty. There's something nice about seeing your lights on, seeing you moving around the yard. Your rooster's decided that four a.m. is a good wake-up time, by the way. There's no sleeping in on this end of Randolph Road now that he's found his voice."

"I was hoping he'd start crowing soon!" The thought of Old Jack finally crowing delighted her. "I love the sound of a rooster heralding the dawn."

"Oh, he heralds all right. Repeatedly. I'll never have to worry about oversleeping again."

"Sorry." She winced, because sleep was a good thing. "Is it really bad?"

"Not now that I've gotten over the surprise of it. Hey, thanks for talking to me. Can I call you tomorrow night?"

She'd love that, but she was tied up the entire evening. "I'm being courted by a group of department-store execs tomorrow night just outside D.C., and then back to Philly for the weekend. And then home."

"Then I'll see you when you get home. Thanks, Elle."

He was thanking her for talking with him. As if what she said mattered to him, to his kids. "Anytime, Matt. Good night."

She disconnected the call and curled further into the oversized chair.

She couldn't let herself get too crazy about all this. She didn't dare. Matt was in a hard place, and she was good with his kids, but that wasn't grounds to jump in with two feet.

She'd had her heart broken once, in full view of the tabloid world: "Fourth Richest Man in America Cheats on Christian Artist Wife with Supermodel."

That gave the Orrie Wimples of the world plenty to talk about.

Alex had hung her out to dry, and she was so focused on wanting a family that she hadn't seen it coming. And when it did, anger and embarrassment had vied for first place, because she should have known better. She grew up knowing better.

Alex had wanted her when they were both struggling loners. But once he had more zeroes behind his bank balance than should be humanly possible, he could be with anyone. Why on earth would he stay with her? A bitter truth, hard to handle, yet totally understandable.

Once burned, twice shy.

Maybe she was hypersensitive because her father had done the very same thing, but if hypersensitive made her more cautious, she was OK with that.

chapter thirteen

Matt wasn't sure he was doing the right thing. He didn't approve of parents taking kids' sides against authority; he believed in a logical order. Kids should do as they're told. And his kid—

He glanced at Randy's frowning face in the rearview mirror.

Was a brat.

He knew that, so why was he following Elle's advice? Because something seemed amiss, and talking to Elle gave him more confidence in his discernment. If nothing else, the requested meeting would show Randy that his father wanted him to get a fair shot, the same standard he expected Randy to follow.

He parked and climbed out of the front seat, reached back and opened Randy's door. "Ready?"

Randy glared at him, folded his arms across his narrow chest, and sat right there.

"The best way to get this out in the open is to talk about it, son."

"Nobody listens."

Matt leaned closer. "What do you mean?"

"'Zactly what I said. Nobody listens. If you try and tell grown-ups something, they just get you into trouble."

"Mrs. Hanna wasn't like that."

Randy's face softened. His eyes went wide. "Not her, no."

"Come on." Matt put out a hand. "Together, you and me. I've got your back."

Randy peered up at him.

Three pairs of school doors opened, and streams of kids started dashing to the school buses looping the parking circle.

"Randy!"

"Hey, Jake!" Randy climbed out of the car quickly enough now and dashed across the sidewalk.

"Why weren't you here today?" The dark-haired boy looked from Randy to Matt and back again. His expression went from happy to nervous. "Are you in trouble, Randy?"

"Heck, no." Randy blew off his status as if it was no big deal. "I just had to stay home today. With my dad."

That wasn't exactly true, but Matt didn't have time to fine-tune Randy's answers. And if Randy was saving face to his little friend about his punishment, Matt wasn't going to publicly call him out. "Randy? Gotta go."

"Sure." Randy looked back at Jake. "See ya."

"Hey, Randy." Hesitant, the other boy reached out and touched the sleeve of Randy's shirt as Randy started to move forward. "Thanks for trying to help me." He said the words softly, as if embarrassed.

Randy looked everywhere but at the other kid. "'s OK."

Randy's voice came out kind of gruff, and as the smaller boy dashed off to his waiting bus, Matt moved forward. He swung the door wide and walked toward the principal's office.

He'd forgotten how quickly school halls emptied at dismissal time. By the time they'd reached Mr. Atkins's office, silence filled long halls where noise reigned supreme moments before. Matt tapped on the principal's door, and when Mr. Atkins called him to come in, he opened the door and stepped inside.

Mrs. Kominski was seated near the principal. She sat straight and tall in the chair, and while her lips smiled, her gaze stayed cool. "Mr. Wilmot. Randy."

Randy, who never wanted to be close to anyone, hugged close to Matt's side.

"Have a seat, won't you?" Mr. Atkins motioned to the two chairs side-by-side facing his desk.

"Glad to." Matt made sure Randy was settled, then took the reins. "First, thank you for meeting with us. I've always found that the best way to correct a problem is to accurately assess what's gone wrong."

"I think Randy's behavior has given us a few clues about that," Mr. Atkins noted. "It's not like this is Randy's first visit to my office."

"True," Matt agreed, and then he reached out and held Randy's hand in front of both the teacher and the principal. "But you and I both know that this infraction and Randy's reaction are out of the norm, and it's only fair for Randy to be able to hear what happened from the source. In this case, Mrs. Kominski." He turned her way. "We're all busy, and I don't want to take up too much of your time, so if you can tell me what happened yesterday, Mrs. Kominski, I'd be glad to listen."

She pretended cooperation. "Randy was given a direction. He didn't follow it. He was then seen giving another child answers to a test. When asked to stop talking, he continued feeding the other child answers. And when I reiterated my direction to stop talking and return to his seat, he told me he'd do it when he was done."

Before Matt could turn his way, Randy stood up and faced her, hands clenched by his side. "I didn't give Jake any answers, and you know it."

The teacher rolled her eyes. "I do hope it doesn't come down to needing cameras in the classroom to prove a teacher's words over an errant child's profession of innocence. Randy, you and I both know it happened exactly as I said. Twenty-two other students witnessed it. Do we have to convene a jury of your peers?"

Patronizing and demeaning.

Her attitude surprised Matt, but Randy's words surprised him more. "You know Jake can't do your stupid old test. You know it, and you won't help him, ever." He turned to the principal. "Jake's a nice kid. He doesn't hurt anybody, ever. He doesn't make even a little bit of trouble, but he can't read. He tries and tries, and he just can't do it. And then he cries when she gives him tests and stuff, because he doesn't know what it says. That's what I was doing yesterday. I didn't have to give Jake any answers, not a stinkin' one. I just read him the problems on the paper, and he answered them all by himself. A kid shouldn't get in trouble just because he can't read, should he?"

Halfway through Randy's spiel, Mrs. Kominski began to look uncomfortable. And when Mr. Atkins redirected his attention to her, two dark splotches of color stained her cheeks. "Is this Jake Rodriguez we're talking about?" the principal asked.

"Yeah, that's him!" said Randy.

"Yes."

"Were you aware that he was unable to read the test paper, Mrs. Kominski?" The principal asked the question in a very quiet voice, the kind of voice that meant he wasn't happy.

"A lot of second graders have trouble reading, and the proper thing to do in that instance is raise your hand and ask for help." She met the principal's gaze, but she wasn't nearly as cool and cryptic as she'd been moments before.

"Jake used to ask for help," Randy told the principal with all the honesty of youth. "And Miss Godfrey used to help him, but Mrs. Kominski told her she'd spent enough time on the little apple-picker, and that she needed to help the other kids in class."

The principal opened his mouth, then closed it. He stood. "Matt, please have Randy rejoin his class first thing tomorrow. And if you'll both excuse us, we're going to continue this matter in private."

"Of course." Matt extended his hand to the principal. "Thank you for the opportunity to sort this out."

"You're welcome." Then the older man turned to Randy. "Randy, I want you to know I appreciate what you tried to do for Jake, and I know you're a really good reader." He tapped Randy's file for emphasis. "Would you like to partner with Miss Godfrey and Jake for reading time? That might be a really big help to him."

"Yeah!"

"Randy." Matt sent a pointed look from Randy to the principal.

"I mean yes, sir!" Randy's wide smile said the idea excited him.

"I'll arrange it. See you tomorrow, Randy."

"OK!" Randy waved as he and Matt went through the door, and it was a very different kid who marched back down the now-empty halls of Cedar Mills Elementary. Shoulders back, chin up, Randy strode toward the parking lot as if someone had just handed him the grand prize at a carnival.

And all because grown-ups had listened to him.

It didn't make him less of a brat, Matt knew, but it did show the strength of character developing in the young boy's mind. The courage to right a wrong for the son of a migrant worker was a wonderful thing, and his boy had it.

But aside from Randy's moral victory, Matt knew that Mrs. Kominski must have been the person who contacted Gloria the night before. No one else knew about the suspension. He'd handle that issue privately with Mr. Atkins, but for now, he planned on getting a forty-pack of chicken nuggets and having a celebratory feast with his boys.

He'd call Elle once the boys were in bed, even though he knew she'd be out. He'd leave her a message telling her what went down and thanking her for the advice.

He'd rather thank her in person. See the look on her face when he told her the results. And then give her a big ol' hug for believing in his kid.

Later, he pulled up Elle's number from his contacts list and was surprised when she answered the call. "Hey, I thought you were busy. I was going to leave a message."

"I told them it was urgent and excused myself from the room. How'd it go?"

He recapped the meeting quickly and wasn't quite prepared for her reaction. "How dare she? How dare she treat a little kid like that, just because he's different? Or challenged? She called him an apple-picker? I'd like to show her a thing or two about hard work and industry and—"

"Whoa, girl. Don't hold back. Tell us how you really feel."

His interruption made her laugh, but the laugh sounded rueful. "I cheer for the underdog, Matt. Maybe because I was the underdog, or maybe it was the ten years in the fast lane of nouveau riche and gilded society, but this kind of thing sets me off."

"So I see." He paused a moment, then said, "Thank you. Thank you for helping me see what to do. You have a way of clearing the cobwebs, Elle. Keeping things simple. I really appreciate that."

"You're welcome."

Somehow the thank-you didn't seem like enough. Not nearly enough, but she was in Baltimore, and he was in Cedar Mills. "I know you have to get back to the corporate bigwigs, but thanks for answering the phone."

"Well, I wanted to, Matt."

His heart did a weird little twist. "I'm glad, Elle. Good night."

"Night, Matt."

He hung up the phone, lay back on his bed, and stared at the ceiling.

A text buzzed in. He glanced down, thinking it was Elle, but it wasn't. It was Kim Sedgewick wondering if he and the boys could do a cookout this weekend.

He stared at the text, then quickly typed, "No, sorry. Busy."

He hadn't encouraged her attentions. She was one hot chick, and she knew it, but he had absolutely no interest in her, despite her repeated attempts.

But Elle…

He smiled, picturing her.

Elle wasn't afraid to give as good as she got. She met things head on, no nonsense, and he did, too. He liked that about her; he liked that the boys' craziness didn't fluster her. She took charge and led the way, and they followed. For the first time in years, his boys seemed to blossom, as if they were coming into their own, and a lot of that was because of his neighbor.

She makes you see things, too. Are you ready to handle what that means?

He cringed slightly. She wasn't afraid to hold that mirror up to his face either. She stood her ground, and he wasn't exactly used to that.

But the gentle order she brought to things around her…Matt figured that might be the best trade-off ever.

* * *

First the teacher.

Now the priest.

Who else did Gloria have on her squad? Matt wondered the next day when he saw the middle-aged man standing on his front step. Undoubtedly the parish priest was there to ream him out for not getting the boys to church every single Sunday.

Great.

He moved to the door, embarrassed. He'd made a promise to Carrie and to the priest that married them ten years before. Why was he having such a hard time keeping it?

He opened the door. "Father. This is a surprise." He prepared himself for the expected backlash. Gloria knew everyone in Cedar Mills, she handed out money freely, and she wasn't afraid to stake her claims anywhere. Even in church, it appeared. "Come on in."

"I should have called, but I was out this way to pay a sick call to someone, and I thought I'd just pop in." Then Father Murphy patted Matt's shoulder as if Matt were a kid, "And listen, I want you to know I appreciate how hard it is to get three boys up and dressed and into church."

The priest was complimenting him? For real?

"My mother had a time of it," the priest continued as he moved into the living room. "There were six of us, and my father died when my youngest sister was in diapers, so it all fell on Mom. Sunday mornings were a mix of screaming fits and prayerful adoration, an odd blend of worship, if I do say so myself. Anyway," he took a seat on the couch as Matt settled into the chair opposite him, "Gloria's been on the phone to me several times."

When Matt started to speak, the priest waved him off. "Let me finish. I can just imagine how you must be feeling, and I'm not here to forward Gloria's agenda. I'm here for the boys. Parenthood is a balancing act with two parents, Matt. On your own, it's an overwhelming three-ring circus of missteps and success, but here's what I'd like to suggest." He leaned forward, his arms on his knees, hands clasped. "Let's get the older two boys into faith-formation classes. We've got summer sessions starting right after Independence Day, and if we can get them into the summer intensive program, we can catch them up on what they need to begin their sacraments next year."

"You mean like Communion?"

"Yes." The priest nodded. "We can get them ready for reconciliation and their First Communion. With a year of learning behind them, the Mass will mean more."

"So they might not be as bored."

"Yes!" The priest clapped his hands because Matt got it. "One without the other is hard at their age, but they're at a perfect time to begin discernment. Right from wrong, good from bad, and how choices affect us. And that's what these first years show them, how God wants us to take responsibility for our choices, good and bad, and then deal with them."

"It sounds all right," Matt told him, because it did, actually. "How do I do this? Do I sign them up?"

"Georgia Wilkes is our faith-formation director. She'll call you this week and get the paperwork in order. And in the meantime…" The priest stood. Matt followed suit. "I love seeing you in church with them. That's the best example a parent can set, but I don't want you beating yourself up over this. God wants a joyful congregation, a joyous noise." The priest's grin said he thought joyful noise was a good thing. "So you bring them as you're able, and we'll see about the sacraments. And at some time, I'd like to see the little guy baptized, Matt. At your discretion, of course."

Embarrassment made Matt wince. "I should have done it right away when he was born. Carrie would have wanted me to. But—" He shrugged, admitting his mistake. "I didn't, and then it became a battlefield with Gloria, and that seemed like a stupid reason to get a kid baptized. Something that important shouldn't be because you're ordered to do it."

"Those were harsh times and harsh realities you were facing," Father Murphy agreed. "But it's a new day, Matt. A new time. And we don't have to hurry that process. We could do it next Easter, if you like, at the Vigil Mass with others receiving the sacraments. We've got plenty of time to talk about that." He stuck out his hand and gave Matt a hearty handshake. "I'm glad you were here, and I'll have Georgia call you. She can e-mail you the paperwork. You fill it out and send it back, and we'll get Randy and Todd registered."

"You know their names."

The priest just smiled, but it meant something to Matt that the kindly pastor knew who they were and called them by name, as if he cared more about them than Gloria's cash flow.

"Thanks for listening, Matt. I'll be in touch."

"OK." Matt folded his arms, then loosed them and thrust his hands into his pockets, unsure what to do. "Thanks, Father."

"Don't mention it."

As Father Murphy strode to his car, he paused to wave to the boys in the backyard. They waved back, laughing, and went on with their game.

He hadn't come to yell at Matt. He came to welcome him and the boys. He came to extend an opportunity, and to make Matt feel better about himself and his lax ways.

The kitchen timer buzzed that their pizza was baked. Matt went into the kitchen, pulled out the pizza, and set it on the counter to cool.

He glanced at the calendar and realized that even as busy as he was right now, he could carve two hours on Sunday mornings. Not only could, but should. He took a black-tipped marker and wrote *church* across the four upcoming Sundays on the calendar, and when he stepped back and saw the notation, he smiled.

It wouldn't be easy, the boys proved that.

But Matt was pretty sure it might be worthwhile.

chapter fourteen

Home.

Elle breathed relief as she pulled into her driveway after a long two weeks on the road. The first thing she did was scan the Wilmot yard. The warm, sunny late-afternoon showed no activity. Of course Matt would be working, and the boys…

Could be anywhere, doing anything.

He'd mowed the wide field separating their properties. It looked so much better trimmed down, and was it her imagination, or did that seem more inviting? To have the field separating them freshly mowed, making it easier to cross.

Or maybe the guy is just sick of the bugs and rodents running amok.

She shushed the internal warning. She preferred to think that Matt had mowed on purpose. Her phone rang, and Kate's number flashed in the display.

"Elle! Are you home, or did I catch you in the car? The girls have been missing you like crazy, and yes, we took care of the stupid chickens. Every day. And I'm happily making omelets for supper. Free food!"

"Thank you for taking over here." Elle glanced toward the henhouse as she spoke. "They look marvelous. I just pulled in. Haven't even unloaded yet. And I can't wait to see you guys, either. Doing these sales trips is wonderful, but I'm totally wiped."

"Did they love *Beauty of the Lilies*? I can't imagine they didn't."

She'd held her breath as the meeting time with the executive officers approached, but their enthusiasm for her latest work laid her concerns to rest. "They did love it, and they're confident about the sales potential, whereas I just want to see people smile when they look at it." She yawned, a little surprised by the quiet. Was that because she'd expected a welcoming committee from next door?

Silly, Elle.

"You sound tired."

She yawned again, then stretched. "I can't wait to crash. A busy bunch of days, working both ends of the clock. Sleep can't come soon enough."

"Then I'll bug you about the upcoming ice cream social when you're awake tomorrow."

"Or save us both the hassle and don't bug me at all," Elle told her. As she started up the steps, she frowned at the widening circle of yellowing grass and puddled water in the backyard. "I'm fine, I'm busy, I'm OK on my own."

"Blah, blah, blah."

Elle set her small bag down to unlock the back door.

A smell stung her nostrils, sharp and pungent, the smell of…

Burning wood.

Turning quickly, she looked for the source. "Kate, hang on. I smell something."

She moved back down the steps and turned.

Nothing seemed amiss. She brushed it off as a distant neighbor's campfire. This time of year, lots of folks burned tree-fall debris in their fire pits, and it was a beautiful day for yard work.

"Kate, I'm here, it's—"

She started to say "nothing" when the scent came again, stronger and harsher. Not the clean smell of nature's wood, but a mixed smell, noxious and nasty. She turned again and was pretty sure her heart leaped into her throat.

Matt's house was on fire.

Flames licked the back, along the edge of the back porch and the second-story windows. She yelled to Kate as she raced east. "Call 911. The Wilmot house is burning!"

She raced across the freshly mowed field as a golden arc of flames shot from the back of the house. The sound of breaking glass was followed by a mushroom-shaped plume of smoke from the upstairs rear windows. "Todd! Randy! Amos! Where are you?"

Running up the front steps, she threw open the door, glad it was unlocked. "Todd! Where are you? Todd!"

No answer. The smoke from above was infiltrating the first floor. She looked frantically both ways. Her cell phone jangled. "Hello."

"I called for help. Where are you?" Kate's voice was urgent.

"In the Wilmots', looking for the boys. Kate, I can't find them. What if?" She couldn't finish the thought. It was unbearable. But didn't children often hide from fire, burying themselves in closets trying to keep the life-sucking smoke at bay? What if they were upstairs?

"Maybe they're not there," Kate suggested.

Elle raced from room to room, yelling. "They have to be here, but where? Construction guys all work late this time of year. The kids are always here with a sitter until Matt gets home." Rushing through the house, she found nothing, but a combination of sounds drew her attention. Sorting them out, she realized one was the increasing roar of the fire raging overhead. A sudden burst of smoke down-swept into the lower story as the fire moved through floors and walls. At any moment, she could have the upper half of the house raining down on her.

But the other sounds tweaked her, too. She hung up on Kate in order to listen.

The canned, tinny sound of people talking. TV voices. Crossing the kitchen, she yanked her sweatshirt up and over her mouth to screen the building smoke. She pulled open a door, screaming their names.

Like a bad comedy, three, then four frightened faces looked up at her from the basement rec room. "Run," she yelled to them, holding the door wide. "Fire! Get up here now!"

Junie grabbed Amos and raced up the steps with him. Todd and Randy followed close behind. Shutting the basement door, Elle followed as they ran across the kitchen and through the breezeway, into the fresh air of the outdoors. Herding them to her yard, she turned just in time to see the upper front wall of the living area blow out. Glass popped, and fire snapped, like a well-chewed piece of gum. She gathered the children under her wide-branched oak, cuddling them to her. All four huddled against her as approaching sirens vied with the freight-train roar of the fire for their attention.

"It's all right," she soothed, keeping her voice deep and soft as she cradled four terrified children who'd almost lost their lives. "I've got you. I've got you." She leaned her lips against Amos's soft head, a kiss of supreme gratitude. What if she'd been ten minutes later? What if Kate hadn't called, and she'd already gone inside? What if—

"For everything there is a season, and a time for every matter under the heavens."

She held them close, breathing prayers of thanksgiving because she had made it there in time. Just in time. She dropped her face to Todd's head and breathed. "It's all right."

* * *

Matt tipped back the bottle of iced tea and drank gratefully. It had been hot and dusty all day despite the rains earlier in the week. He and Spike Thompson had been grading a terraced lot set in the hillside of the new development. The sharp slope slowed their progress. Eyeing the steep angle of the lowest regression, he was glad he wouldn't be the guy mowing the grass.

He glanced at his watch. Six fifteen. He should be done and home by seven thirty at the latest, and maybe he and the boys could welcome Elle home with a trip for ice cream. A village cone on a late spring night sounded real good.

His phone vibrated. "Wilmot Excavating."

"Matt?"

The voice on the other end was agitated and unfamiliar, which usually meant his kids were in trouble. "Speaking."

The next words put his heart literally into his throat. "There's a fire at your house. A bad one. Someone just called it in."

"Who?" he shouted, jumping from the grader and racing for his truck. He yelled to the other man to follow.

"I don't know. Charlie told me to find you. He and the boys are there now."

Charlie Entz was the local fire chief. It must be his wife Matt was talking to. "My boys. How are my boys?"

"I don't know. I haven't heard a thing."

Dear God, they had to be OK. They had to. Gunning the engine as Spike leapt into the passenger seat, he said one word. "Fire."

Spike didn't swear.

He prayed.

He clenched his hands, face set, eyes tight. Matt tried to join him, but couldn't. If there was a God, and he was pretty darn sure there wasn't, he wasn't hanging out in Cedar Mills waiting to put out fires.

With his foot jammed to the floor, he wheeled around the turns and bends between the subdivision and his home with the skill of a racecar driver, glad for tight suspensions.

First responders blocked the eastern end of Randolph Road. Screeching to a halt, he was approached by a young fireman. "Road's blocked, sir. House fire about half mile down."

"It's my house." He half-choked on the words. "I've got to get there."

"You're Wilmot?"

When Matt nodded, the young fireman moved quickly. "I'll move the rig, sir. Go on ahead."

"My boys?"

The young man looked blank, then nervous. "I don't have any information, sir."

Frenetic activity surrounded his house as Matt and Spike drew near. Men scurried purposefully, laying hose, climbing ladders, radios humming, voices barking over the roar of the fire. Stopping behind the last truck east of the house, Matt and Spike raced down the road on foot, then up the drive. Matt grabbed the first yellow coat he could. "My boys?"

The man gestured right at the same time that Matt heard a familiar voice. "Dad!"

Turning, he saw them huddled beneath the big oak in Elle's yard. He ran that way, Spike by his side. He had no idea when he started crying, but he saw the tears on Spike's face before feeling them on his own. Later Spike would protest that he hadn't shed a tear with his friend and boss, but he'd be lying.

"You're OK. You're OK." Muttering the words over and over, Matt couldn't hold them close enough or long enough as he knelt down. Like newborn pups, they wiggled beneath one arm and against the other, jockeying for position. At some point his eyes met Elle's.

"What happened?"

She shook her head, one arm still firm around Junie, seated close beside her. The girl was strangely silent as she trained a numb gaze on the raging fire next door. Matt hollered for a medic, and one of them hurried his way. "I think she's going into shock," he told her.

The EMT squatted down, asked Junie a couple of questions, then took her hand to help her stand. "I'll take her to the ambulance and check her out," she told Matt and Elle. "Her parents are on the way."

Once Junie was being looked after, Matt turned his attention back to Elle.

She looked unnerved.

Matt didn't blame her, because he was plenty scared himself. "Can you fill me in?"

She shook her head. "I don't know. I'd just gotten home and smelled smoke. I turned, and it was coming from the upstairs windows in the back."

"Upstairs." Matt thought hard. There was nothing upstairs that should start a fire.

Todd grabbed his arm. "Miss Drake saved us. We didn't even know the house was on fire. We were watching TV in the basement—"

"And all of a sudden someone was screaming!" Randy jumped in, not to be outdone. "We got kinda scared, and then the door opened up—"

"And like all this smoke was swirling around—"

"And it was her, telling us to run!" Randy finished. "So we did."

"And then the windows started breaking…" Todd's voice slowed as the dangerous aspects began to unfold.

"And she pulled us out the door, running so fast!"

"Well, I was a state finalist in middle distance." Elle touched a hand to Randy's cheek in a gentle show of confidence. "We're safe, and that's all that matters. Houses can be rebuilt. As long as you're OK and Junie's OK, we're fine, boys."

Matt met her eye in silent gratitude, then pressed his lips to Randy's hair. With one arm he squeezed Todd closer; the other cradled Amos. "I don't know how to thank you."

Elle looked uncomfortable at the thought. "Don't, please. I was just in the right place at the right time."

"Well, I don't see that as any accident or coincidence, ma'am." Spike spoke firmly.

Elle looked him in the eye. "Me, either."

Gratitude swelled within Matt. She'd run into a burning building to save four children. She'd risked life and limb to rescue his family. She—

He stretched forward, boys and all, and gathered her in for a hug. Amos grabbed hold, Todd hugged her fiercely, and even Randy slipped an arm around her neck. "Thanks for saving our lives," he said gruffly, as if it still tested his belief system to trust her.

Spike joined in until Amos struggled in protest. "I can't breathe. Help!"

With a choking half laugh, Matt released her and dropped his chin to Amos's head. "Thank you."

She looked at him.

He looked at her.

Beautiful. So amazingly, utterly beautiful.

He didn't know how he'd missed it before, maybe because he was too busy slapping Band-Aids on his guilt-spattered ego.

She pushed up off the ground and clasped Todd's hand to pull him up beside her. "Let's take them to my place, OK? We can get them settled for the night."

Matt stood too, holding Amos snug in his arm. "To stay?"

"Unless there's somewhere else you've got in mind?" She waited for him, one arm firm around Todd's narrow shoulders.

"Dad's doing well, but their place isn't big enough for all of us. And having the four of us underfoot isn't exactly a walk in the park." Was she crazy, inviting them all to bunk down at her place? Crazy and nice, he realized. And it would keep him close to his machinery and the alarm system. Still— "It's such an imposition."

"Tell me something I don't know." Elle winked at Todd. "We can use the house tonight and then clean the in-law apartment tomorrow. It's only four rooms, but it's right next door to your base of operations. I know I don't like leaving my shed without someone to watch over things. I expect you feel the same about all that pricey equipment."

"I do."

Todd's thin hand reached for hers before Matt's words were out. Then he turned, mesmerized by the gruesome sight of the blackened house before him as the firefighters worked to contain the flames. "I think we need to get them away from this, Matt," she added softly, dropping her eyes to the boy in a silent message.

"You're right." Handing Amos to Spike, Matt hauled Randy up into his arms and started across the yard. Once downwind of the Wilmot house, the sting of smoke grew sharper.

Clutching his boy, he moved woodenly, the shock of the possibilities setting in.

They could have been gone. All of them. Every one. Todd, with his tentative nature and Carrie's brown eyes. Randy, the little troublemaker, whose blond buzz and twinkling gaze made him a terror to watch under ordinary circumstances. And Amos, so innocent and sweet, his round face always trusting.

He focused on the woman before him, her arm around the shoulders of his oldest son.

She'd saved them. Somehow, someway, she'd gotten there in the nick of time.

God?

An hour ago he'd have said no way. Now he wasn't so sure.

Later, he'd hear the details. Probably dozens of times. But for now, he thanked God for the angular woman walking before him, her short bob ruffled by the fire wind.

He thanked God for the sweet, sensible woman who was Elle Drake.

chapter fifteen

"They're settled, then?" Elle raised her eyes as Matt came down the stairs at the back of the house. He looked troubled and exhausted.

"For the moment. I've got Randy and Todd in the first room. Amos is with me. You're sure this is all right with you? Really all right?"

"Would I have offered otherwise?"

He studied her, then shook his head. "No. I'm just kind of surprised when people go out of their way these days."

"Coffee?" She pointed to the one-cup brewing system before tipping her head toward the ongoing action next door. "I don't think we grown-ups get to sleep for a while."

"I'll hold off on the coffee. I've got to get over there." He pulled on his scruffy work jacket, and even though he was tired and worn, the determination in his eyes and the strength in his jaw said Matt was willing to see things through. That was a quality Elle appreciated. "Elle, I owe you."

She waved him off. "Go. Check things out next door and be careful. Please."

He looked at her.

She looked at him.

He made a rueful face. "This wasn't exactly the first date I had in mind."

Talk about an understatement. "Me either. Although as I've grown to know you and the boys, I'm not as surprised as you might think."

He stared at her, and she thought for one long moment she'd made him mad, but then he smiled. "In our case, forewarned is forearmed. I'll be back."

"I'll be here."

He started to leave, then swung back once more. "I drove like a crazy man to get back over here," he told her. "All I could think was, where are the boys? Are they all right? Are they OK?" He breathed deep, still watching her. "Finding them with you under that tree was the most beautiful sight I've ever seen, Elle. The most beautiful, ever, by far. I—" He swallowed hard, watching her as he struggled to speak. Then he took a deep breath. "I just wanted you to know that."

His house was crumbling to ashes.

His children had been traumatized, but they were safe and sound, tucked in bed.

He'd called her beautiful.

This wasn't the silly romantic setting she'd been mulling for two weeks. It was more real life, like a true, firsthand glimpse of how crazy life can be with three rambunctious little boys and their gray-eyed, hardworking father.

Elle decided she could handle real-life just fine as long as everyone managed to survive.

* * *

"Matt!"

Matt heard his mother's voice just as the roof of the house began to cave. The second story collapsed with a groaning, thunderous *crack!* as embers burst skyward. He raised a hand so she could find him, but couldn't turn away from the sight unfolding before him.

What if Elle hadn't gotten home when she did? What if she'd gone into her house and never noticed the fire?

"Matt, there you are! Where are the boys? Are they OK?" His parents launched questions as the fire chief approached from the other side.

"Got a minute, Matt?"

"The boys are fine, Mom. Dad. They're fine."

His mother hugged him, burst into tears, and hugged him some more. "Hey, it's OK, Mom." He hugged her back, because he understood the firestorm of emotion all too well. "Everyone's safe; everything's fine. It's OK."

"But what if they weren't all right?" She raised tear-soaked eyes to his. "What if something happened to those precious boys and me too busy to take care of them?"

"Matt, I'm better now," his father cut in. "Let us take the boys back to our place. You can live there while we figure this all out. I'm so sorry, son."

They looked as guilty as he felt. Their guilt was misplaced. His? Not so much. But right now the fire chief needed to talk to him. "Charlie, go ahead, give me what you've got. Do you have an idea how this started? Did my boys…," he hated to ask or suggest the boys might have monkeyed with something, but their track record indicated it was a real possibility. He didn't keep matches in the house, and the grill lighter was hung in the garage, out of reach, but then he hadn't expected Todd to take a joyride in a Bobcat, either.

"We won't know the cause for a while, Matt, but as soon as we have an idea, we'll tell you," Charlie assured him. "I've called in an emergency enclosure team. They'll stake off the yard and install temporary fencing so that no one goes near the building."

"If the boys are with us, they won't be tempted." Matt's father clapped Charlie on the back. "Charlie, you guys did a great job of keeping this contained."

"You did, Charlie," Matt agreed. "And we're grateful. It could have been so much worse." If the fire had spread to the massive equipment barns in the back field, their business could have gone up in smoke, too, but even that loss would be sustainable, as long as the boys and Junie were all right.

"Where are the boys, Matt?" His mother gripped his arm. "I want to see them."

"At Elle's."

"Elle's?" She looked up, puzzled.

"Elle Drake, next door. I've got the boys tucked in over there. Go see her, Mom."

She looked surprised and a little uncomfortable, so Matt encouraged her. "Go see them. Elle can take you upstairs so you can peek at them and make sure they're settled. I need to stay here, but Elle would prob-ably love some company. She's staying put with the boys." He turned back to Charlie. "Do we have an update on Junie? She looked wiped out when they moved her to the ambulance."

"She'll be fine. Just stunned. Like the rest of us when something like this happens."

Charlie was spot-on, but as Matt looked around, he didn't focus on the complete loss of his house and belongings. It didn't matter as much as he would have thought, and that surprised him.

The boys were all right. Junie would be, too. And Elle... Funny, cryptic Elle Drake had charged into a burning house, risking her life to save his because if anything had happened to those boys, well...his life wouldn't be worth living, and he knew that. "Your guys are amazing, Charlie. Thank you."

"Part of the job, Matt. I'm just glad those kids got out. It's mighty hard to hear smoke detectors two floors up when you're underground."

The sound-barrier effect hadn't occurred to Matt. There were smoke detectors on all levels of the house, including the downstairs rec room, but the two floors of separation had minimized the warning. "Something to think about when we rebuild."

"If you do a basement room, make sure you've got an audio system hardwired with a backup battery. That way if something happens two floors away, you're not insulated from the noise."

Good advice. "I'll see to it, Charlie."

As the efforts of the Cedar Mills Hose Company brought the fire under control, the pace of the firefighters and police began to slow. A van filled with Ladies Auxiliary members rolled onto the grass field and stopped. Several women climbed out. They pulled trays of sandwiches and cookies from the back of the van and flipped out a folding table to hold the food.

Working together, two of the women set up institutional-sized insulated coffee carafes and a water dispenser, then arranged cups, stir sticks, sugars, and creamers alongside.

"I'm getting you coffee," Dan Wilmot said. "And some for me, too." Matt's father crossed to the van while Matt watched the fire crews.

The macabre sight of the house humbled him. How quickly life could change. He knew it more than most, but a little thing like not being able to hear smoke detectors had almost cost him his family.

Close. So close.

A car screeched to a halt on the road in front of Elle's, and the two people inside didn't just climb out.

They raced out of the car and toward the fire.

Gloria and Al D'Amico, Carrie's parents, and they didn't look worried. They looked mad. Fighting mad.

He didn't want to do this now, but Gloria and Al would leave him little choice. He accepted coffee from his father, knowing a bad situation had just grown worse.

"You almost killed them this time, Matthew!" Gloria got right up in his face, and Al was right behind her. "I warned you. Others warned you. And did you listen? No! You never listen to anyone!"

"Now, just a minute." Matt's father set his coffee down on the bumper of a pick-up truck and faced Gloria. "Matt's done nothing wrong here."

"Nothing wrong?" Gloria didn't screech the words. She repeated them in a harsh, menacing tone, the kind she used in front of juries. "He's leaving three small children in the hands of incapable sitters, he has no rules or regulations to keep these boys in line, and he's risking their lives daily with his lax attitude. I've already buried a daughter, Daniel. I have no intention of doing the same thing with my grandsons."

Raw, consuming anger broadsided Matt.

She blamed him for Carrie's death.

She thought he was lax and incompetent. She thought—

Does it matter what she thinks? Truly?

He didn't want it to matter, but he knew Gloria. If she thought she could gain control of his kids, she'd do it in a heartbeat, just to show him how much better she was at everything. "I'm not going to do this, Gloria. Accidents happen, and we're just glad everyone's OK."

"You've got no call to act like this, Gloria." Matt's father folded his arms across his chest. "I know it's upsetting, but the boys are fine, and the house can be rebuilt."

"I don't care about his stupid house." She clipped each word for effect. "I care about my daughter's children. My grandchildren. How close we came to losing them because of your ineptitude."

Her accusations actually made him feel less guilty. Junie had turned out to be a solid babysitter for those nights he had to work late. She played with the kids. She read Amos stories and built Lego castles with the older boys.

But Gloria wasn't done. She moved closer, eyes narrowed. "I am filing for custody of those boys, Matthew. And don't think I won't stand a real good chance of getting it." She waved a small notebook in the air. "I still have friends in this town, and I've got reports and eyewitness accounts of every dangerous situation that's occurred the past two years. And plenty of judicial friends as well. None of them will take this lightly, and even if I lose, I'll keep you so tied up in court that you won't know which way to turn. Do I make myself clear?"

Anger rose up inside him, fast and furious. People were watching. The kindly women from the Ladies Auxiliary looked stunned. A few firefighters moved closer, as if to protect him, but then—

Oh, then—

A hand touched his. Soft, strong fingers clasped his and intertwined. "I'm pretty sure there isn't a judge in Ohio that will break up our family. Is there, Matt?" Elle squeezed his hand lightly and met his gaze with a look of such tenderness that her touch and her words seemed delightfully real.

"*Your* family?" The look of anger Gloria aimed at Elle put Matt's protective instincts on high alert. "Stay out of this, whoever you are."

"I'm Elle Drake. I live right there," Elle indicated the gracious old farmhouse with a look, "and I'm about to become the boys' stepmother and Matt's wife."

She was?

Matt kept his mouth closed as Elle held Gloria's gaze, unflinching, and for the first time in a long time, Gloria seemed at a loss for words. The effect was unfortunately short-lived.

"That's not true." She tried to dismiss Elle with a wave. "I'd have heard, believe me. I hear everything."

Elle acted relaxed, but Matt felt the tension in her hand, her arm. "We've kept things low-key on purpose, haven't we?"

She looked at him, and what else could he do but nod? "We sure have."

Elle squeezed his arm with her other hand. He covered that hand with his, hoping they looked like a happy, newly engaged couple.

"You're lying." Gloria moved closer, still menacing. Her husband touched her arm.

"Gloria. Let it go. It's not worth it."

"Not worth it?" She spun around and nailed her husband with the same fierceness she'd shown Matt. "Carrie's babies aren't worth fighting for? Protecting? You're willing to walk away from our grandsons and turn them over to her?"

The weary look on Al D'Amico's face said this had been a long battle.

"Why would you walk away from your grandsons?" Elle asked.

Al looked at her, surprised and confused.

So did Gloria.

And Matt's father studied Elle with an expression that said he was impressed, and it took a lot to impress a Wilmot.

"They'll always be your grandchildren," Elle continued. "Heritage and love are part of being a family, aren't they? That's intrinsic to their well-being. I'm just glad I get to be part of it."

Her words defused Gloria. Matt knew his former mother-in-law; he understood that she probably wasn't done with her campaign to interfere with the boys' and his life, but Elle's presence and words had taken her by surprise.

Him, too.

The Ladies Auxiliary looked absolutely delighted by their good news, which meant it would be all over town by morning.

A wedding.

Married.

To Elle Drake, his next-door neighbor.

If this was a dream, he needed to wake up and figure out what was real and what wasn't. But he wasn't dreaming, and Elle had just saved his sorry hide again because Gloria turned and stalked back toward her big, black luxury car. Al hesitated as if torn, then followed her.

"Well." Dan Wilmot crossed the few feet separating them. "Elle, is it?"

"Yes." With Gloria and Al gone, Elle looked a little less sure of herself. "Nice to meet you, Mr. Wilmot. I've heard a lot about you."

"Nice to meet you!" Dan told her, then grabbed her in a big hug that meant his father was perfectly all right with the situation, except it wasn't real. None of this was real except the smoldering ashes of his burnt-out home. "Welcome to the family! Matt's mother is going to be so pleased to hear the news. She's had this on her little prayer list for a while now, a good strong woman to watch over Matt and those boys!"

"And heaven knows they need it," Elle agreed sweetly. "And of course being married increases the odds of success. A two to three ratio is always better."

"Exactly!" Dan beamed as if they'd just solved a major world problem. "When's the wedding?"

Matt turned toward Elle. "I was wondering that myself."

"No date's been set yet." Clearly Elle was good at improvisation. "I've been gone, and I'd just gotten back from an East Coast tour when all this happened."

"Well, I'd make it sooner rather than later. Gloria's got a head of steam worked up over all this, and having a mother on hand would make a big difference."

Having a mother on hand would make a big difference…

His father was right.

It would make all the difference.

People had told him that when Kim showed interest during the past year, but the thought of Kim putting anyone's needs ahead of her own had kept him at bay.

But Elle…

Elle was amazing.

Elle made the boys laugh. She made him laugh. She made them think about things other than themselves. She made them cookies, made them work, and most of all, she expected them to rise to a challenge. To be good. To be kind.

And when they were around her, they tried to meet her expectations. Married. To Elle.

He gripped her hand tighter as they made their way over to her house. His father moved ahead, and Matt took advantage of the moment to slow Elle's steps. "You seem to excel at getting me out of trouble."

Elle winced. "I couldn't let her rake you over the coals like that. Who does that kind of thing, when someone's house is burning down alongside them? Sorry." She made a face of regret and sighed. "Now we'll have to wiggle our way out of this, and that's going to be a tangle, but I figured it would quiet her down. And it did work," she added with a quick, small smile.

"What if we don't wiggle our way out of this?"

"What?"

She tried to stop their progress, but Matt kept her hand in his and kept walking.

"Matt."

"You said yourself it makes perfect sense."

"I said no such thing," she hissed as they drew closer to the house. "We barely know each other."

He smiled into her eyes and saw the answering flicker of acknowledgment and interest. Real interest. "A lifetime gives us plenty of time for that, I guess."

"Are you crazy?"

He was, kind of, because her off-the-cuff idea was growing in appeal.

"Maybe. Or maybe you came up with the best answer possible." They'd reached the door. He put a finger to his lips. "We'll hash this out later."

"There is nothing to hash out."

He winked, because the more he thought about it, the more he liked the idea.

"Matt, I—"

He kissed her.

He kissed her long and slow and with a gentle firmness that said they had a lot to talk about.

Later.

And when he stopped kissing her, he cupped her face with his two hands and whispered, "That wasn't so bad, was it?"

* * *

It was wonderful, and he knew it, which meant she should take him down a peg, but his parents were excitedly waiting inside her back door. "We'll discuss this later."

He grazed one finger across her lips. "I'm looking forward to it."

Insufferable.

Confidence bordering on cockiness.

Righteously good-looking.

And he couldn't possibly be serious. Could he?

One look at his face said otherwise. He held the door open, and his parents met them with open arms.

"Elle, I'm so happy for you! For both of you! For all of us!" Matt's mother hugged her. "You know when Matt first told me that you were helping with Todd, I wondered if there might be a spark. Oops!" She grimaced. "Bad choice of words. There was a note in his voice I hadn't heard there in a long time. I'm so glad I was right!"

"Me too."

"Welcome to the family, Elle," Mary Lou continued. "Now, you can call me Mom or Mary Lou, whatever suits you is fine with me. And I just have to tell you," she moved closer, and her face took on a more serious expression, "you saved more than those children tonight. You saved our family, Elle. We all knew this was a trying time. Daniel's health, a crazy busy season, and Matt's problems with childcare."

"Life hands us some tough turns, doesn't it?"

"It does, but God's often got a backup plan, and that's you."

Elle was pretty sure God would disagree, since she'd just told a big, fat lie to Matt's former in-laws. And his father. And in front of a lot of townspeople. Confession was clearly in her future. "Mrs. Wilmot," she began.

"Mary Lou," the older woman insisted and grasped her hands. "I might not be as good about going to services as I used to be, but I'm changing that right now. And Daniel will go right along with me."

Daniel looked a little surprised by her edict, but he was wise not to argue.

"Elle goes to St. Casimir's, Mom."

"The Polish Catholic church?"

"Yes."

"How perfect."

Matt reached over and squeezed her hand, purposely. "That's where we met, actually."

His mother beamed. "Well, there you have it. God's hand in this from beginning to end. I am so excited I probably won't sleep, but it's late, and we all need sleep. Elle." She reached out and hugged Elle again, smiling as tears welled in her eyes. "Thank you again. For saving the children, and for loving my son."

This was getting harder and crazier as the moments ticked on. What had she been thinking when she butted into Gloria's attack?

You wanted to protect those you care about. That's not a bad thing.

She hugged Matt's mom and then his dad, all the while remembering a different quote, one that talked about tangled webs and deception. And when the older Wilmots had said their good-byes with promises of seeing them tomorrow, she sat down hard on a kitchen chair, folded her arms on the kitchen table, and dropped her face into them. "What was I thinking?"

Matt stood for a moment, then pulled out the chair next to her. "That you wanted her to stop yelling at me, I suppose."

"Well, there's that," she admitted, her face still buried in her arms. "And I kind of wanted to punch her, and that's not very ladylike, so I lied instead."

"You were kind of good at it," Matt admitted.

"That's not a compliment, Matthew."

He couldn't help it. He laughed and pulled her more upright. "Stop burying your face and talk to me."

"No. You're insane."

"I've heard that before. It's not true, by the way."

She looked from him to the backyard and back. "You sounded out there like you're actually considering this."

"I am. So should you."

Her eyes went wide. "Why?"

"You like me."

"Oh, bother."

"Maybe even like me a lot, at least it seemed that way when I kissed you, Elle." Her flush made him smile. "And you like my kids."

"Your middle child thinks I'm a witch. I'd hardly call that good mothering material."

"He's far too opinionated for a seven-year-old. You'll bring him over to your side eventually."

"Matt, I—"

"Listen." He stood and pulled her up with him. "You've had a crazy long day. Me too. So let's put this to rest for the night, OK? We'll revisit this tomorrow. And then the next day. And the one after that. You did offer the use of the apartment, remember?"

Oh, she remembered all right. But that was when they were just next-door neighbors, and Matt didn't know she was crushing on him like an eighth grader at a spring dance.

He hugged her then, the kind of sweet, all-encompassing hug she could get used to, all of her days, and when he let her go, she had to force herself back. "We have a lot to discuss."

"And time to do it."

She took a deep breath. "Tomorrow."

"In between shopping for clothes."

Clothes.

She'd never thought of that. Matt and the boys had absolutely nothing but the clothes on their backs. "I've never shopped for kids' clothes before."

"Talk about a baptism of fire." Matt touched one hand to her cheek, and the feel of his thick, callused skin reminded her of how hard and long this man worked to provide for his family. "If you don't have time, Mom will go with me, I'm sure."

She raised a hand to cover his and watched his smile grow wider. "I'll make time."

"Good."

They stood like that for long, slow ticks of the clock. Then Elle stepped back. "You go cuddle with Amos."

"Good night, Elle."

She took a deep breath, wondering how on earth one life could change so quickly and completely in less than eight hours. "Good night, Matt."

chapter sixteen

"I don't think we should eat the food. Pretend you're sick or something," Randy whispered to Todd the next morning.

"We've got to eat something," Todd answered sensibly. "And I'm not a scaredy-cat." He started down the stairs, and Elle ducked back into the kitchen as if she hadn't heard a thing. He came across the front room and stopped in the kitchen. "Where's my dad, Miss Drake?"

She pointed east. "He and Amos woke up early. They're talking to people about the house, what needs fixing once everything's cleaned up."

"A lot." He sank onto a kitchen chair, and his little face looked as drawn and worried as it had weeks ago. "I looked out the upstairs window, and it's like ruined, isn't it? I don't know where we'll live."

His voice broke.

Randy peeked around the corner. When she looked that way, he ducked back behind the wall, but she saw enough to know he was worried, too. "I do."

Todd looked up.

Randy peeped around the doorway again.

"Follow me." She opened the back door, waited on the sidewalk, then led the way to the apartment on the far side of the house. She opened the door and let them walk in. "What do you think?"

Todd looked around as he moved forward. "Is this a place?"

"Well, yes." She met his gaze. "I'm not sure what that means, Todd. Everything's a place, isn't it?"

"You know, like a place to live," he explained. "Like how Ben Wojtzak and his mom live in a place that's not a house."

"An apartment."

"Yes!" He smiled up at her, but then the smile faded as he remembered why they had to live in a new place.

"That's exactly what it is," she told him and Randy. Randy walked ahead, then paused and glanced around as if scouting the place for possible dungeons. When he got to the second room off the kitchen, he got excited. "There are two bedrooms, Todd!"

"Good." Todd watched as Randy sidestepped into the second bedroom.

"Is two bedrooms a thing?" Elle asked.

"He likes to stay with me," Todd told her in a soft voice. "I keep saying I want my own room, but I'll wait until Randy's big enough to have his own. So if there's two bedrooms, Dad can have one with Amos, and Randy can be with me."

Thoughtful and kind with a little bit of his dad's protective nature.

She hadn't seen that in Todd initially. Maybe it had been buried beneath the uncertainty, but she recognized the trait now. "That's nice of you, Todd."

He shrugged one shoulder as if making a big deal bothered him. She added humble to the list of fine qualities.

"We really get to stay here?" He followed Randy, then turned, puzzled. "Why do you need two places to live?" he asked. "The other one is real big, and you're all by yourself."

Leave it to a kid to get right to the point. "It's actually too big," she agreed. "But what I needed was a plot of land with a big enough barn and shed to put my kiln, so while the house was too big, the setup outside was perfect."

"Your what?" Todd wondered.

"Kiln. My big oven."

Randy stopped dead in his tracks and didn't look quite so comfortable all of a sudden.

"Do you boys know what I do?"

Todd shook his head, and he didn't look all that relaxed, either.

Randy stood still. Very still. Then he took a long step closer to his big brother. "Do you cook things? Like…big things?"

"I don't cook them, Randy."

He stared at her, still distrustful.

"I fire them."

Todd frowned. So did Randy.

"I'm an artist. A potter. I make dishes."

Randy sidled closer to Todd, unconvinced. "Nobody makes dishes," he muttered, as if she were trying to trick them and he was too smart to be fooled. "You buy 'em."

Elle squatted to his level. "But before they get to the store, someone has to make them, don't they?"

He shrugged one shoulder as if maybe they did.

"That's what I do. I make dishes out of a special clay, and then I fire them in the oven. So it's kind of like cooking the dishes, except my oven gets very, very hot. It's no place for kids, ever, so you guys have to stay away from the shed and the barn, OK?"

Her edict seemed to suit Randy just fine. "OK."

Todd looked beyond her, to the south-facing window. "Can you show us?"

"Can you both be super good?"

"Why?" Randy arched impish brows.

"Because the dishes are breakable. And very expensive."

"I'll be good," Todd promised.

"Me, too." As they crossed the yard a few moments later, Randy spotted Matt. "Dad!" He bellowed across the grass field. "We're going to see the big oven!"

"Good!" Matt called back, and even from this far away, Elle could see his grin. "Supper!"

Randy ground to a halt until Todd grabbed his arm. "He's messing with you."

"Maybe she put a spell on him."

Elle bent low again, determined to put a hard stop to Randy's imaginings. "I am not a witch. I have never even seen a witch because there is no such thing. Now do you want to see my work shed or not?"

"Yes," said Todd.

Randy nodded a little more cautiously, and when she opened the door on the kiln side, his eyes went round. "Wow."

"Cool, right?"

He stared around, then stepped in. "Can I touch stuff?"

"Not this time around, but I'll tell you what. Once we get your lives organized again—" Two blank looks stared at her. "Clothing. Shoes. Book bags, books, toys."

Randy looked out the far window as if just realizing the extent of their loss. "Do you think all my stuff burned?"

Elle tiptoed around a delicate subject. "I don't know, and we can't go looking through stuff until everything cools off."

"But it probally burned." He spoke softly as he stared across the big field. "If stuff was upstairs, it probally burned, right? Because the upstairs is like, gone."

From the look of the destruction in daylight, she couldn't doubt his assertion. "It might have."

A tear snaked its way down his cheek, then another, until he shed a stream of silent tears as he stared at his burnt-out home.

"Randy."

She reached for him, but he shook her off and raced for her house, chin tucked, sobbing. She watched him go, unsure what to do.

"He kept his box upstairs," Todd whispered.

She turned back to Todd. "His what?"

"His wooden box," Todd explained softly. "It had all his special stuff in it. His rock collection, and the Starting Lineup guy Dad gave him because he loves football so much just like Dad, and his extra sticks of gum, and Mom's picture. He used to talk to her at night, when Dad thought he was sleeping."

"Oh, Todd." She put a hand on his shoulder as Randy charged through the back screen door. When it banged shut, she wondered if she had what it took to make a difference to him.

Todd had wanted and needed a friend from the beginning. He was a lost soul, and they'd already forged the framework of a relationship.

Amos was little enough to just need a mama, and with no memory of his own mother, he'd love easily.

But Randy carried his anger like a coat of armor, stiff and unyielding. He was little when his mother died, and he might not actually remember her either, but he was convicted enough to cling to her image and create a relationship with her.

Maybe she was foolish to think seriously about Matt's offer. And maybe in the light of day he'd realize his own folly, and they'd quietly let things go.

She and Todd left the potter's shed and went back into the yard. Matt was crossing over, pretending to chase Amos. The preschooler laughed out loud, dodging this way and that, trying to fool his father.

So much joy and too much sorrow.

Matt looked up and saw them. He waved, scooped up Amos, and headed their way. "You guys ready?"

"For?"

"Shopping?"

Elle swept the destroyed house a quiet look. "Are you done there?"

"For the moment. They're sending your mother out tomorrow to do the write-up. I didn't know your mother was an insurance adjustor, Elle."

"Add it to the elongated list of things we don't know about each other." She kept her tone pointed on purpose. Maybe he'd realize they were being silly. Maybe the light of day had knocked some sense into him. Maybe—

"That'll give us plenty to talk about once it snows, when we'll have plenty of time, although our snowplowing contracts keep me pretty busy in a bad winter." He tucked Amos onto his shoulders and moved toward the house. "Let's go get breakfast at the Sugar Maple because I don't expect you've got Fruity-O's or bagels."

"An accurate assumption."

"So let's grab food, then take the boys shopping, and by then we'll probably need psychotherapy."

"You're exaggerating."

His grin said he wasn't.

"It can't be all that bad. Not with two of us." Three kids, basic clothing, piece of cake.

Elle had never been so wrong in her life.

chapter seventeen

"You go and get Amos fitted for shoes," she prodded Matt when they arrived at the store. "I've shopped with Kate's girls a bunch of times. The boys and I will grab shorts and tops, then join you in the shoe department."

"You'll be OK?" Doubt clouded Matt's expression, and his frown lines only deepened when Randy and Todd smiled up at him. "I've done this before. You're being either brave or foolhardy, Elle."

"We'll be fine," she insisted. "It's not rocket science; it's a bunch of summer clothes, and kids like to shop for new clothes."

"They do?" Matt asked.

"We do?" Todd echoed. He looked at Randy. Randy looked back. His dour expression indicated he didn't like shopping for anything, ever.

"The faster we get this done, the faster we can figure out household stuff," she told Matt. "And I bet Kate or your mother will take charge of these guys while we get everything you need for the apartment. You tackle Amos; then we'll join you in a few minutes."

"Be good." Matt leveled the boys a stern look before toting Amos to the shoe department on the other side of the store.

Amos waved to Elle. She waved back and moved the cart forward. "OK, let's do this."

No boys. Not to her left, not to her right, and nowhere to be seen. Randy and Todd had disappeared faster than ninjas in a video game, and Elle had no idea there were so many good hiding places in a department store. What had she been thinking?

She called, not too loudly, because she really didn't need Matt to know that she couldn't be trusted with his children for less than a minute.

No one answered.

She searched.

Nothing.

She hunted high and low. But no Randy and no Todd.

Clearly they needed to die, but that did seem kind of *Extreme Stepmother, Prisoner Edition,* so she thought about what her mother would have done. Pretending she was making a store announcement, she cupped her hands megaphone-style. "The entire plan for a delicious chicken nugget meal is about to be scrapped. In its place will be bowls of sticky, cold, congealed oatmeal if you're not back here on the count of three. And if you think I don't mean it, you are sadly mistaken. One…"

She glanced around. An old woman smiled knowledgeably. A middle-aged man gave her a suspicious look.

"Two." The elderly woman was now openly chuckling behind a plastic rain cap. The man had moved on, but a young mother met her eyes with a look of understanding. Nothing akin to children had appeared in her field of vision.

"Two and a half…" *Come on, boys, you're making me look bad!*

"And, theeereee…" Stretching it out, just as her mother had done thirty-some years before, she gave them every opportunity she legally could and still have a vestige of self-respect.

"Here we are!"

"OK!"

They tumbled toward her, racing down the aisle, the swinging pants rack in the background providing mute evidence as to their hiding place. Todd reached her first. "Are we really going out for nuggets?"

"I love them the best!" Randy's voice chirped in tune.

"Like the very best?" she wondered.

Randy bobbed his head. So did Todd. "Yeah, we love 'em."

"Then think about that the next time you're tempted to disappear or mess around. That was your one allowable indiscretion." She hoped her firm expression got through to them, because she meant every word.

"We have a ton of stuff to get done, and you two need to be right here helping me. Got it?"

Randy gulped. Todd looked around. "Do we have to get stupid clothes?"

"You need clothes, Todd. We have to replace what got ruined in the fire."

He waved a hand to the left. "No, I know that, Miss Drake…"

"Call me Elle."

"Huh?"

"What?" Randy looked at her like her head had just exploded.

"If we're going to be living so close together, and hanging out, you should call me Elle."

"Like your first name?" Todd squeaked.

"Like…" She made a face at him. "Yes."

"But we don't do that."

"Now you do."

"Wow," Randy breathed. "Is it that easy?"

"Is what that easy?"

"To change the rules."

She grinned and ruffled his shaggy hair. "This time it is."

"OK, Elle." Todd tested the word and grinned wide. "My grandma makes me get clothes that aren't very comfortable."

"Some occasions call for dressier clothes. Nice pants, shirts. Like church and school."

"Is that all we can get?"

"Nope." She pointed over their heads. "Each of you go pick out four play shirts."

"Superheroes?"

"Sure."

"Yankees shirts?"

"Gotta love pinstripes."

Todd beamed at that. "Me and Dad are Yankees fans, but Randy likes Cleveland."

"Really?" She laughed. "Randy, I'm a Cleveland fan, too. Have you ever gone to an Indians game?"

He shook his head.

"Well, your dad and I will have to check the summer schedule. There's got to be time to get up to Cleveland for a weekend."

Todd stared at her. "Our dad can't go anyplace in the summer because it's too busy."

"Ever," Randy added.

"I see." Matt might reconsider the seriousness of her proposal when she reamed him out about not making time for the boys. Which meant she should do it gently. "I'll talk to him. And if he can't go, I can take you myself."

"What?"

"Really?"

"Would you?"

"Would you what?" Matt's voice surprised her from behind. He set two pairs of little-guy shoes into the cart, and a dozen packs of underwear in assorted sizes. "I figured I'd get the basics. You guys are slow." He noted the empty cart with a glance. "And should I ask what you're promising?"

"Probably not."

He sighed and directed his attention to the boys. "Is it something I'd let you do?"

"Not if you knew about it," Todd admitted.

"Not with a girl!" Randy exclaimed.

"Go get your play shirts," Elle interrupted them. "I'm setting my phone for a two-minute buzzer. You." She pointed to Randy. "Size eight. And you," she shifted her attention to Todd. "Size ten."

"How'd you know?"

"Phone app." She held the phone up. "You're losing time."

They laughed and hustled to the rack, and each one had four shirts in less than two minutes. "Same thing, only shorts this time, that shelf."

She showed them the shelves of shorts. "Red, blue, or black. Same sizes. Go."

"I can't believe it's working," Matt whispered as they scrambled for the shorts. "I'm kind of in awe."

"That's only because you didn't see them disappear for the first ten minutes. The only thing that saved me from a police intervention was threatening their food supply."

"Whatever works, Elle." He grinned and handed Amos a pack of fruit snacks from the box he'd set in the cart. "Food can be a great incentive. What did you promise them that I'm not going to approve of?"

"Uh, um…" She picked out clothes for Amos as she put off the question. "Boys, socks next. Not too many, it's summer. Get six for each of you."

"Any kind we want?"

"Yes."

Todd had six pairs in record time, all exactly the same. Randy busied himself studying superheroes, dinosaurs, and firemen-trimmed socks, so she had Todd pick out socks for Amos.

"Pants for church and school. Two pairs. But these you have to try on. And what about sports clothes?"

"Sports clothes?" Matt asked.

"Soccer? Baseball? What are the boys signed up for over the summer?"

"I haven't been available to drive them around in the evening, so—" He kind of muttered the next sentence. "I don't have them signed up for anything."

"I see." She measured the boys' hopeful looks and Matt's discomfort and decided to go easy on all three of them for the moment. "You mean nothing, *yet*."

The boys shifted their attention to Matt. "I might mean that, except my schedule hasn't eased up in the last fifteen seconds, Elle. I'm still pretty unavailable at night for the next few months. Having Dad out has messed with our production. I won't be around to drive them, not early enough, anyway."

"I am."

Surprise arched Randy's brows. Todd grinned.

"And you wouldn't mind?"

"I love sports. I was All-County and All-State in track and field. I played stopper for the varsity soccer team for four years and only stopped playing in college because arts schools don't field athletic programs." She laid a handful of polo-style shirts on the top of the cart. "Of course I wouldn't mind. And if it's too late to sign them up for this year, we can get them into an indoor over-winter program to develop skills for next year."

"So I could play baseball?" Todd sounded hopeful and excited. "For real?"

"And I could maybe play soccer with my friends?" Randy asked. "Like on a team?"

"Yes and yes."

Todd hugged her. Randy hugged Matt. Amos threw his fruit snack wrapper on the floor, which meant they were wearing on the four-year-old's patience. Matt picked it up and put it into his pocket. "We're on the brink, Elle."

"One pair of sweat pants and a jacket for each of you and we're done."

"I can't believe we get to pick our own clothes," Todd whispered to Randy, but in a voice loud enough to be heard by half the store. "Maybe she doesn't know we're not s'posed to."

"Don't tell her!"

"I won't."

Matt scrubbed a hand to his neck. "I never thought of why shopping was a problem. I just knew it was. Gloria insisted on taking them back-to-school shopping each August, and they kind of dreaded it and probably acted like brats."

"There's no excuse for being brats."

"No," he agreed as he lifted a restless Amos out of the seat. "And she was very generous with them."

"Did she take Amos, too?"

"Nope." He tweaked the preschooler's nose as he sat him down, and Amos made a mad dash for his big brothers. "Carrie died having Amos. I think being around him is hard on Gloria."

Hard on *her*?

Elle's heart went out to the little boy. No mom, a busy dad, and shrugged off by his grandparents. "He's precious, Matt. I would have given anything…" She stopped herself before she said more.

Her arms had ached for a child and been deprived. She'd have traded her fame and fortune for one moment of motherhood.

It hadn't happened.

And now Matt was offering her the chance to step into that role, the role she'd been denied. To become a mom to his three sons, with all the crazy that came along with the job. And she was actually considering it.

"They could use you, Elle." Matt put his hands on the full cart and kept his voice low. "Me, too. I know it's not all lovey-dovey like the first time around, but we've both been there, done that, and it didn't come out all that well, did it?"

Not all lovey-dovey.

She appreciated his honesty, because imagining a man like Matt falling in love with a woman like her was downright silly. She'd known that all along.

So she pretended her heart didn't break a little with his casual announcement, and thanked God for the practicality of the moment.

God and Matt were offering her a chance to seize her dream of motherhood. To be Matt's wife and the boys' mother, to have a house full of children, her goal fulfilled.

They'd need to talk.

Elle wasn't stupid, nor thick-skinned. She'd been cheated on once, and it wasn't about to happen again. Matt needed to know that.

"I gotta go potty!" A serious and intense expression claimed Amos's face.

"Me, too!"

"Me, too!"

"Whoops, I'll meet you over by shoes. You got this OK?" Matt picked up Amos as he nodded toward the cart.

For the moment, yes. As she watched him and the boys head to the far side of the store, she realized she'd have to know where the bathrooms were in each store, because for all intents and purposes, she was about to become…a mother.

When they rejoined her in the shoe department, Matt set a tall stack of men's clothing into the cart.

"You're not trying them on?" she asked. "Any of them?"

"Why would I?"

"To see if you like them? If they fit? If they look good together?"

"Girl stuff," he scoffed. "No one cares what I look like in the cab of a dozer. I always buy the same jeans, in the same size, some faded, some regular. Less hassle."

"Being a man is ridiculously easy."

"That's because women shop things to death." His expression challenged her to find fault in his logic, and she couldn't. "They agonize over color, style, how it looks, are they skinny enough."

"I'm thin enough."

"I'll say." He was pulling a hoodie from a rack as he said it, but turned in time to see the hurt expression on her face. "I just insulted you, didn't I?"

"It's fine."

"It's not." He tossed the hoodie into the cart and set his hands on her upper arms. "You're lovely just the way you are. You're the one who said you were thin. I shouldn't have agreed, I see that now."

She blushed because he was right, she was overreacting.

"So let me just say I think you're perfect, Elle."

"That's a little over-the-top."

"Is it?" He held her gaze, and his eyes said it wasn't. "I'll be the judge of that."

He couldn't be serious, and yet he looked serious and sincere, five minutes after reminding her they shouldn't worry about lovey-dovey emotions. He let her go and grabbed Amos just as the little guy turned to head toward the exit door. "Gotcha."

"Let's go, Dad!" Amos pointed to the door. "I wanna pway!"

"After we get shoes for your brothers," Elle told him. "And Dad."

"If you're good, I'll get us a bag of suckers," Matt promised.

"My favowite ones?"

"Yes. But only if you're good."

Amos took Matt's big, strong face into his little hands and leaned close, a silhouetted miniature of his big, strong father. "I'll be so good. I pwomise." He crossed his heart like Randy sometimes did, only Randy rarely meant it. She was pretty sure Amos did. "But can we huwwy? Like super fast?" And then he kissed his dad and grabbed more of Elle's heart.

By the time they got out of the store, Matt had spent a ridiculous amount of money, the boys were tired and whiny, and it wasn't even close to noon, but when Matt drove up Elle's driveway, the skeletal sight of their house settled the older boys down.

The smell of wet, burned wood overtook spring scents. And when Matt's mother called and asked if she could take the boys to the zoo for the afternoon, Matt agreed. She bustled in the back door just as they finished the second round of chicken nuggets.

"Boys!"

"Grandma!" All three hurried to hug her, and when Matt's father followed her in, they charged him, too.

Matt stepped in front of his dad. "Do you guys remember that Grandpa had surgery not too long ago?"

"Yes."

"I remember."

"That means he can't carry you or wrestle with you or pick you up and throw you right now. Got it?"

"Yup!"

"Got it!"

Matt turned to his father. "You sure you're up for this?"

"I've got the boss with me." Dan winked and sent the older boys out to the car. "She won't let me get away with anything."

"We'll bring them back after supper," his mother said. "That will give you two time to figure things out."

"Thanks, Mom." Matt shut the door and, turned to Elle. "Alone at last."

She held up a list of household items he needed to buy.

"More shopping."

"Really?"

"You want to work tomorrow, right?"

"I *have* to work tomorrow," he told her.

"Then we can get to know each other at the store. The apartment's got furniture, but no TV, linens, or kitchen or cleaning stuff."

"Setting up a house is a pain." He reached out and opened the door for her, but as she moved by, he wrapped an arm around her waist and pulled her back. "But." He smiled into her eyes as if she was the prettiest thing in the world, or maybe his attention just made her feel like the prettiest thing. He dropped his gaze and then his lips to her mouth in a kiss that was too long and too short. "I sure do love having such good-looking help by my side getting it done."

"Matt."

"Hmm?" His smile deepened, and he let one finger graze the side of her cheek. "If I have to put things back together, Elle, I'm glad to be doing it with you. And that's the truth of the matter."

Sweet and sincere, but she wouldn't fool herself with thoughts of romance and love. She'd learned her lesson there.

Still, there were things they needed to talk about, but not now. They had half a dozen hours to outfit the apartment with everything Matt would need to start rebalancing his life, which meant they'd talk once that was done.

chapter eighteen

Elle Drake was amazing.

He was getting married.

By noon the next day, Matt had texted her three times over almost nothing, just because he wanted her to know he was thinking about her. The big boys had gone to school, Amos was at day care, and Elle was working on a project in the barn, so why did he keep bothering her?

Possibly because you're afraid she'll come to her senses and change her mind, because why would a beautiful and talented and financially comfortable woman want to take on a crew of rowdy boys and their workaholic father?

For no reason he could think of as he directed the shovel operator excavating the new recessed skating rink the town had voted to install.

His phone buzzed with a text from Jason. "You're not seriously considering marrying your neighbor, are you? What are you thinking?"

Jason with the Mrs. Brady–type wife and one princess daughter. He had no clue what Matt experienced on a day-to-day basis, and because Jason didn't handle drama too well, his quiet, organized lifestyle suited him. Matt's reality was quite the opposite, and everyone in the eastern half of the state knew it.

"I thought it was just a stupid rumor," the next text read. "But now Mom and Dad are talking about it like it's a done deal. What's up with that?"

He called Jason back straightaway. "Yes, Elle and I are talking marriage if she doesn't wise up and back out of the deal. So shut up, OK?"

Jason never shut up, an inherent flaw in his personality. "You don't know this woman. None of us know her, but I know what folks used to say about her."

"I know what they used to say about you, too. Fortunately, we all mature, some more slowly than others. She's wonderful, Jason. The boys love her. Moreover, they respect her."

"You couldn't find a nanny, so you find a wife instead? This is a stretch. You know it. I know it. She's not exactly your type, Matt."

He had a type? Since when? He'd dated exactly four girls before meeting Carrie, and they'd married right out of college. "I was married long before I was old enough to have a type, Jason. You of all people should be happy for me. A woman in the house means fewer emergencies for me to handle."

"A convenient marriage."

It wasn't…and yet, it was. "It suits us. Both of us."

"Can't you just hire her to babysit and keep your options open? I can't see you settling this way, Matt. Not in the long run."

Anger ran a rod across Matt's shoulders. "You're talking stupid. I'm supposed to ask a world-renowned artist to babysit? Are you crazy? And marrying Elle isn't settling for anything. You don't have a clue what you're talking about. If she's willing to take us on, it would be the best thing that's happened to me and my boys in a long time. If anyone's doing the settling, it's her."

"Her ex's new wife says he didn't stray from his marriage. He was pushed out, and she just happened to be in the right place at the right time to catch him."

"Of course she was." The burr between Matt's shoulders grew sharper. "She was right there to offer her brand of counseling to a married man, who just happens to be one of the richest guys in the country. Listen, Jase, I don't know what all went down between Elle and her ex-husband. But I do know it broke her heart, so from this point on, I'm asking you and Cindie to ignore whatever his new wife says in the tabloids. It's old news, and Elle is moving on. With me."

"You're serious."

He was very serious, so why was Jason being deliberately obtuse? "Quite."

"And this doesn't seem weird and sudden to you?"

"I'd go with sudden and nice." He thought of how Elle made the boys smile, how she wasn't afraid to wear her long, potter's dress and dance with Amos. "Nothing weird about it."

"Listen. I know she saved the kids, but marrying her is kind of an exaggerated way of saying thank you, isn't it?"

Was that what he was doing?

Maybe.

But if it worked out for both of them, that couldn't be a bad thing. Was need more important than love? When it came to his three boys, it sure seemed to be.

"You're serious, Matt? Really? Because this isn't like you."

"I've got work, Jason. So do you." He hung up the phone, irritated.

For years, people had been all up in his business, as if losing a wife gave them permission to offer advice on what to do with the house, the boys, their lives, their faith, their habits. For four years, he'd spun the plates of life in the air with nothing more than some help from his mother when she was available, and as a full-time school teacher until last year, she hadn't been available all that much. He'd gotten all the advice in the world, freely given, with few offers of actual help.

He hadn't just lost a wife the day Carrie died.

He'd lost a partner in everything. Marriage, parenting, romance, excavating. She'd taken charge of a lot of things so he wouldn't have to, and it worked. Now he had the chance to fix things, with Elle.

It wasn't the same. He knew that. She knew that.

But that didn't make it wrong. Did it?

He texted her again. "Wanna do lunch?"

"Working."

He texted back, "You sure? I'm buying."

"Of course you'd be buying. That's how it's done. But still working."

"Food is essential."

"Which is why I'll see you at supper. Six o'clock."

He stared at the phone. She wasn't going to meet him; she was working, and he should respect that.

But if he was willing to take some time and meet her, shouldn't she do the same thing? Or was his irritation with Jason seeping into his exchange with Elle?

And six o'clock supper?

She must be kidding. He never got home before seven on summer nights. Sometimes later, even. Like a farmer, he needed to make the most of the long summer days, the extended daylight hours. Sandwiching in extra jobs wasn't a golden opportunity this year. It was a necessity, to pull off that payment due late winter. He texted back, "Can't get home before seven, earliest. Maybe later. Mom will come by to watch the boys."

Silence.

No answering text, no snappy rejoinder.

He stared at the phone, waiting, then shoved it into his pocket, aggravated. He didn't bother with lunch, and when Spike brought back a sack of donuts from Petersen's Bakery, Matt wolfed down two and kept right on working because time was money. Everyone knew that.

* * *

Work should never be more important than children, and Elle would be more than willing to explain that to Matt Wilmot, but not in a stupid, impersonal text message.

Luckily, she'd finished her current project before Matt riled her up with his "home late" message. She cleaned up her painting table, picked up her phone, and locked the shed.

She should have gone to lunch with him. Why didn't she?

Because you're afraid to let anyone call the shots. You want control.

Not control, she decided. Just a buffer, an invisible wall erected of necessity. She'd learned to do that a long time ago. She'd let down with Alex. She'd believed his promises, trusted his vows.

Now pragmatism ruled the day. Was it wrong to choose with care? Make well-thought decisions?

No.

It was lunch, Elle. You could have just said yes, and you'd be having lunch with Matt right now, instead of staring at a half-empty refrigerator.

And have Matt think she was at his beck and call? No, thank you.

"Elle? Are you in here?"

She turned at the sound of her mother's voice. "Hey, Mom."

Aggie came through the back door and folded her arms. She held Elle's gaze, which meant she'd heard what went down at the fire. "Are you seriously thinking of marrying Matt Wilmot?"

"Possibly. Maybe. Yes." She met and held her mother's gaze. "He is smokin' hot, Mom. That's got to be a plus, right?"

Her mother studied her reaction, then pointed to a chair. "Sit."

Elle sat. Aggie pulled up the chair next to her, sat, and covered one of Elle's hands with both of hers. "What's going on, and how did this happen? Because the two of you have the gossip network of Cedar Mills quite fired up."

"It doesn't take much for that to happen," Elle remarked. "And nothing's decided for sure, but yes, we're talking about marriage."

"Talking about marriage?" Aggie repeated slowly. "Honey, marriage isn't a business merger." She paused, then sighed as she read Elle's reaction. "Unless it *is* a business merger."

"It's not like that, Mom."

Aggie held her gaze until Elle cringed. "OK, it's not all hearts and flowers either. I had that once. It didn't work out so well."

"Because Alex turned out to be a pig and broke his vows once he realized that money could buy a whole lot more than stocks and bonds."

"Well, there's that," Elle conceded. Leave it to her mother to leap to her defense. She loved that about her. "I think I'm at an age and stage where practicality outweighs hormones."

"There's nothing wrong with hormones. Or romance. Or love," Aggie insisted. "Love is patient, love is kind. There's a reason the Bible talks about love and romance, Elle. Corinthians and the Song of Solomon. They're good things."

She might be right, but they hadn't gotten Elle very far in the past. "Mom, men are not lining up to sing their praises about me. I figured that out a long time ago. But Matt and the boys are a package deal. I think I could be good for them. All of them," she added.

Understanding softened her mother's expression. "Motherhood."

"Have you seen three children who need a mother more?"

"No, but, Elle—"

"Matt and I are still talking," Elle interrupted her. "Nothing is settled, and when it is, you'll be the first to know. I promise. But in the meantime, I could use some prayers, because if I don't marry the guy, I might have to kill him, and that will have its own nasty ramifications. He's beyond clueless."

Her mother regarded her, then sighed. "You're a fixer, Elle. You always have been. It's part of you, born in you. Like Grandma Novinski, you have an artist's heart and a servant's nature, but what if you go into this relationship with all this practical thought, and it doesn't work out? Then those three little boys are brokenhearted all over again."

"So we should never take a chance?" Elle asked.

Aggie frowned.

"I know what you're saying, Mom, but I see so many marriages crumbling around me, including my own. Maybe going into this as more of a partnership is the smart choice. No rose-colored lenses or romantic notions."

Her mother didn't look convinced. "And what if you happen to fall in love with him, Elle? What do we do with all of your practical application then? Or are you blocking the chance at love to keep yourself insulated from hurt?"

"Minimized risk management."

"Oh, dear heavens." Aggie stood and braced her hands on the table, facing Elle. "You'll do what you want, Elle. I know that." Her tone said that wasn't always a good thing. "And whatever you decide, I will be behind you one hundred percent, but when I see my beautiful daughter willing to settle for less than what God intended, it breaks my heart. You are fearfully and wonderfully made, Elinora, and the day they put you into my arms, so perfect and beautiful and precious, was the happiest day of my life. How I wish you saw yourself now the way I saw you then."

She didn't hug Elle or carry on. She grabbed up her purse and strode out. The slap of the wooden screened door left a hollow behind.

The phone rang.

Elle breathed deep, saw the day care number, and answered the call. "Hello."

"Miss Drake, this is Junie Oliver's mother. I've got Amos in daycare here during the day."

"Theresa, right?"

"Yes. Matt's got you down as the emergency contact now."

"Yes."

"Well, Amos has spiked a fever. He was perfectly fine, and then wasn't. Of course, that's not unusual with children."

It wasn't? Elle had no clue. "Did you try his dad?"

"I did, and it went straight to voice mail. Can you pick him up?"

Sure she could, but then what would she do with him? She had no idea, but her brother-in-law was a doctor, and she had a fifteen-minute ride to make a plan. She could do this.

She spent five minutes on the phone with Jeff, then made a three-minute stop at the pharmacy for meds, a children's thermometer, and ginger ale, then parked at the day-care center, which wasn't far from the church.

"Hey, little guy." She knelt beside the small cot in the front room of the gingerbread-style house. "Sorry you're not feeling well. I'm going to take you home, OK?"

"I want my daddy."

"I know. We'll get him. I promise."

"I want him now, pwease." Amos's gaze begged more than his words. "I just want my daddy." Mournful, red-rimmed eyes peered up at her. The little guy clutched the corner of the thin blanket and glanced around as if hoping Matt would appear. "Pwease get him. I don't feel good."

"Of course you don't." The teacher stepped in to help. "And...," she hesitated as if wondering how to reference Elle. "And this nice lady is going to take you home."

Slow, quiet tears slipped down Amos's round cheeks.

Elle's heart broke for him. She'd witnessed his histrionics often enough, and she knew his occasional off-the-wall, attention-grabbing behavior.

But this was different. This was a sick, small child in need of a parent. "Come here, darling." She didn't wait for the little guy's permission, she simply bent down and gathered him up into her arms. "Let's get you home and get you better, OK?"

He didn't fight her, but when they got to the car, the teacher, who had walked out with them, grimaced. "You need a booster seat. Hang on."

She'd forgotten that in her hurry. Kids needed booster seats at this age, and she'd raced over here, totally forgetting a basic necessity.

The woman returned and tucked the seat into the car. "Here you go. We keep a few extras here. They come in handy for times like this."

"Thank you." She secured Amos's belt and got into the car. She pulled out of the day care driveway, watching the road and the sick little guy in the back seat, wondering how she was going to do both.

It took about two minutes for Amos to fall sound asleep, which meant she could pay attention to driving, but was that normal? She didn't know.

She got home, brought him inside, and tucked him onto the couch in her living room.

Should she wake him to give him medicine? Or let him sleep?

He felt hot. That meant she should wake him, didn't it? Or should she have given him the fever reducer at the day care house before he dozed off?

That would have been smarter.

She called Matt's number and got no answer, like Mrs. Oliver had said. She left a message, then texted him, too.

Her landline rang. She answered it as Amos whimpered on the couch. "Hello."

"Elle, it's Mary Lou Wilmot. Theresa Oliver said Amos is sick. Do you need me to take him or come watch him, dear? I'm not one bit busy, and I'd be happy to do it."

Should she admit to Matt's mother she didn't have a clue what to do for Amos, or pretend she was a capable adult?

Amos furrowed his brow in sleep, and that made her decision easy. "Mary Lou, he's fallen asleep with a fever, and I don't know how to give him medication when he's sleeping." Did she sound desperate?

Possibly, but if Mary Lou had a clue about helping the little guy, she'd willingly own it.

"It's a trick, isn't it? You know sleep's important, but you want to get the fever down. I'll come right over, if that's all right?"

"Yes. Please."

She got there in less than ten minutes, and with her help, they woke Amos enough to get his medicine down, and then they laid him right back to sleep.

"Done."

"Done!" Mary Lou smiled at her as she laid a cool, damp cloth over Amos's brow. "It's tricky on your own. I honestly don't know how Matt's managed all these years, Elle. A little maneuver like that is so much easier with two people."

Matt came through the back door just then, looking anxious. He kicked off his boots and charged into the front room. "Amos is sick?"

"There's a bug going around." Elle had gotten that from Jeff on the way to the daycare center. "Fever, aches, and congestion."

"Flu?"

She shook her head. "Jeff didn't say flu. He said a bug. Don't kids get bugs like this fairly often?"

"They do," agreed Matt's mother.

Matt laid a hand against Amos's forehead, then pulled back, concerned. "We should take him in to be seen. I can't believe I missed the call."

"Shouldn't we give the medicine time to work, first? We just gave it to him, and Jeff said—"

Matt didn't wait to hear what her brother-in-law said. "What if he needs antibiotics?"

"Jeff didn't say anything about that, so I don't know." She glanced at Matt's mother. "What do you think, Mary Lou?"

Mary Lou didn't look any too anxious to argue with Matt, but she said, "Usually they want to wait a day or two before prescribing."

"When a kid's sick, he's sick. There's not a lot of sense in waiting," Matt said. Then he shifted his attention to Elle. "Your brother-in-law's a family doctor," Matt told her, as if that made Jeff's opinion negligible. "The boys go to the pediatric practice by the mall."

"I see."

Matt bundled the sleeping boy into his arms and headed for the door.

"Don't you need to call them first?" his mother asked.

"I'll call from the car. I don't want to waste any more time," Matt told her as he angled his way through the door.

He left as quickly as he came, leaving Elle and his mother looking at each other. "Well." Elle picked up the little medicine spoon and the ibuprofen bottle and took them into the kitchen. "Is it normal to rush a kid to the doctor like that? Because Jeff didn't seem all that concerned, and he told me that if the fever didn't come down with the medicine or if it lasted into three days, then he should be seen. He might not be a pediatrician, but he sees lots of kids in his practice."

Matt's mother hesitated before she replied. "I think Matt errs on the side of caution with the boys after what happened to Carrie. It's like he doesn't dare take a chance or let things go."

Elle washed her hands, frowning. "So he rushes them in for medical care at the first sign of illness, but he's willing to work constant twelve-hour days all summer and never see them."

Mary Lou winced. "That about sums it up."

A hot mess of crazy.

Figuring out Matt and his boys was like tackling a Rubik's Cube with some of the colored squares peeled off. Could she do this? Should she do this?

"Elle."

She tried to compose her face before she turned back to Matt's mother. "Yes?"

Mary Lou came her way. "You're probably wondering how fast you can run, and I don't blame you."

"I'm not good with excessive reactions."

"Which is why you're perfect for Matt and those boys," Mary Lou went on. "You've got the grace and calm to defuse the anger and the chaos that surrounds this family on a too-regular basis."

Did she?

Suddenly she wasn't so sure.

Maybe she was getting in over her head. Maybe she was gilding the lily, trying to make things seem right when they were already all wrong.

Mary Lou took her hand. "Matt second-guesses himself a lot. Part of that is his perfectionist nature, but a bigger part is circumstantial. He's angry at God, Gloria's angry at him, and neither one has come to grips with Carrie's death, that sometimes things just happen and we don't have to assign blame. We just have to pick up our yoke and move on."

"He loves those boys."

"Yes." Mary Lou gripped her hand tighter. "But love isn't always enough, and I think you recognize that."

She did, but was she setting herself up for another failure, like her mother suggested? Or was she taking a chance for the dream that had eluded her for so long? How would she know?

"Prayer is my equalizer." Mary Lou picked up her purse and moved toward the door. "I lift my eyes up to the hills—from where will my help come?" She met Elle's gaze once more. "I've always been a church-goer, but Dan and the boys kind of shrugged things off. Then when bad things happen, they flounder and wonder why. I've seen your work, Elle. Seeing your designs is like a window to your soul, and that's the kind of strength Matt and his boys need. I'm not trying to convince you," she added, and she smiled softly as she said it. "I just wanted you to see this as I see it. A new chance for goodness, all around."

Elle had prayed for guidance, for a sign of right versus wrong.

Her answer had just come, via Matt's mother. The school bus pulled up at the end of the driveway to let Todd and Randy off. Randy spotted his grandmother's car and raced up the drive, shouting a welcome.

Todd came more slowly, but smiling—until his gaze drifted to the burned-out house next door. He paused, quiet and still, staring.

It broke Elle's heart to see it.

They needed her. Even the stubborn, dig-his-heels-in father needed her. He might not know it, but she did.

chapter nineteen

Amos had looked really ill when Matt walked into Elle's living room ninety minutes before.

By the time the front office staff slipped him in to see the doctor, the little guy's fever was gone, and Amos was racing mini cars up and around the examining table with more realistic noises than Matt would have thought possible.

A virus going around, the doctor said. Rest and fluids, fever reducer as needed, and he should be fine in a couple of days.

Which was pretty much what Elle's brother-in-law intimated.

He pulled up into the drive, knowing he was destined to eat crow.

Amos hopped out of his seat, dashed up the walk, and yelled, "I'm home! I got a sucker! I'm home!"

Elle stepped out.

Matt did a quick mental assessment as he approached. On a scale of one to ten, one being happy to see him, ten being pack-your-things-and-go, she looked…

An unreadable five.

Now he remembered why he hated fives, because the conversation could go either way. She leaned over the back rail, arms folded against the faded wood, and watched him approach. "What's the verdict?"

A dishonest man would lie to get himself out of trouble, but what kind of man did that?

A smart one.

He waved off the warning and paused as Amos dashed up the steps. "A virus. Wait it out."

"Ah."

He waited, knowing she could and should ream him out, because instead of listening to her or her brother-in-law doctor, he'd charged off, handed over a fifty-dollar co-pay, and been told the same thing Jeff told Elle over the phone. "I panicked."

"You did."

He climbed the lower two steps and paused. "I'm sorry I raced off."

"And ignored your mother and me."

"That, too."

"And interrupted my work session today."

"That's off limits, I take it."

Her gaze slid from the barns housing all kinds of pricey equipment back to Matt. "Respect for work space goes both ways."

"You're right. I'm just not used to…" He trailed off, not sure how to put it and stay out of trouble.

"A woman's work being important."

"Of course it's important. It's just—"

She raised a hand. "We can talk about this later."

"Or I'll apologize and go back to work, and we'll forget it ever happened."

"Option one," she told him as she turned and opened the door. "And you can't go back to work. You've got a kid to watch."

"Where's Junie?"

"I sent her home when your mother decided to take the older boys to her house overnight."

"They'll love that," Matt said as he followed her inside. "They haven't had a chance to do that in months."

"So she said. But this guy," she smiled and squatted low to talk to Amos, "is going to need more medicine soon because that fever's likely to come back, and we don't want him uncomfortable, do we?"

"No."

She pointed to the countertop. "Ibuprofen and acetaminophen there, next to the special spoon with a hollow handle. Your mom brought some freezer ices over, there's Jell-O in the fridge, and he'll need the next dose around six o'clock."

Matt stared at the medicine, then the clock, then her. "You're leaving?"

"Work calls." She indicated the shed, kissed Amos's cheek, and walked out the door and across the yard.

"Can we pway checkers, Dad? Or, I know! Go Fish! It's my favowite!"

"You pick," said Matt as he watched Elle cross the yard to the barn-like building beyond. She let herself in through the door and closed it behind her.

"Can I have a fweeze pop?"

"Can you ask politely?" The minute he said the words, he realized Elle was rubbing off on him.

"May I pwease have one?"

"Yup. Green, pink, orange, or red?"

"Red!"

"You've got it." He snipped the freeze pop in half and set both halves on the table.

"Elle gives me a bowl," Amos instructed. "From up there." He pointed to a cupboard, and when Matt opened it, sure enough, there were bowls inside. Breakable ones. He pulled one out and set it on the table. "Be careful, OK?"

"I will!"

Matt called Spike, explained that he had to stay with Amos, and asked Spike to finish up the final grading. By the time he and Spike had gone over the specifications, Amos had finished his freeze pop and found a deck of cards.

"Whoa, hang on, kid. You're a mess." Matt sponged him and the table down with a wet paper towel, then took a seat. "Do you want to deal?"

"Sure!" Amos counted out the seven cards with slow precision, and when he lost count at six, he had to go back and recount his and Matt's piles. "Seven!" he declared a few minutes later. He grinned up at Matt, so proud of his accomplishments.

"You did good, Amos."

"Fanx! You go first, Daddy!" He peeked at his cards when Matt asked for a five and shook his head, triumphant. "Go fish!"

Matt fished for nearly a half hour, but by the time they got done with game number two, Amos looked flushed. Laying his palm against the little guy's cheek, Matt knew his fever was climbing again. He gave him medicine, put his nighttime diaper on him, then cuddled his littlest son on the couch while the Cleveland Indians put a hurting on the visiting Detroit Tigers.

He couldn't remember the last time he sat and watched a baseball game on TV.

Guilt nudged him. He should be laying out a prep plan for the week-end's work or writing a schedule, or assigning crews for the coming week of jobs, but that would mean moving Amos, and it felt downright nice to sit in the peace and quiet of the small apartment living room, holding his son, watching a game.

By the end of the fourth inning, guilt won.

He tucked Amos into bed, opened his laptop, and laid out a schedule for the upcoming weeks. The long hours of June daylight tempted him to keep working, but when he heard the sound of the barn door closing, he shut down the laptop and walked outside as Elle crossed the yard. She spotted him and raised a hand to her hair as if hoping it looked all right, a winsome and feminine thing to do.

"You set me up," he said when she drew closer.

She ignored his statement. "How's Amos?"

"As predicted. We played, his fever came back, I gave him the meds, and he fell asleep in my arms."

"Giving you time to relax and embrace the best feeling in the world, I expect."

He looked at her carefully and sensed the complicated emotion behind simple words. "You never had children."

"Five long years of intensity ending in epic fail." She took a while to look at nothing in particular. "Nothing worked, and that seemed so wrong. In this day and age when everyone could get pregnant, we couldn't. Not and stay pregnant, anyway." She shrugged, still not looking at him. Distress darkened her sweet, pragmatic face. "It didn't matter how much money we had or which specialist we consulted, the end was always the same. No baby."

"I'm sorry, Elle." He was, too, because her expression told the story of heartbreak that went beyond the explanation. "That had to be hard."

"Lots of things are hard," she supposed, gazing out. "When things got bad, I buried myself in my work, and Alex cozied up with a swim-suit model. Did you know that they're married now?" she asked softly. "And expecting a child."

He knew that—Alex Caulder's happiness made regular headlines—but seeing Elle's flash of pain made it all too real.

He reached out an arm and drew her closer. "That bites."

"Yup." She leaned her head against his shoulder and sighed, and when she did, his protective nature came out. Elle was a strong, caring person. She deserved happiness. What kind of God denied happi-ness to faithful people? That made no sense to Matt, which meant the whole God-thing was vastly overplayed in order to give people a false sense of forever-after nonsense.

He chalked it up to simplistic foolishness, but he didn't dare say that around Elle. For a smart woman, she claimed an innocent faith, but maybe she needed that to get through life's down times.

Not him. He got by with focus and hard work, much like his father before him.

He breathed deep. She smelled like strawberry and chemicals. "Nice scent," he whispered.

She laughed softly. "Hazards of the trade."

"You haven't shown me your work yet."

"You saw it online. You told me so. Remember?"

"Not the same as in person, is it?"

"Not really."

He rubbed his nose against her hair. "Can we go see it now?"

"No."

He kissed her temple. "Soon?"

He felt her cheeks move when she smiled. "Yes."

"Is it secret?"

"I showed the boys, so it can't be too secret."

"Good point." He kept his mouth against her skin, then whispered, "Why'd you set me up tonight?"

"Because you needed it." She turned then and faced him. "Because you have the most amazing miracles right before your eyes, and you think work is more important."

This year it was more important than ever, but only he and his father knew why. The outstanding loan wasn't common knowledge, and Matt wasn't about to throw his father under the bus, so he kept his silence. He indicated her barn with a glance. "And yet you went back to work this evening."

"Enforced bonding time."

"Elle." How could he explain what fell on his shoulders? How much needed to be done this year to make up for last year's parade of storms? "You do your work in a controlled environment. You don't have to worry about snow or wind or torrential downpours sweeping in from the Ohio Valley and wreaking havoc with days of almost finished work. Delays. Government red tape. Zoning and planning approvals. Building inspectors who don't show up, blocking progress."

"Every job has variables and timelines. But they're only kids once, Matt, and they're hungry for attention."

"You don't think it will be easier with two of us?" he asked.

She held his gaze. "If we're both fully invested. And if we respect each other's time and commitments."

"Here's the problem," he told her frankly. "I have the pressure of a whole company resting on my shoulders right now. Everything you see there," he pointed to the storage barns beyond his skeletal house, "falls on me to produce as much income as we can physically handle this year after getting thoroughly roughed up last year. No one expected Dad to get sick and need surgery. Payroll has to be met, utilities must get paid, and that can't happen if jobs don't get completed on time. Excavation and grading is usually the first and last step in getting those mortgage payouts and loans initiated. Without us, nothing gets done, and we're on a finite schedule, weather dependent. That's not easy to juggle."

"Your father's ready to come back, and your brother should be sharing equally in the workload."

She was right, but it wasn't that simple. Was it? "Jason's good at what he does, but he's never been good at stretching himself thin."

"Is that because he's not good at it or because he knows you'll shoulder extra rather than risk failure?"

He couldn't deny he'd wondered the same thing, but it stung coming from Elle. "You have to let us handle this."

"Off limits?"

"No." He hesitated, though, because in a way, it was. Because it was their business, their family business. "It's been the three of us for over a decade, Elle. My dad bought out my uncle eleven years ago, and it's been me, him, and Jase ever since. This year's particularly tight because of Dad's problems."

"Your parents are nice people, Matt."

They were, so he nodded against her hair as he pulled her closer again and realized he was starting to get used to the funny, chemical smell. The thought of smells brought him to another subject. "Your leach lines need to be redone. That will take care of your drainage problem in the backyard."

"I know." She leaned back and frowned up at him. "I hate the thought of big equipment back here so close to my work. And yes, I'm sure it's a ridiculous worry, but I couldn't bring myself to just get it done. My mother thinks I'm whacked."

"Mothers are often right."

She smacked his arm, and he smiled against her hair, then her cheek. "I'll do it myself. I won't go near your pottery barn or shed or whatever you want to call it, and I'll do it right, OK? If you watch the boys."

"Bartering. I like that."

"Yeah?" He turned her and smiled into her eyes. "I could arrange a trade of this or that, darlin'." He teased her mouth with his lips and lingered there a while. "So what do you think, Elle? Will you marry me? Help me raise these crazy, fun little boys? I'd be most beholdin' to you."

She laughed and caught his face in her hands. "Stop kissing me."

He shook his head, thinking he'd never had a better summer's evening. "I can't."

"Matt."

"But—"

"You sound serious."

"I am." He locked his hands around her middle. "You want me to make some changes. Commitments."

"I think it goes with the territory, Matt."

"And it goes both ways," he told her. He indicated the attached apartment where Amos was sleeping. "My heart broke the day that little guy was born, Elle. It didn't just break, it shattered, because burying Carrie and taking on the boys and work and life wiped me out. It was like being knocked upside the head by a two-by-four, and the reality never got better. Nothing ever seemed right. I can't do that again, Elle."

"Do what?"

"Risk losing you to pregnancy. It hit me upside the head once. I don't ever want to have to face that again."

She frowned. "I think we covered that topic. Five years of shots and interventions and chronic disappointment left its mark. I have no wish to go through any of that again, Matt. Ever."

"You're OK with just having the boys?"

She slanted a teasing smile his way. "And their father."

He laughed and pulled her into a hug, a hug that could have lasted forever, except she stepped away. "I think we better see about that marriage license, Matt."

She was right.

Being here, holding Elle, kissing her, felt too right to be wrong, but he understood what she meant. "Tomorrow. We can be married next week at the town court."

"Tomorrow is fine, and we're not using a justice of the peace. We'll arrange for Father Murphy to do the wedding according to his schedule. In church."

"Well, we met there." He met her smile with his. "I guess that makes sense. Can you arrange things?"

"I can."

He brushed his mouth against hers once more. "Quickly?"

She sighed, and that sigh just about undid him. "Yes."

"Good." He kissed her forehead and waited while she walked into the kitchen of the main house. "Good night, Elle."

She hesitated just long enough to make him a little crazy, then smiled. "Night."

She shut the door, and he waited until he heard the turn of the lock before heading back to the attached apartment.

He yearned for her, as if someway, somehow, they were meant to be together. It was different than his romance with Carrie, and he didn't want to compare the two women or the relationships, because he was a different man than he'd been a dozen years before. Older, more committed, wiser in some ways, and more experienced.

But his feelings for Elle were strong, no matter what his stupid brother said.

She brought out something in him, something that made him want to be a better man, a better person. A better father.

And no matter what anyone said, that couldn't be considered a bad thing.

chapter twenty

"You are here on a clandestine cause," Elle told her mother, sister, and Matt's mother the next afternoon. "Your mission, should you choose to accept it, is to help plan and implement a very small wedding."

Matt's mother squealed. Kate beamed. Aggie studied her carefully, then looked down and opened a new page in her electronic tablet. "I will take notes. When?"

Elle had spent an hour that morning talking with the church office and the priest. "Next week so we can sneak it in before Kate has this baby."

"I'll explain to the baby that he needs to exercise patience," Kate said. "Elle, this is so exciting!"

"You are so good for my son," declared Mary Lou. "And for these precious boys. And I've even gotten Matt's father to come to church with me since he met you, Elle. He was always too busy, but maybe being sick and then the fire?" She shrugged. "He's taking baby steps back, and about time, too."

"How big is this wedding?"

"Just family, so small."

"Under fifty people."

"I should hope so." Elle poured a glass of tea and sat down with them. "Do you think the Polish ladies would cater the dinner for us?"

Aggie paused in her note-taking and looked up, surprised. "They would love it, Elle."

"So would I." She'd fought her mother on so many things with her first wedding, so invested in getting everything upscale and right, the rising young artist polishing her star.

There was something good and solid about being ten years older with a better understanding of faith, family, and community. "I was thinking a family-style serving at the tables—"

"Lovely!" Aggie typed quickly.

"And perhaps a Thanksgiving menu even though it's summer?"

"Perfect!" The Polish Ladies Group was famous for putting on Thanksgiving-style dinners as fundraisers.

"And I'd like Janek's Bakery to do the traditional pastry table with just a small wedding cake."

"Elle." Aggie paused her typing and peered over her glasses. "It sounds lovely, but are you doing this to make me happy? Or you?"

Clearly they both remembered the endless tussles over her first wedding day. "Both," she admitted and laughed. "But mostly I'm doing this for the boys. This is a big step for us and them, and I want the wedding to represent all the goodness of marriage and faith. There'll be plenty of day-to-day crazy in our lives as we all adjust, but Todd and Randy are old enough to remember this. I want it to be just right. We're meeting with Father this weekend, the date's cleared with the church, and Matt got both Todd and Randy signed up for summertime religion classes. We're too late for summer baseball for Todd, but there's a six-week fall league I got him into and a recreation soccer league for Randy. Evenings are going to fill right up, so if we can make the wedding nice but simple, I'd be grateful to all of you."

"I'll do phone invites to save time," Kate offered.

"And flowers?" her mother asked. "Which florist?"

"You're better at that than I am," Elle told her. "Can we do simple clusters of lilies on the tables, nothing majorly expensive or crazy, done in my pots?"

"Beautiful and meaningful," agreed her mother, making note. "Can we use the church hall?"

"It's being painted over summer break from school, but Father suggested using a park pavilion."

"And of course those are all booked since the first week of January," said Mary Lou, and Elle agreed.

"Yes, but they had a cancellation at Bradley Park, so I grabbed it. It's just the right size, and the park will be shady."

"So, flowers, food, church, hall, guests. Music and a dress," Aggie announced.

"I thought I'd just wear one of my summer dresses," Elle said, and when her mother looked dubious, she sighed. "Mom, it's not like it's a first wedding for either of us, and Matt's just going to wear a suit."

"A brand new suit because everything was lost in the fire," Matt's mother reminded her. Then she leaned forward and grasped Elle's hands. "I've never had the pleasure of shopping for a daughter's wedding dress, Elle," she added softly. "Gloria wanted absolute secrecy about Carrie's dress, and Cindie's mother took her to New York, so that was never a possibility. If you decide to get one, I'd like to come with you and your mother. If that's OK?"

A dress.

Every ounce of her being hated the thought of dress shopping because no matter how pretty and lacy the gown was, it was still plain, old Elle inside.

"And if you're being careful to make the rest of the plans go seamlessly, it seems like a new dress is the perfect finishing touch," Kate added. "You're right about the boys remembering, but part of that will be wedding pictures. If you're wearing same old, same old, that takes a little of the shine off, don't you think?"

She didn't want to agree, but Kate was right. "All right, but we can't dawdle. Or fuss. Or—"

Her mother laid cool, soft fingers on her arm. "It will be fine. I promise."

She knew her well. She recognized the raw self-image Elle saw in the mirror. She might not understand it, but she knew it was there. "OK. How about Monday while the boys are in school?"

"Monday is perfect," Mary Lou declared.

"Works for me." Kate reached out and hugged her awkwardly. "I am just so happy for you and Matt. And glad that Kim Sedgewick got nudged out of the running."

"Kate." Aggie frowned over her reading glasses.

"Mom, it wasn't as if the entire town didn't know she was tracking his cell phone."

"Tell me you're kidding," Elle said. "Is there an app for that?"

"If there isn't, there will be: 'hashtag crazy ex-girlfriend'," Kate joked, but then she turned serious. "Which brings me to the D'Amicos. Do they know you've scheduled the wedding?"

Elle shook her head. "Not as yet."

"It's a delicate situation," Aggie noted.

Mary Lou disagreed. "It shouldn't be. I've tried to talk to Gloria, several times, but she's angry at everything, so I don't see it as delicate anymore. After four years, it's become self-serving."

"She lost a lot." Aggie stopped typing notes and peered up, over the glasses. "She lost her daughter, her only child, and what a heartbreak that must be."

"It is." Mary Lou admitted. "But doesn't God teach us to extend kindness and compassion to children? Matt and Gloria were never close, and I see blame on both sides. Two stubborn, successful people, butting heads. Carrie was the glue that held them together, so without her, there was no buffer zone. But when it comes to children, shouldn't we put their best interests first?"

"Always," said Elle, and that earned her Mary Lou's smile. "Each child seen as a gift, a miracle. There's no reason not to put them first."

"And that's my problem with Carrie's mother," Mary Lou told them. "She's grown so angry that she wants to take those children from Matt. She's got people watching, taking notes."

Aggie was sipping tea as Mary Lou spoke. She stopped, the glass halfway to the table. "No one would do that. Would they?"

"She is doing that, right now, and has been," said Mary Lou. "So it's gone beyond normal grief and loss; it's become a war. Her threats the night of the fire weren't idle." Matt's mother turned her gaze to Elle. "She meant every word, and Gloria is successful enough and powerful enough to try to follow through. And of course we'd fight to maintain custody, but who wants to waste all that time, money, and effort on a court case that shouldn't exist?"

She laid her hand over Elle's. "You took the wind out of her sails when you spoke up, because if there's a wife and stepmother in the picture, that weighs heavily in the system. No one wants to break up a family unit. And she was all set to capitalize on that fire." Mary Lou lifted her shoulders. "Who thinks that way?"

"Troubled souls," Elle told her. "When your soul is weighted in anger, it's hard to see the light. Let's give her time."

"I've given her time," Mary Lou declared, and Elle glimpsed an older version of Matt's stubbornness. "I've tried to see it her way for years, but it's only gotten worse. We don't even dare invite her to birthday parties anymore because she's so mean-spirited. Todd's afraid of her, Randy listens to every single word she says, and Amos—"

"Just loves everyone."

"Yes." That made Matt's mother smile. "He's a gentle heart, that one. So whatever Matt decides to do about Gloria and Al is fine with me. I'm tired of fighting with them."

Finality thickened Mary Lou's tone, the same thing she heard when Matt touched on the subject of Carrie's parents, but they were still the children's grandparents, and that meant something. In her family, that meant a lot, but right now she needed to focus on the wedding—as unbelievable as that seemed—the boys, and her work. But someplace in there, she'd try to figure out a peace offering. The note in Mary Lou's voice indicated it wouldn't be easy.

* * *

"Why did I not see our first date as being an ice cream social at the church?" Matt whispered as he drove to St. Casimir's on Friday night.

"One of God's little ironies," Elle muttered.

Matt almost pinched himself to see if this was really him, attending a normal hometown event like this, but when the boys started squabbling in the back seat, it became real enough.

"I've avoided these things like the plague since I came back home," Elle told him as they pulled up to the broad parish center.

"Why?"

"A huge room full of people who had exactly what I wanted," she told him. "A family. And here I was, alone, my marriage annulled. Too much salt in that wound," she explained, "so avoidance was key. Every time Kate asked me to come along, I made sure I had something else going on, even if it was shampooing my hair."

"Clean hair being essential to life as we know it." Matt grinned as the boys piled out of the back of the SUV. "Corral Amos, would you?"

"Away from the road, little man." Elle caught Amos's shoulder and steered him toward the curb. "Up there with Daddy, please."

The bigger boys made a beeline for the main doors. Amos skipped ahead, half-dancing. "I wuv ice cream!"

"Well, who doesn't?" Matt nudged Elle's shoulder with his, smiling as they mounted the steps. At the last moment, on the very top step, he grasped Elle's hand.

She paused. Looked at him.

He met her gaze with one of his own and a raised brow that waited for her.

She gulped. Then felt the light pressure of his fingers holding hers. A gentle squeeze of comfort, before walking into the storm.

She'd made a life not caring what people thought, so why did she care now? What old buttons were being pushed by walking into this small-town function with Matt at her side, holding her hand?

Disbelief, she decided. She didn't want to see the disbelief on people's faces, knowing a handsome guy like Matt Wilmot could have walked in with anyone…and chose her.

Opting for innocuous, she asked, "What kind of ice cream do you like?"

He grinned. Just out and out grinned at her and gave her hand another understanding squeeze. "Vanilla."

"For real?"

"Cross my heart."

"But that's so boring."

"Nevertheless." He raised a pointed brow.

"Just plain vanilla? Not like, vanilla with strawberries? Or cherries? Or chocolate fudge swirl? Just plain vanilla?"

"I'm a man of simple tastes." Another squeeze to her hand. "But I know what I like."

He held her look then, in a way she wished he wouldn't in a public place. Gazes locked, neither one could break away, break the spell. Her heart ran rampant in her chest, and an adrenaline surge made her palms go damp.

All over a few little words and a squeeze to her hand. How was she going to react when the man meant business?

"Elle! Matt! I saw the boys, and I knew you guys were here. Why are you lurking in the doorway?" Kate noted their locked hands, stopped, and grinned. "Never mind. I think I figured it out. Come on over here. We've already fed the bulk of the crowd, and I'm afraid we ran out of strawberry. But there's tons of chocolate. And vanilla."

Matt grinned lazily. "Perfect."

He seemed oblivious to the looks cast in their direction as they wound their way across the busy floor. The boys were in line ahead of them and waved eagerly as Matt and Elle took their place at the end.

"Look, Dad! We're way up here already!"

Matt gave Todd two thumbs-up. "Way to go. Save me some, won't you?"

"Why? Will they run out?" Todd eyed the group of people between him and his father with a hint of worry. Amos squirmed by Todd's side, then broke away and came running back to Matt. He hoisted the boy, one-armed, refusing to let go of Elle's hand. "Naw. They've got plenty. We'll meet you at a table."

Todd nodded, then widened his eyes as the first server filled his dish with ice cream. Randy followed suit. Matt eyed Amos. "So, you're waiting for us?"

He nodded, eyes round at the sight of so many people surrounding him. Elle offered, "What kind do you want, honey? Chocolate or vanilla?"

His answer was absolute. "Both."

"Then both it is."

* * *

A beautiful night, a family night. An odd first date, made more wonderful with his sons' joy and delicious ice cream sundaes.

Living the dream of normal.

Once the boys were asleep later, Matt walked Elle back to her side of the house.

She laughed at him for doing that, but when he kissed her, long and sweet, she stopped laughing.

She sighed, making him wish away the short days until the wedding.

Matt wasn't stupid. He understood wants and needs, and it had been a long time since he'd been with a woman.

He'd had opportunities, and he'd been tempted a few times, but each time he thought of the consequences. His life, the boys, their reputation. Maybe he owed Gloria a thank-you note, because her vendetta made him consider everything in terms of the boys. Otherwise, he might have more regrets on his plate, and he had plenty enough already, thank you.

He hesitated by Elle's door, then walked the short steps back to the attached apartment. He paused, then dropped down on the bottom step, frog-song surrounding him.

What was he feeling?

He had no idea. Couldn't put it into words. Not and make sense anyhow.

He liked her. A lot. Enjoyed being with her, looked forward to seeing her. And he'd felt an old surge when he'd taken her hand. A surge of warmth and protection. And more, he admitted to himself.

She wasn't Carrie. Elle wasn't anything like Carrie had been. His first wife had been small and pretty. Tough, too. But he'd been drawn to look out for her, care for her, her size bringing out all the protective instincts he had.

Yet, oddly, he felt that way toward Elle, as strong as she was. As talented as she was. As smart as she was. Feeling protective of a woman who looked him eye to eye and stood her ground unabashedly was a new experience. A very new experience.

But it was one he was enjoying.

And he wasn't as oblivious as he seemed. He'd heard talk over the years. Rumors. Aspersions. Careless people noting how blessed Aggie was to have Kate, so delightfully normal with her perfect, little family, when Elle was just so...different. Outspoken. Independent. Unafraid to compete with the guys on the athletic fields, and wildly talented and successful artistically.

The ugly duckling, someone had said back in high school. He'd laughed back then, before he knew her. And felt the shame of that laughter now.

No, she'd never be a swan. Or a little dove. But it didn't matter, not to him. She made him laugh, made him think, made him want to be a better person, a better friend, a better...

Husband. He wanted the chance to be a better husband than he'd been before. A chance to love and care for a wife who touched his heart and soul in a way he would have thought impossible. To cherish, honor, and protect once again.

The chance to do all that with Elle Drake.

They'd agreed to tell the boys tomorrow night. Todd would be accepting, Amos was happy by nature, and Randy...

Matt sighed because Randy would give them a run for their money, just because he could. But if he was a betting man, he'd put his money on Elle, because if anyone could lock horns with Randy and come out OK...

It was his future wife.

chapter twenty-one

Matt called a family meeting the next night. "Boys, I need to talk to you. Actually," he reached out and grasped Elle's hand in a show of solidarity she welcomed, "we need to talk to you."

"About what?" Todd crossed the yard, a mitt on one hand, a baseball in the other.

"I didn't do it." Randy's denial was complete and emphatic.

"Famous last words," Matt whispered for Elle's benefit. "You're not in trouble. We wanted to talk to you about living here. Permanently."

"It's too small."

"I want my room back."

"OK."

They answered in order of age, top to bottom. Matt squeezed Amos in a hug, his quick acceptance a blessing. Then he shook his head at the older boys. "Not in the apartment, boys. In the house." He cleared his throat. "Elle and I are going to get married. We'll live here, in her house. Yes, Randy, you'll have your room, and you can set it up any way you want to."

Randy stared from one to the other, and if hot looks indicated barometric pressure, a growing storm front was encroaching.

"And, Todd, you'll have yours as well. Unless you want to share with Amos."

"You're getting married? For real?" Todd asked. He kept his gaze on Elle, and when she nodded, he smiled.

"I want a room of my own. Please."

"There are plenty of rooms for all of us."

"No, there's not," Randy argued. "There's only four. Daddy will have to stay in the apartment."

Elle blushed and hated herself for doing it. Matt stayed calm. "Once we're married, I'll sleep in Elle's room. Mommies and daddies always share a bedroom. That way we can talk about the kids, share our days…" Elle was grateful when he left it right there.

Randy seared Elle with a look. "She's not my mommy."

"Will you kiss and stuff the way you used to with Mom?" In contrast, Todd's voice was curious.

"Oh, sure." He nudged Elle with his shoulder. Then he addressed his middle son. "Elle knows she's not your mommy, Randy. But she'd like to be your friend. And she does make good suppers."

"Do you love her?"

Leave it to Randy to get to the crux of the matter. Elle went rigid. She didn't want or need promises of love. She'd seen the breakdown of that firsthand, the meaningless vows, spoken as needed. Nothing more.

A partnership was better. Much better. Less drama and more bargaining room. When the heart got too involved, the head didn't stand a chance.

"I do." Matt grazed her cheek with his hand and smiled as if he meant it, but there was only so much little boys needed to know.

"Really?" Randy studied them both as if hunting for the weak spot.

"Yeah, Randy. Really."

He said the words easily, and that hurt, because Elle knew the truth. Matt had made himself clear. They didn't need "lovey-dovey" stuff. She grabbed hold of the practicality of the moment when Todd turned her way.

"Do I get to pick my room first? I'm the oldest."

"After your dad and I figure out which one we're using, you can have first pick. Dad is older, after all."

"But you're the oldest. Aren't you?" Todd gave her a quizzical look, his glance darting from her to his father in frank measurement.

"Todd, over the years, I've discovered it's never good to ask a woman about her age. When you're a grown-up, a couple of years here or there doesn't matter."

"But she's older." Randy went for the jugular. "She looks older."

Brat. Elle decided to nip it in the bud. "I am two years older than your father. But that doesn't matter once you're a grown-up."

"It doesn't?"

"Nope."

"OK." Todd looked at Randy, then tugged on his arm. "Can we go to the fort now?"

"You guys are OK with this?"

Todd shrugged. Randy kept his mouth closed in a tight, prim line. Amos wiggled to get down.

Matt nodded his satisfaction. "Go play. Ice cream in an hour. Then bed."

As they scampered off in the direction of their pseudo-fort in the trees, he eyed Elle. "How'd I do?"

"Aaaaaaaagh."

"That rough, huh?" He smiled in sympathy.

"You handled it beautifully. I, however, couldn't get beyond the fact that Randy was ready to ship you off to the apartment rather than have you share a room with the wicked witch of the west."

"That was an interesting twist."

"But you handled it. Even to saying things you didn't mean. I get that they're kids, Matt, and we need a united front, but I don't want them to think we've lied to them. Honesty is important to me. Very important."

He assessed her with a deliberate look, a look that made her go soft inside. He leaned over, kissed her long and slow, then stood. "I meant every word, Elle. Every one." He winked and went off to mow the front lawn, as if pledges of love were a dime a dozen. These days they were, kind of. People used the word "love" with abandon, never thinking how dreadfully important the true emotion was.

She touched her fingers to her mouth, savoring his words, his kiss. She gathered the outside dishes and carried them inside, tired of labels. This—*this thing*— between her and Matt didn't need a name.

It was good and mutually beneficial on both sides, and there was a lot to be said for that.

* * *

She met her mother, Mary Lou, and Kate at noon on Monday at Jennifer's Bridal, three blocks south of St. Casimir's.

She didn't want to, and as she parked across from the bridal store, the twin windows filled with princess-styled gowns tempted her right back into the car. But then Mary Lou popped out the door, and Kate waved from inside, so she had no choice. She strode into the shop, wishing she were anywhere else, because Elle hadn't been froufrou back in the day, and nothing had changed. If there'd been more time, she would have ordered something simple shipped in and been done with it.

But there wasn't time, not really, and Mary Lou's excitement was almost contagious. "Elle, this is Paulette." Mary Lou drew a young woman forward. "She used to be our neighbor before she went and got married."

"Elle." Paulette extended her hand and smiled. "It is so nice to meet you. I love your work. I have a subscription to Hyland Manor, and every time there's a new Elle Drake piece, they send me an e-mail alert. Buying your work and putting it in my house is my guilty pleasure."

Her sincere words bridged what could have been an awkward beginning. "Paulette, what a nice thing to say."

"Just the truth." Paulette motioned toward the bridal display room to their left. "I know this is a quick wedding, and it's also a second wedding for both of you. The moms took a few minutes to fill me in."

Of course they did.

"But," she continued, "we've got an extensive selection of gowns that are appropriate and beautiful along this display wall. And we'd be happy to take care of any alterations you might need."

"This quickly?" Elle wondered, and Paulette smiled.

"Yes, ma'am."

"Well." Elle stared at the rack, then inspiration struck. "Mothers." She turned and faced both Aggie and Mary Lou.

"Yes?" Mary Lou faced her, eager.

"Yes?" Aggie's voice was more cautious.

"I'd like you to pick the gowns." She waved toward the elongated display and then herself. "I've never had an eye for this kind of thing. My artistic talents stopped at fashion, so if you two wouldn't mind picking out dresses, Kate and Paulette can help me get into them. Is that all right?"

Mary Lou looked as happy as Elle had ever seen her. "I'd love it!"

Aggie seemed OK with it, too. "I actually think that's a good idea. You tend to have preconceived notions about what looks good and what doesn't. I'm in."

"Me, too!"

Elle thought it would be an all-afternoon event.

It wasn't.

When she tried on the eighth dress, she knew, and when she wore it out of the fitting room, both mothers sighed, and when they did, Kate pumped a fist in victory.

"Elle." Aggie rose and crossed the narrow area. "I don't know what you think, but I've never seen you look more beautiful, darling."

"It's stunning and simple and breathtakingly beautiful." Mary Lou moved to her other side. "This chiffon, so soft. And the flow of the gown when you move is marvelous."

"I love it." Elle looked into the mirror and couldn't believe she not only said the words—she meant them. "It's absolutely perfect, isn't it?"

Her mother smiled up at her, a smile that said more than casual words, and gripped her hand. "Yes. It is."

chapter twenty-two

Elle was a beautiful bride. An amazing, wonderful, and beautiful bride, and when she caught his gaze from down the aisle and smiled, just for him, at him, warmth flooded Matt.

This was good and righteous and…he stumbled mentally, not sure of how many good words were too many, and when Amos raced from the altar and paused in front of Elle, she handed her lilies to her sister, reached down, and scooped him up. Snuggling his littlest son on her hip, she proceeded down the short aisle in a slightly unconventional manner.

Matt was pretty sure that was indicative of their life to come. Him, Elle, the kids.

Perfect.

"I, Matthew Daniel Wilmot, take you, Elinora Gwendolyn Drake…"

He smiled at Elle as he repeated the classic words midway through the Mass.

"…for richer, for poorer, in sickness and in health…"

He gazed into her eyes and meant every word.

"As long as we both shall live."

And when he finally got to kiss his bride, three children hugged them both.

And it was good. At last.

She was swept away from Matt as they entered the foyer of the park lodge. Pictures had taken longer than expected, and everyone had worked up an appetite, but that was all right. The boys had been surprisingly well behaved, and Matt's parents were taking them home from the reception so he and Elle could go off on their abbreviated honeymoon.

But he liked having his wife by his side. Then suddenly she was gone, whisked away, surrounded by women and girls of all sizes and shapes.

Someone took his arm. He turned and came face-to-face with Elle's great-aunt. "Aunt Martha."

She nodded and smiled, then spoke in a warm, thick accent. "You come here and stand. We will wait to enter the party room. Soon, they will bring Elle to you with the new marriage cap upon her hair." She raised her hands up as if tossing something aside. "Gone is the veil of innocence, to be replaced by her life as a woman. She officially becomes your wife." She patted his shoulder for emphasis.

He could have joked or teased about the pointlessness of the church if this capping ceremony magically made Elle his wife.

But he couldn't. The old woman was so pleased, so sincere. He nodded, then asked, "Did you make the cap?"

She beamed, pleased that he understood the custom. "I did, yes. I make it special for our Elle. She is big, yes?"

He laughed out loud. "I hadn't thought so. Did you make an extra large cap?"

She winced, shaking her head. "I'm sorry. I do not mean big. I mean tall. I get excited, my English...it comes, it goes." She shrugged her shoulders delicately.

"Yes, she's tall," Matt eased the way for the old woman. "And I know the cap will be beautiful."

A very pregnant Kate sailed by just then. She took Spike's hand and led him into the main room. She wore her sister's veil, the ivory tulle flowing down her back, ending inches lower than it had on Elle. He heard the MC announce the attendants and watched as Kate and Spike circled the room in time to the music, their movements smooth. He hadn't even known Spike could dance.

A flurry behind him drew his attention. He turned. "Elle."

She stood before him, the gathered dress rippling in soft folds to the floor. Gone was the veil. In its place was a sweet old-fashioned ivory cap. Appliquéd with bits of lace, the soft cap adorned her short bob with a femininity she normally eschewed. He took a breath. Stepped forward. And suddenly understood what Aunt Martha had said. *"It is now that she truly becomes your wife."*

* * *

Elle felt the intensity of Matt's look as he turned. Saw the love and amazement in his eyes. Then the warmth and desire.

The combination took her breath away. As he stepped to her, she froze, feeling suddenly awkward and tall. Very, very tall. And when he reached out his arm for her, it was all she could do to touch it. Place her arm in his. But it was either that or throw up on his feet.

Then suddenly his other hand covered hers. A gesture of love and protection. A mark of strength. Leaning forward, he touched her lips with his own, whispering words for her ears only. Soft words of love and promise. Faith and protection. Care and desire.

The announcer called for them, introducing them as a married couple. Beaming, they stepped into the banquet hall filled with family and friends, joyous with applause.

She saw none of it. Heard none of it. Her eyes were on him and him alone as they danced around the circled floor. *Matt's wife.* She closed her eyes briefly, savoring the moment. Then felt his mouth on hers, gentle but insistent. She leaned back, smiling at the unspoken message.

His wife.

They ended the dance in front of their parents and graciously accepted the salted bread and sips of wine as they were offered.

Then a toast, to a hundred years married. Neither one joked of the incongruity of that at their ages. The song was sung, and glasses raised to their health, to their home, to their children.

Elle paused at that one. Kept her eyes averted. But Matt understood what so many did not. Reaching over, he turned her chin. Met her eye. Then whispered, "My gift to you is my children, Elle. Three little lives that I could never entrust to another until you came along. Now they're ours."

She cried at that pronouncement and had Kate fussing with her makeup for the next five minutes.

"Stop, already," she finally protested, laughing and batting her sister's hands away. "Shouldn't you go have a baby or something?"

"As soon as we fix your mascara. No more tears!" the younger woman ordered, her voice both light and gruff. "I thought you were the unemotional sister. The tough one."

Elle looked across the room, filled with the closest family and friends, her new husband, and *their* boys. She smiled and sighed softly, crazy-happy. "Not today."

* * *

"It was a beautiful day, Matt."

"Yes. It was." Matt angled the car into the small parking garage near the hotel. He climbed out and came around to her side.

Her Uncle Sam had delivered their bags that morning. She had nothing to hold, nothing to use as a prop or a diversion. Suddenly nervous, she felt his hand on her arm. Then on her waist. Carefully he spun her, humming, dancing her across the concrete floor of the garage.

"Matt." She laughed at him, enthralled by this side of him. Carefree. Happy. Loving.

"Yes, wife?"

They were almost to the exit, the warm lights of the old inn beckoning them.

There was no chorus of frogs here in the city. The soft whir of the occasional car, the distant sound of a siren. Different sounds. Night sounds. City sounds.

But his words blocked them all out of her consciousness. And the kiss he bestowed upon her in the doorway left her breathless. Weak-kneed and expectant. She looked at him, read his eyes. Felt the grip of his hands at her waist. Heard him whisper into her hair. Words of sweetness and promise. Words of love.

She leaned back into his arm, her heart racing, a million thoughts coursing through her head. Fear vied with hope, anxiety with joy.

But she couldn't quite say those words of love he wanted to hear. To put it all on the line once again. It was safer for both of them if she stayed that little bit detached.

It might seem foolish. She *had* married him, after all. And tried to convince herself that it was for all the staid, stable reasons they'd discussed. Convenience, security, a bonded family for the boys. Right up until Matt had gone and proclaimed his love for her. In front of the kids, no less. Why had he done that?

Looking up, the answer was there on his face. Right in front of her. His eyes warm, the obvious look of desire. The words of affection he wasn't afraid to whisper in her ear.

The ones she couldn't say back. Not and feel safe. In control. Because somehow she knew that loving Matt Wilmot was bound to be an out-of-control experience. And she didn't dare risk it.

Not yet.

* * *

Matt took Elle's hand and led her into the classic, pricey hotel.

Behind the scrolled chestnut desk, a well-dressed young man smiled as they approached. Matt matched his smile. "We're Mr. and Mrs. Wilmot. We have the Bridal Suite."

Offering a pen, the young man was the soul of propriety. He handed them the key, then nodded to the old-fashioned elevators. "Everything has been settled in your room as requested, sir. If there is anything you need, just use the house phone." At Matt's nod, he continued, "And congratulations to both of you."

Matt smiled, a hand of comfort around his wife's middle. "Thank you." As they crossed to the elevators, he angled his head to Elle. "You OK?"

She made a face, then confessed. "Nervous. Anxious. Scared to death?" She met his look. "You'd think I was…"

He put a gentle finger to her lips once they were inside the elevator. "I'm nervous, too."

"Right." She rolled her eyes.

"I am. I want everything right for you. Perfect for you. I don't want to fail you in any way and have it bring up old memories. Bad ones."

"Matt, you couldn't. You're…"

Once again he shushed her, with his mouth this time. And neither one was aware that the elevator had stopped until it had almost started again. Laughing, they exited, pressing the hold button. Outside their room, he reached for her. Held her. "You make me forget myself, Elle."

"Really?"

"Oh, yeah. I don't know if that's good or bad."

She did a quick intake of air. "Why would that be bad?"

"Because I'm not so sure I have the same effect on you." He held her gaze with a look of question.

"Oh, Matt." She reached out a hand to his cheek, then smiled as he nuzzled his mouth into it. He liked making her smile. "How could you possibly doubt it?"

Seeing her face, the look in her eye, he decided to settle for that. However hurt she'd been the last time, he'd go the distance to show her he was there for the long haul. The heavy lifting. He cocked a brow to her.

"You do at least like me, don't you?" He kept his voice teasing. His touch at her waist was light.

She felt the flush rise yet again. "Matt. You mean so much to me. The chance to be with you, mother the boys…"

"I'll remind you of that when Randy blows up a rocket in the living room. Or Amos wets the bed."

She angled her head to him, looking puzzled. "Matthew?"

"Hmm?"

"Did you want to stand in the hall all night and talk about children?"

His grip tightened. "No."

"Then let's go inside, shall we?" Easing away, she nodded to the keycard in his hand.

He smiled. "Let's."

chapter twenty-three

The summer flew by.

Elle's life became a whirlwind explosion of chronic busyness. She loved it.

Most of the time.

She registered the older boys for a nearby adventure-based day camp and sent Amos to day care four days a week so she could fulfill her work commitments. Those arrangements got them through summer, while Matt worked relentless long days, leapfrogging from project to project. Had he always been this busy? And if so, how had the boys survived?

By the grace of God, Elle decided midsummer: Before they'd go through another summer like this, she and Matt would have a long, serious talk. If money was the issue, if lack of funds pushed him to work at breakneck speeds, then it shouldn't be a problem, because she had money. That wasn't exactly a secret; her success and her commissioned projects were already showing up in mailboxes for pre-holiday shopping. She had figured out quickly that there were two subjects to stay clear of over the summer. Matt's current work schedule and Gloria D'Amico. For the time being, she'd let it ride, because in every other way, things worked beautifully between them. So beautifully that she blushed sometimes, thinking of it.

And then scolded herself for acting like a lovestruck teen. But a happy one.

Daniel returned to work in July. That should have helped, but it seemed to open the door for both of them to take on more work. Was it greed or necessity that drove Matt? Elle wasn't sure, but when the older Wilmot did the same thing, she realized they were cut from similar cloth, and neither one seemed willing to slow down.

But they needed to, or they needed Jason to take on a full share, because they weren't the only ones minding a clock.

Her work was constructed around deadlines, too. She understood the concept. Maybe Matt was right, perhaps the seasonal aspects of his job pushed Wilmot Excavating extra hard through the limited nice weather. Once winter hit, outdoor construction would grind to a halt. The waiting for spring would begin. No doubt Matt would have more time for the boys then. If she let him live that long.

Her mother called her the third Friday of September. "Are you home with Amos today?"

"I'm *with* Amos." Elle smiled at him through the rearview mirror, and when the little guy grinned back, she enjoyed a surge of love so delightfully rich it probably should have been ruled unlawful. "We're on our way to see a traveling dinosaur exhibit, but we should be back home by one. What's up?"

"I wanted to run some Christmas ideas by you, but it can wait until next week. If I swing by on Monday afternoon, is that all right? I hate to interrupt your work with all you've got going on, but you know I like to plan ahead."

Elle knew the truth in that and couldn't fault her for it because she was the same way. "Crazy has become my new normal, and who would have thought that six months ago?" She kept her voice easy, but her mother knew her too well.

"You're running Todd to baseball practices two nights a week and Randy to soccer two nights a week, and First Communion classes for both of them. When do you get time to just be you, Elle? You're going to make yourself sick."

"Says the single mother who raised two busy and diverse girls while working full-time."

"I grew into the role, though, and that makes a difference. It wasn't sprung on me overnight."

"Mom, I'm fine. We're fine." Elle wasn't one hundred percent sure she was right, but she was new in this role, and didn't any important role require adjustment time? "I know our schedule is ridiculously busy, but I wanted to make sure the older boys got a chance to test out their sports in the off-seasons so we could get them on teams next spring and summer. You know how much I love sports."

"I know this, of course."

"And Matt's working crazy hours."

"This isn't exactly news, Elle, nor is it a new circumstance." Aggie sounded aggrieved. "Everyone in town has known this right along. But now he's got you to manage the children, and does he slow down? No."

"Mom." Elle turned the corner and parked along the shady street leading to the natural history museum. "We knew this would be a busy year. He has commitments to keep, commitments he made before we were married."

"And a fair number he's made since. I live in this town, Elle. I see the insurance numbers, and I know who bids on what. I don't want him using you as nothing more than a built-in babysitter so he can make Wilmot Excavating bigger and richer and more of a local monopoly. I had plenty of excuses from your father, believe me. But here…" She paused and took a breath. "I didn't call to complain about Matt's work schedule. That's between you two. I did call to insist on helping. Let me do some running around for you. I'm not doing a thing at night except meeting with the Quilters Club on Tuesdays. I'd like to help."

Her mother loved keeping busy, and she was good with the boys, so this was a definite win. "If you want to take the Wednesday night baseball practice run, I won't complain."

"I'll take Wednesday and Thursday so I have time with both older boys," her mother decided, and Elle was smart enough to accept graciously. "I didn't get you back here, closer to family, to have you be worked to death. And this will give the boys a chance to know me."

It would, and Aggie Drake was a fun person to know. "Perfect. I'd love the help, actually. And their fall sessions only go through November. Then we have a break until mid-January."

"No one with school-age children considers December a break, Elle, but you'll discover that yourself. Plays, concerts, volunteering at school, holiday gatherings, parties, church services, special Masses, and Advent vespers. Let's look at December as an entity unto itself, and we'll figure it out after Thanksgiving."

"Is it really that busy?" Elle asked the question, and her mother's tone gave her the answer.

"It was four weeks of running with two girls. I cannot imagine it's gotten better when you throw in a preschooler on top of elementary school functions. But we're family, and I love doing things with boys at long last, so it will be fine. I'll be there to help, and I will love every moment."

"And I'll be glad of it. I'd love to have a couple of evenings at home, just getting things organized for the next day."

"A necessity for any mother," Aggie agreed. She hesitated, as if she wanted to say more, but she didn't. "I'll see you on Sunday at the nine o'clock Mass. I enjoy sitting with my new grandsons. And their parents."

Elle had taken over the fall weeknight schedule without complaint, but on Sunday morning they went to church as a family, no matter how nice the weather was, how much work Matt had, or the fact that he wasn't Catholic and hadn't bothered going to church when he was younger.

Life was different now, and he was older and more mature. And Elle left him little choice, because it was the right thing to do.

When he reached out for her hand during the Lord's Prayer...when he held her palm to his, just so, their fingers entwined, and prayed those Christ-inspired words out loud, she prayed for their bond to be solidified in faith, hope, and love. Day by day, week by week, she felt like they were gently, lovingly reaching that goal.

*   *   *

"You're keeping Randy so busy, he's having a hard time making trouble," Matt whispered as they set out harvest-style front-porch decorations two weeks later. "He's doing well in school, he's rarely in the hot seat, and he's got a better attitude."

She tipped a smile up to him as she arranged pumpkins and gourds around the lowest straw bale. "Shush. You'll jinx it. Can you reach that scarecrow behind you?"

"This one?" Matt gave the straw-filled decoration a once-over. "No self-respecting bird would find him scary. He's way too happy."

"He's cute, right?" Elle snugged him into the back bale, next to his straw-filled wife. "And look here." She pulled out two little scarecrows and set them in the front. "A family."

"We've got scarecrow guys?" Todd had been kicking the soccer ball around with Randy when he noticed what they were doing. He dashed their way. Randy followed, dribbling the soccer ball like he was born to play. "Can we do a graveyard, too? Like with tombstones? Like the spookiest one ever?" Todd added.

"And spiderwebs?" asked Randy.

Todd bumped knuckles with his brother. "And ghosts?"

"Talk to your father. I'm in charge of porch decor. He's the graveyard guy."

"Dad, come on!" Todd grabbed Matt's hand, excited. "Me and Randy could paint the tombstones. I know how to make them look really scary!"

While the boys conferred noisily over their ideas for the scariest tombstones ever, Matt turned her way. "Are you OK with a graveyard?" He indicated the cute, country, harvest-style porch with a grimace. "It's not exactly along the same lines, I know."

"I was one of those kids who loved going out trick-or-treating," she confessed. "I'd have loved a scary graveyard complete with cobwebs and fake smoke. And eerie voices would be good, too."

"I've had enough smoke to last a lifetime," Matt noted. "But I don't mind making tombstones with them. You OK out here?" He bent over and settled his mouth against hers, and if it took a little time to answer, well…who could blame her?

"Go. Do not let them use power tools that can remove limbs, OK?"

"Got it."

The boys followed him over to his work barns, whooping and hollering the whole while. Elle stood, leaned over to get the wicker basket of gourds, and paused, light-headed.

Her vision went blurry, and her breath caught, and it felt like her stomach rose up to greet her throat for a long moment.

And then everything felt normal again.

Head rush...

It had happened a few days before, too, when she walked out of the shed, but she'd been working for hours, eyes down, focused on the task at hand, so that seemed fairly normal. And the cool, damp fall weather riled up sinuses.

She finished the porch as the buzz of Matt's power saw sounded from across the trimmed lot.

Matt had dug out a walkway from the backyard to the excavation barns, and he and Spike had leveled a truck load of concrete into an easy-to-care-for sidewalk. The old house had been cleared away, and eventually, a new excavation office would be built in its place.

She paused by the back door. Where the four-room apartment had been, they'd hired a local craftsman to convert the space into an open family room accessible from the kitchen. They were leaving one bedroom and turning the other one into a full bathroom and extra storage and closet space. Once finished, the new great room would take the strain off the long, wide living room in the front of the house, and the distance would give adults a place to gather and talk, while children played in the room out back.

She loved the plan and almost had to pinch herself as it took shape to make sure she wasn't dreaming.

A beloved wife and mother.

Everything she'd ever wanted, hoped for, or dreamed of had come true. No matter what happened, she'd never ask for anything more.

* * *

Matt stared at the November calendar, counted the weeks, then studied the computerized spreadsheets before him.

Four months.

The balloon payment was due in March. If they finished the current projects, they had a shot, as long as they laid everyone off three weeks earlier than usual. And that was if their commercial customers and the town paid them in a timely fashion, and construction companies were noted for delaying winter payments until the spring influx of money rolled in.

Wilmot Excavating didn't have that option this year. His father walked in as Matt examined the calendar for leeway.

He found none.

"It's tight, Matt. If I pull my personal money out of my retirement account, we can cover this."

"And have you pay a twenty percent penalty?" Matt wasn't about to consider that. "No, we'll do OK if we can register payments and cut staff that extra three weeks." He hoped he sounded more confident than he felt, because pulling in those payments was out of his control.

"I should have consulted you," his father told him. Regret speared his voice, and Dan Wilmot wasn't the kind to admit his errors freely. "I saw a good deal, and I jumped on it, figuring we were flush, so it was worth the gamble. I should have known better. I mean, we're talking a seven-figure payment. When last year got washed out—" He sighed, and the muscle in his cheek twitched. "I knew we were in trouble. And then to have the old ticker go bad on top of it." Dan stared at the computer screen as if wishing he could make it all go away.

"You couldn't help getting sick, Dad."

"Well, I might not have gotten sick if I hadn't put all that stress on us."

Did the stress of this equipment expansion put his father's health in jeopardy? Matt didn't know, but he didn't want his father to spend the next four months worrying. That couldn't be good for a bad heart. "We'll do this, Dad. I know it. But we should bring Jason on board. It's not right to keep him outside the loop."

Dan refused instantly. "Jase isn't like you, Matt. You jump in, both feet, and handle things. Jase will just get angry and remind us that he should have been consulted from the beginning."

Jase would be correct, Matt knew. But there was little good in rehashing that now. "And projecting our winter income at that level," he pointed to Matt's spreadsheets, "that's banking on several companies who are notoriously late with payments." Dan breathed deep. "If we need to, we'll wipe out my account. The twenty percent can be my punishment for putting us in a precarious position. We don't want to mess with our credit rating, and you've done your share and more, Matt." He put a heavy hand on Matt's shoulder. "This is on me now."

"Dad, I—"

Daniel pulled on his heavy jacket and walked out.

Matt stood, moved to the window, and watched him.

His father had run this business for nearly four decades, first with his father, then his brother, and now his sons. For three generations they'd slowly grown the company until it was the largest excavation firm in eastern Ohio.

Dan had made a bold move at a bad time, and he'd kept it to himself until he'd been hospitalized. It was only then that Matt realized the pressure he was under.

And now Matt was under the same pressure, and Jase went home every night, free from worry.

That wasn't fair, but it was kind of how it had always been. Concern for Dan's health kept Matt from rocking the boat now, but Elle was right. If Jason was going to be a partner, he needed to invest himself fully. She'd stepped up to the plate all summer and fall, but she'd made it clear that next summer there would be more family time.

And she meant it.

Four months.

He closed down the computer, pulled on his coat, and trudged home. They could leverage the loan by mortgaging the business, but that would throw up red flags for their credit standing. Lots of businesses were hard-hit by last year's weather conditions, but a drop in credit ratings made customers nervous.

They were better off letting the customers think everything was fine. And when heavy lake-effect snow was forecast for the following two days, he knew their construction season was most likely over, and plow season would begin, and that realization sounded like a death knell.

The money brought in by clearing municipal and commercial lots wasn't a drop in the bucket compared to the upcoming payment, and if their big commercial construction customers waited until spring mortgage loans were released, they would be nearly forty percent short of the balloon payment.

Elle's got money. She's opened up her life to you. She's shown you her accounts. Ask her for a short-term loan to get you through.

He couldn't.

Even if it seemed like the smart, sensible thing to do, what if she took it the wrong way and thought he married her for her money? She'd been burned once, and badly, in the full view of an entire country. Alex Caulder's actions had shaken her to the core. He knew that. No way was he about to shake her confidence in him. He and his father would handle this because they had to. But he wasn't looking forward to the next few months.

* * *

"Do we have to go to Uncle Jason's house for Thanksgiving?" Randy groaned loud and long from the bottom step. "He always makes us stay in the playroom."

"Forgive me for noting this, but that doesn't sound like a huge hardship for a few hours, Randy."

"Dad, you know what I mean." Randy scowled. "We can't go outside because it's wet, we can't watch TV because it's bad for us, we have to eat on the basement table—"

"The upstairs table only seats ten people, and there's nothing wrong with kids eating downstairs."

"It is Thanksgiving," Elle reminded him softly, when Randy stormed off. "Maybe next year we can have everyone here, and all share the same table. Or at least tables on the same level."

"Cindie doesn't handle noise well. She's sensitive, and boys can be rowdy. We've done it this way for a while."

Elle didn't back down. "Change is a part of life," she told him. "And the boys might be less rowdy on their own turf. It's just a suggestion," she added as she wrapped up a second pie. "But I don't see looking back on Thanksgiving as a hateful holiday being beneficial to anyone, and to dread it every year can't possibly be fun. And it kind of messes with the theme of the day, don't you think?"

He came up behind her and nuzzled her cheek. "I think you'll manage to make me see your point, which is, by the way, a good one. I just didn't have the energy this year to make it a battlefield."

"Why, Matt?" She turned to face him. "Why the craziness this year? Or is it like this every year, and if that's the case, we need to make adjustments. It's not as if we need the money." She kissed him then, sweetly and gently. "We're not hurting for anything, so I don't get it. Unless there's a problem with the business. And in that case, we should talk about it. If my business were in trouble, you'd be the first person I'd tell."

But her business wasn't in trouble. It was flying high, making her one of the most sought-after artists in America and the U.K.

No, this was his problem for the moment. He'd promised his father discretion, and he needed to keep that promise. He returned the kiss and made light of the situation. "My wife keeps me up at night. Once I catch up on sleep this winter, I'll be fine."

She studied him, and he felt like a first-class jerk for putting her off, but then she tucked her head against his shoulder and held him. He didn't know he needed holding until she did that. "They say the first year of marriage is the toughest." She leaned back and met his gaze. "I want to make you happy, Matt. That's important to me."

He tugged her back into his hug, his embrace. Guilt rose up to choke him, because how in the world could she imagine he wasn't happy with her? "Elle, I swear to—"

"We don't swear, Matt."

He laughed softly, loving the feel of her in his arms, the scent of her, pie crust, and soft soap, all mixed up with a dash of pumpkin spice. "Well, then I promise you, I've never been happier. I love my wife, I love my boys, and I'll be glad when we're not living in a construction zone, but that was the best use of the house insurance money. But I'll enjoy some peace and quiet when it's finally done."

She leaned back and studied him.

She knew something was wrong. He read the knowledge in her eyes, but she let it go when Amos skipped into the room wearing his paper Indian headdress from his preschool Thanksgiving dinner the day before. "Are we weady?"

"R-r-r-ready," Elle told him, stressing the sound. "Like a pirate, remember?"

"R-r-r-r!" Amos slapped her a high five. "I'm r-r-r-ready to go!"

"Good job." Matt let Elle go and hoisted Amos. "Can you give a shout out to your brothers to get in the van?"

"Yup!" Matt set Amos down, and he raced back toward Randy and Todd.

"Can you grab that pie, Matt?"

"Sure."

"And Matt?"

He turned, caught between a rock and a hard place, with no clear exit in sight.

"Whatever it is, I'm here for you. OK?"

"We're fine, Elle." He shrugged and jutted his chin toward the outdoors. "Winter's a tough season to get through. We hate shutting projects down, we hate waiting, and if this week's lake-effect snowfall is an indicator, we've got a busy winter of being up all night plowing, more often than not."

"Can't we hire someone to run your plow?" she asked softly. "I'd gladly cover their pay to have my husband rested and relaxed at home with his family."

Tell her.

Tell her what's going on. If this were Carrie, you'd have told her.

The truth in that thought stung. He'd have told Carrie as a confidant because she had no money. She wouldn't offer to fix it and get them out of trouble.

Elle would.

Elle *could,* and that bothered him, which was stupid, right? And he'd promised his father to keep it hushed.

You promised your wife, too. In those vows you spoke. Are you making promises too lightly, or just making promises you can't keep?

"Ready?" She faced him directly as she lifted the second pie.

"Sure." He couldn't figure this out now; there wasn't time. He ignored her question about hiring someone to do the plow work. He'd never had to ask anyone for help in the past; he'd always paid his own way. No way in the world did he want to change that now.

chapter twenty-four

"St. Who?" Randy turned quizzical eyes up to Elle's as they roasted marshmallows over the wood stove grate a few weeks later.

"St. Mikolaj." Elle rolled the word like her Polish grandmother used to. "We call him Nicholas here. St. Nicholas. But a long, long time ago, he was a bishop in Turkey, far away across the Atlantic Ocean." She pointed out the spot on the nearby globe. "He would go to people's homes, dressed up all regal and fancy in his bishop's robes, and he'd bring the children special things. Treats, little gifts. Candies, fruit. He wanted to show them how proud he was of their good behavior. Show them that the Lord loved them."

"That was a really nice thing to do," Todd told her.

"It was," Elle agreed. The noise of the work crew doing the finishing touches on the new family room competed for the boys' attention. She raised her voice slightly. "Tomorrow is his feast day. In my mother's country, children would put a shoe by the door, and St. Mikolaj would stop by and fill the shoes with treats. Just like he used to in the old days."

"Really?" Now Randy sounded excited. The idea of treats without a job attached was enough to win his interest. "Can we put our shoes out?"

"Well, now, I don't know," Elle demurred, looking at him thoughtfully. "Have you been good?"

His sweet face brightened with sincerity. "I've been trying harder."

She gave him a spontaneous hug. "That's true. You have. And you, Todd?"

"I work extra hard in school to stay in the Blue Group. Miss Fischer said she never saw a harder worker. And I helped Mr. Ogilbene carry all the stuff from the old school closet to the dumpster."

"That was nice," she admitted. When she turned to ask Amos, she noted that he looked a little odd. Tired maybe? "How about you, Mister?"

On cue, he threw up.

The other boys made sounds of disgust, then pretended to be gagging themselves as the noxious smell filled the living room. Elle raced for the kitchen, grabbed a big pot, and thrust it under the sick boy's chin. "Use this, honey. I'll pour you a bath. And don't you worry about a thing. It's just a stupid old stomach bug that's got you."

Amos sobbed, retching. "I don't like bugs," he wailed, his face a caricature of complete misery.

"I know, darling. I know. It'll be better soon. I promise."

Wrong.

It got worse. Much worse. By midnight the other two boys were vomiting, but at least they made it to the bathroom. Amos's record was shaky at best.

"You OK?" Matt tucked an arm around her shoulders, turning her face to his. "You look a little green yourself."

"I'm fine," she answered, trying hard to be convincing.

He felt her forehead. "No fever, but you don't look right, Elle."

"Probably a touch of what they have, grown-up style. You know. You feel woozy but don't actually get sick."

"I can call Spike's brother to come help with plowing and stay here with you."

Elle looked at the thick-falling snow, coming down at a rate of two inches per hour. "Your zero-tolerance contracts won't be happy if you put slow guys on their jobs. I can handle this. It can't last too long, right?"

He looked uncertain as he hugged her. "The washer's going; the dryer's almost done. I'll probably be out most of the night, but call if you need me. If Dad and Jason weren't already on site—"

Heavy weekend snow in December played havoc with all kinds of events and put local retailers into a panic. "Go. We'll be fine. And if we're not, I'll call. I'll get the boys settled with ginger ale and mindless TV, and then I'll crash right along with them."

"You're sure?"

"Go to work."

He did, looking unconvinced. By midafternoon he was home, the plowing contracts done. The thin afternoon light promised more snow by morning. "If this keeps up, there'll be no worry for a white Christmas."

She nodded, trying to smile. He took one look at her and frowned. "You stay on the couch. Or better yet, go take a nap. I've got the boys covered, and no one's going to be worried about supper from the looks of it."

She did as he suggested, taking herself up to the soft comfort of their bed where her swimming head could rest against the feather-stuffed pillow.

She slept for over two hours, the noises of boys who were obviously feeling better piercing her consciousness around suppertime. Then something shifted the side of the bed gently. She blinked her eyes open. "Matt."

He smiled and laid a gentle hand to her forehead. "Still cool. Good. How're you feeling?"

She thought about that. Then gave him a quizzical look. "As long as I lie perfectly flat, I'm fine. Just real light-headed and woozy when I stand. Or sit up quickly."

He nodded. "I know. That's exactly how I felt when I had this kind of bug a couple of years back, the last time it made the rounds of the Wilmot house. The boys are definitely feeling better. Randy and Todd, at least. Amos is still peaked. No appetite. But the other ones are having bologna sandwiches for dinner."

"That's supposed to be gentle on their stomachs?"

He shrugged. "I figured they'd be the best judge. They're really chowing down."

"You might be sorry," she warned. "I think dry toast would have been a better start. Or crackers. You don't want to test agitated tummies too harshly."

He waved it off. "They kept the ginger ale down all day. They'll be fine."

Famous last words that he came to regret by eight p.m. when both older boys were running to the bathroom once more. By the time morning came, he'd gotten about three hours of broken sleep. Still he worried more for his wife than for himself. "I said sit down."

"Matthew. Stop fussing. It's just a little bug. I can't spend my life in bed."

"One day doesn't constitute a life," he retorted, pouring her some green tea. "Drink your tea and relax."

At the sight of the tea, she curled her lip. "It smells funny."

Matt's forehead furrowed. "Does it?" He lifted the cup to his face and inhaled. Then shrugged. "Smells like it always smells, Elle. Green."

She shook her head. "Not to me, it doesn't. The bug must have messed up my sense of smell. When you're done plowing, can you stop by school and pick up the boys' homework? That way we can get it done this afternoon."

"You're up to this today?" The sounds of rambunctious voices and monster trucks on the floor of the living room permeated the air.

She leaned back and gave him a tired smile. "Just don't stay gone too long."

*　*　*

By that night, the boys were back in the groove, full force.

Elle wasn't.

She put on a good front, but the queasy fatigue dogged her through the next week. Determined to push through, she had Matt take Amos to day care so she could start laying plans for her coming year's work. She grabbed her wool coat, tugged it around her shoulders, and crossed the cleared path to the potter's shed. She unlocked the door and swung it in, determined.

The combinations of smells broadsided her.

Putting a hand to her face, she walked in slowly. Noxious scents accosted her. Moving toward the workroom, she felt her stomach lurch and knew that this time she was going to be sick. Hurrying to the bathroom, she made it just in time.

Drained, she sank down to the tiles, her head swimming. Dropping it between her knees, she breathed slowly, trying to sort things out.

The boys had thrown off the bug in a couple of days.

She was on day seven and feeling worse, with Christmas just over a week away. The thought of their first Christmas together, and all the fun stuff she'd planned for the family as a whole, swam before her. Tears stung her eyes. Her body, normally responsive, felt weak and spindly. The thought of the distance from the shed to the house loomed monumental. She closed her eyes, leaning a tired head against the tiled wall.

"The Lord sustains them on their sickbed; in their illness you heal all their infirmities." The words came to her softly. Psalm 41. A song of beauty and glory.

There was still shopping to do. Wrapping. Tree trimming. Decorating. Cookies and treats to be made and frozen. She drew a testing breath. Straightened, just a little. Then stood.

Better. Not good, but better. Making her way out of the shed, she went back to the house and lay down on the couch, knees weak and stomach upset. Then she called Jeff's practice. "Listen, I know you're not supposed to see family members, but I can't shake this stomach bug, and I don't want Matt to get all worried, and I know I should have found a primary care doctor when I came back to Cedar Mills, but I didn't."

"Come on in," Jeff told her. "Roxanne's got an afternoon opening, and we'll set you up as a new patient once you're feeling better. If it's something more than a virus, she'll send you on. I'll let the front desk know."

"OK." She felt better knowing Jeff's partner would give her a professional opinion. "I'll head right over."

* * *

"You look wiped out." Jeff's partner sent her a sympathetic look as she entered the room and took a seat on the examining stool. "Jeff said this started when the boys were sick last week?"

"Yes. Only I'm not shaking it like they did."

"That happens sometimes." She noted something into the notebook computer on her lap. "Did all three of the boys have the virus at once? That couldn't have been fun."

"Go big or go home," Elle said. "It must be affecting me differently, maybe because I'm older. I can't eat, I get dizzy, I fall asleep midafternoon, and everything smells bad. Food, chemicals, art supplies. I actually threw up in my work shed this morning. I walked in and was overwhelmed by the odors I've worked with for nearly twenty years. Nothing smells right, even smells I normally love."

Roxanne considered her for a moment, then patted her shoulder. "I'm going to run a couple of tests, Elle. Nothing major. You sit tight."

She lay back on the exam table, resting her head, and promptly dozed, until someone pricked her finger. "Hey." She gave a tired frown to the young woman grasping her hand.

The nurse smiled. "Hey, yourself. Give me just a couple of minutes here, and I'll leave you to your nap."

"I'm not really tired," Elle protested.

"Of course you're not." The nurse smiled down at her, finished her tasks, and left, whistling Christmas carols.

The doctor returned a few minutes later, sat back down, and smiled at her. "Caught a little nap, I heard."

"How crazy is that?" Elle asked. "I can be in the middle of something and fall sound asleep. It's ridiculous. Can you give me something for it? Because with those three boys, I have to be totally on my game, and I'm not even close."

"Nope."

Elle stared at her. "There's nothing you can do? Because I don't think I can go on like this."

"Women do it all the time." Roxanne assured her, looking amused.

Elle didn't see an ounce of humor in the situation. "Women do what all the time?"

The good doctor leaned forward. "Have babies."

Elle stared at Roxanne. Her mouth dropped open. She narrowed her eyes, then looked at the doctor. "That can't be. After I spent five years doing everything known to modern science to make it possible, the doctors in Massachusetts assured me it was quite impossible. How did this happen?"

Roxanne tapped the pretty wedding band on Elle's finger. "I'm guessing the way it normally happens."

Elle blushed. "Not that. I mean…how?"

Roxanne shrugged. "It's not my area of expertise, so I've got no answers for you, but I can assure you, it did happen," she finished cheerfully. "I'm going to refer you to an obstetrician just around the corner. She specializes in high-risk obstetrics. Now don't get yourself all riled," the doctor ordered, seeing the look Elle gave her. "I'm doing it as a precaution because of your age and medical history. I have no reason to believe anything is less than fine. Your HCG count is high, and you're very symptomatic. It's always been said that a well-set pregnancy makes its presence known. You have three boys at home, right?"

Elle nodded, fairly dumbstruck. A baby…*a baby*…after all this time.

"Then I'm praying for a girl." Giving Elle a hand up, she shook her hand heartily. "Congratulations, Mom. And, Merry Christmas."

Merry Christmas.

A child, a new life, within her, the culmination of all her hopes and dreams, a total surprise. She drew a deep breath and realized she felt better—so much better—because she was sick for the very best reason of all. She was carrying Matt's baby.

chapter twenty-five

If Matt had seen Gloria's car, he'd have bypassed the office, but he didn't see it, and here she was, arms folded, waiting for him inside the small construction office in the first barn. "Gloria. What can I do for you?"

Susan shot him a sympathetic look and busied herself with online files because the narrow space didn't offer a whole lot of choice for giving them privacy.

"I want to take my grandsons Christmas shopping."

Matt had known this was coming. He thought she'd call, like usual, but since his wedding, nothing Gloria did was usual. "There's not enough time before Christmas," he told her, and when she raised her chin, he prepared for battle. "They've got faith-formation classes Tuesday after school, we've got Advent vespers on Monday evenings, and Elle's mother and aunt are doing Saturday cookie-making lessons with them. All three of them are doing a stint in the Living Nativity, and we'd love to have you come to that. And you're more than welcome to come see any of their games once the Christmas break is done. But there's no good time to take them out shopping before Christmas because it's just over a week away."

"Then I'll settle for a less-than-good time."

The last thing Matt wanted to do was argue with her. He'd just had a significant bid rejected by a new developer, the hydraulics on one of the big plows had blown out, and the steep grade of one of the newer private subdivisions had ruined the brakes on a plow truck. He looked at Susan. "You've got the boys' calendar there, don't you?"

She flipped open a calendar page on her computer, then leaned back to allow Gloria line of sight. "Sunday looks fine." Gloria tapped a finger to the screen. "I'll pick them up at noon."

Matt shook his head. "Sunday is family day now. Church in the morning together, and then we spend the day together. Unless there's a storm and I get called out to plow."

"Your wife's idea?" Gloria bit out the words. "Because God knows you never did something like that on your own."

It had been Elle's idea, but Gloria's tone challenged him. "I spent four years raising those boys on my own. I must have done something right, at least once. Don't you think?"

He didn't think her expression could go darker.

It did.

"I think their guardian angels had a workout, that's what I think!" Gloria declared. "Are you refusing to let me take the boys shopping?"

Matt had caved in the past because guilt over Carrie's death pushed him to assuage Gloria's feelings. But dropping in unannounced this close to Christmas put severe limits on the timetable. "I am, yes, but not because I want to. And you know Elle's invited you over to the house."

"Her house."

"Our house," Matt corrected, trying to stay reasonable. "Come over for dinner on Sunday. Spend the afternoon with us. You and Big Al," he added. "Elle's mom will be there, and her sister's family. We're celebrating having the new family room done in time for Christmas."

Gloria gazed out the window beyond him, and Matt knew what she saw. The big farmhouse, snug in the snow, banks of golden light spilling out of the windows. He knew it because the sight made him smile every time he came home, no matter how hard the day had been.

"The boys would love to have you there."

"And so would you, of course." Gloria turned from the inviting scene beyond the office window. "To keep an eye on me. Monitor what I say."

There was no arguing with her. Matt saw that clearly. He stepped back, hands up, palms out. "I've got to clear up a couple of things and get home. The older boys have a brief Nativity practice tonight, and I promised to drive them."

She glanced back at the house again, almost as if…intrigued.

But then she squared her shoulders and marched out, letting the door slam shut in her wake.

Susan cringed. "Sorry. She walked in right before you got here, or I'd have sent you a warning."

"Gloria's noted for impeccable timing." Matt moved to the back office. "I'm going to clean up a few things, then head home. Did Jason stop in?"

Susan shook her head. "No."

Of course he didn't. Jason was way too accustomed to having Matt handle the majority of the paperwork and follow-through. While that was partially Matt's fault for letting it happen, his brother wanted full partnership in the business. But that meant a full share of the responsibility, and right now, that wasn't happening. "I'll call him. Again."

Susan stood and pulled on her jacket. "Good luck."

He'd need it. "Thanks."

By the time he'd wounded Jason's ego and taken care of a few things, it was almost five thirty and the boys had to be at practice by six fifteen.

He loved that the boys were busy and seemed more motivated and content. And they were getting into a lot less trouble, so that was a total bonus.

But it was hard to leave things undone at the end of the day and head home to manage their schedules when so much fell on him at work.

Elle would remind him of the whole sparrow thing, how God took care of things.

And that was all well and good, but God wasn't writing checks for that monster loan or new hydraulics and brakes.

Check your bad attitude at the door. You're not upset at Elle and the boys. You're upset with circumstances beyond your control. Not their fault.

So he walked in, hung his jacket on a hook inside the back door, and saw Elle, first thing. "Hey, how are you doing?" Just seeing her look better and happier inspired his smile. "You look better."

"I am." She gripped his hands, and when he pulled her in for a hug, she clung tightly. "I'm so much better, Matt."

He laughed, because that was a very important thing to check off his worry list. "Good. Sometimes it takes us grown-ups a few extra days."

"Or months," she suggested, drawing back.

Months?

"Approximately five and a half as near as I can tell, but we'll know more when we go to the official doctor on Tuesday." She took his hand and laid it against her tummy. "We're pregnant, Matt."

He stared at her, processing the words, her expression, and the symptoms he'd lived three times before.

Pregnant?

How could that be? How was that possible? She'd specifically said they couldn't get pregnant. Ever.

His mouth went dry. His palms began to sweat. "You said we couldn't get pregnant."

Pure delight brightened her pretty blue eyes and brought sweet, pink color back to her ivory cheeks. "I know. I tried so hard back then, and nothing worked. And now..." She dropped her gaze to his hand against her stomach. "This. It's like a miracle."

Miracle. Right. How'd that last miracle work out for you, Matt? Oh, let's see, you lost your wife and faced life with three little boys alone. Totally and desperately alone.

He couldn't find enough breath to form words, and that was probably a good thing because what he wanted to say wouldn't sit well.

He felt tricked. Deceived. Betrayed. He stared at her, at his beloved wife, a woman who'd come to mean so much to him, and couldn't believe she didn't get it.

He drew his hand back and stepped away, still watching her, wondering how she could do this. He'd told her how he felt. He'd explained his emotions. She'd agreed that they would have no children because, yes, he was crazy afraid of negative outcomes. He'd lived them. He didn't want to ever test fate again.

It took her a few seconds to sense his reaction, and when she did, he literally watched her shining joy fade, like the last whisper of light on a dark December day.

"You're not happy."

Talk about an understatement. He stared at her, stared hard. How did she not get this? "You said it was impossible."

Emotions scrambled her features, but as she studied him, his face, his gaze, his posture, she retreated. And then she put her hand…her beautiful, strong potter's hand…over her womb in a gesture of protection he knew too well. "It was, for years. And now it's not."

He couldn't do this.

Musical notes signaled the end of a favorite TV show, and the scramble of feet indicated the boys were heading their way.

He backed up farther, grabbed the door, and stalked out. No way could he deal with three cute, inquisitive faces and mind his tongue right now.

This can't be happening. Pinch yourself. Or shake. Wake up!

But it was happening, and he knew that because Elle's look of joy was the same one he'd witnessed on Carrie's face, in Carrie's gaze, three separate times, and no matter how commonplace babies might be to some, his joy had ended in a stark, cold funeral.

And he would have never willingly put himself in that position again.

chapter twenty-six

Alone again.

It didn't matter that Matt lived in the house, because physical presence only went so far. His heart—and his soul—had moved farther away, clothed in anger.

They went through the paces of being married, but the sweet warmth, the laughter, the humor, the gentle lovemaking on a cold, winter's night...gone. All gone.

And when the time came for her doctor's appointment on Tuesday morning, Elle got into her car and went into town alone.

* * *

Vitamins. Advice. Books. Scheduled appointments.

All the things she'd watched others go through, the step-by-step motions of growing a child, now hers. She wanted to be thrilled, and for the baby she was ecstatic, but at what cost came her joy?

Her marriage.

And by Tuesday she'd taken the sting of Matt's rejection and turned it into a defense mechanism. She'd been left before, and she'd survived.

She'd been double-crossed, cheated on, and had her personal life splayed across national newspapers and TV stations.

She'd done OK.

Her mistake was trusting that Matt was different. Believing his words of love. Having faith in the intangible.

So be it.

She had three beautiful boys who were growing to love her and an unborn child, a swimmer in a secret sea, gaining strength in her womb.

She'd be fine. Just fine. Because she had to be.

* * *

Matt watched from his office next door as Elle's car pulled away.

A part of him wanted to dash after her and say it was all going to be all right, but it wasn't all right. None of this was all right.

Had she lied to him?

He couldn't believe she'd do that, but if her story was true, then how could things completely change like that? He didn't know a lot about women's issues, but a body didn't go on autopilot and self-correct. Did it?

You think she tricked you?

His conscience reamed him, big time.

Elle is about the most honest, aboveboard person on the planet. Put two and two together, Einstein. She spent years trying to get pregnant with someone else. Sometimes it's all about the combination of elements involved. Not the process.

That thought tweaked him.

Could it be that way? That somehow, because he was the father, things worked out?

The simplicity of the answer almost made sense, but it didn't make the thought of going through pregnancy, watching his beloved wife risk her life, any easier. If anything, it made it harder because he didn't expect happily-ever-afters anymore. He knew better. It wasn't like he could relax and enjoy the moment-to-moment progression.

"Wherever you're supposed to be," Susan motioned toward the window overlooking the barn and the big backyard. "I'd get in my truck and go there, because you're not doing any good here, staring at the snow."

He looked at her and blurted out the words. "Elle's pregnant."

Susan's face transformed the way every woman's did when they heard those insidious words. "Oh, Matt. How wonderful!"

He'd rather throw up than pretend it was wonderful. It wasn't wonderful. It was frightening and scary and—

"Are you seriously being a moron about all this?"

He jerked back slightly, affronted. "What do you mean?"

She studied him, then sighed. "Here's your problem, Matt."

Great. Someone else with all the answers. Just what he'd hoped for.

"You want control. You have it here," she swept the office a glance, "and even though you pretend you want Jason to help more, you like control. When things get wrenched out of your hands, you react because you can't let go and let God."

God again?

He took the boys to church. He made his way through a service that meant little. He smiled and uttered the responses that came so easily to Elle, but he did it for her and the boys.

He didn't need prayer, or church, or a pie-in-the-sky notion of supremacy and Providence. The whole idea was overrated, but he liked the idea of family unity, so he went. End of story.

"You're still mad at God because you lost Carrie."

"I'd have to believe in him to be mad at him, wouldn't I?"

Susan shrugged. "You want things your way. And yet when life hands you the most awesome opportunities, you let something as perfect and holy and magical as new life waylay you. That's just dumb."

"I'm not dumb."

Her expression said otherwise, and she pointed west. "You have the most amazing wife in the world, a warm, funny woman who goes the distance for you and those boys. She didn't just save *them* last summer, Matt. She saved *you*, only you're not wise enough to know it. You can fire me for speaking my mind, but if you're too dense to see what's going on in front of you, how wonderfully perfect your life's become, then I'm happy to let you know. If you have a lick of common sense in that head of yours, you'll follow her and apologize. And then treat her like gold, because after all that moron put her through in Boston, Elle Drake should be treated like a princess."

"Elle Wilmot."

She held his gaze and didn't hold back. "If you want to claim her as your wife, then go treat her like a wife."

"You have ravished my heart, my sister, my bride, you have ravished my heart with a glance of your eyes, with one jewel of your necklace."

The passage from their wedding came back to him. He'd bonded with the words then because the phrasing fit his feelings toward Elle. And while he'd been ready to lay the responsibility of this twist at Elle's door, he'd been a very willing participant in love's sweet moments.

He grabbed his jacket and headed to the truck. When he got into the driver's seat, he realized he had no idea where Elle had gone or which doctor she was seeing. He called Susan quickly. "How many obstetricians are there in town?"

"There are two practices," she told him. "One on Benton, and one right around the corner from Jeff's medical practice. It's on Walnut, facing Pine. You have to park around back. That's a practice that covers pregnancies that need extra monitoring."

"High risk."

She didn't try to deny it. "Yes."

He swallowed hard, thrust the truck into gear, and drove as fast as he could into town to find his wife. He'd made promises to her, repeatedly. He'd pledged he'd be there for her in times of trouble, through thick and thin, and then at the first crossroads that didn't go his way, he'd bailed.

He needed her forgiveness, but more than that, he needed her love. But first?

He had to find her.

* * *

Reams of paperwork.

Elle went through the sheets on the clipboard one by one, filling out forms and answering questions. Medical history, past doctors, family history…

She'd done this many times over in Boston, using some of the best infertility minds in the country, repeatedly.

And here she was, newly married and expecting a baby.

"Mrs. Wilmot?"

"Yes." She stood. The nurse motioned her into a small anteroom. She recorded Elle's weight and organized a collection of test tube vials.

"Are you light-headed or squeamish about giving blood?"

Elle made a face. "I was poked and prodded for years in Boston, trying to get pregnant. So now that I am, nothing you do will possibly bother me. I'm going to have a baby!"

The nurse laughed. "That's the best attitude! Well, I'll go easy on you anyway, just because I've had my chocolate today and I'm feeling magnanimous. This has to be a thrill for you."

Oh, it was. Sheltering this life within was the greatest blessing on earth. How she wished Matt felt the same way, but that was his problem. Not hers. "It is."

"OK, don't look if it bothers you." The nurse drew the blood quickly into the labeled containers and then sealed everything. "I'm going to take you back to the room where Dr. Gartley will see you."

"Elle."

She turned, surprised. Matt stood in the doorway separating the waiting room from the clinician's station. She gazed at him, and for the life of her, she didn't know what to say.

"How is everything?"

She hesitated, still surprised that he'd come. He'd never asked where she was going. Or which doctor. Of course, in Cedar Mills, there weren't a host of choices.

"We're just doing the preliminary tests now," the nurse told him. "Are you Mr. Wilmot?"

He nodded. "Yes. I'm the father."

The words sounded alien to Elle. He didn't want to be a father again. He'd made that clear. She'd just spent five days tiptoeing around him, pretending in front of three impressionable boys that everything was all right.

It wasn't all right. He'd bailed at the first sign of trouble, and it really wasn't trouble at all. It was a blessing, plain and simple. And Matt

Wilmot was a stupid man for not seeing that.

"Can I come back with you?" He asked Elle the question, and her first instinct was to say no. Then she realized that was a fairly adolescent response, so she nodded and stood.

Matt reached out to take her hand.

She busied it with her purse, as if she didn't notice his move. Maybe he was ready to play nice. Maybe he regretted his actions, or perhaps he was realizing his part in this whole thing, but none of that mattered.

She'd believed his promises. He'd sworn his love. He had said he was a heavy lifter. Oh, she remembered all of it, but in Elle's world, actions spoke more loudly than words. Alex had proven that for all the world to see. He'd broken her heart and shrugged it off like it was nothing.

Matt Wilmot would never get the chance to do the same.

"Right this way." The nurse led them back to an examining room. And when Dr. Gartley ordered an ultrasound, Elle's heart chugged to a stop.

"Is there something wrong?"

The doctor looked over at her. So did Matt. "Why would you think that?" the doctor asked.

"Because is it normal to do an ultrasound at this stage?" Elle met the doctor's gaze.

"Purely diagnostic," the doctor assured them easily. "I think you're a little farther along than we expected. This way we'll know for sure."

"If there's something wrong you have to tell me, OK?" Elle instructed the doctor. "I can handle it."

"We can handle it," Matt said. He came up alongside her and laid his big, rugged hand against her cheek.

Too little, too late.

She'd curled up alone in their bed the past several nights, while Matt stubbornly took the room downstairs. She'd cried herself to sleep, wondering how things could have gotten so messed up. Unexpected joy slipped into their lives and pushed happiness out the window. It made no sense.

And here he was, touching her cheek, as if everything was all right.

It wasn't. And maybe it never could be again, because trust wasn't something you messed with. Ever.

"So, lovebirds."

The doctor's voice brought Elle's attention around, but she didn't correct the obstetrician. "Oh, Matt. Look!" The form of a tiny baby took shape on the screen, the rounded head, the curve of a body, and there, right there in front of their eyes, two tiny hands reached out while thin legs bent and kicked.

A baby.

"Oh." She couldn't take her eyes off that screen if she tried, and Elle didn't try, and she didn't apologize for the tears slipping down her cheeks, wetting the cotton gown. "I can't believe I'm seeing this," she whispered, and when Matt gripped her hand…

She gripped his right back.

And then the doctor readjusted the probe. "Well, if one gets you that excited, what do you think about this?" The picture muddied, then cleared.

Another head appeared, to the right of the first baby. "I suspected as much by your numbers," Dr. Gartley told Elle and Matt as their mouths dropped open, "but I wanted to confirm it with a visual. Congratulations. We've got twins."

Twins.

Two babies. Two precious children to add to their family.

"Twins?" Matt's voice came out like a croak, and Elle was ready to smack him if he said anything he shouldn't, because right here, right now, was the most blessed moment of her life.

"I can't believe it."

"Me, either." Matt sounded shell-shocked, but he kept her hand snug in his. And then he turned his gaze back to the doctor. "A twin pregnancy can be more dangerous than a single pregnancy, can't it?"

And there it was, focusing on the negatives when God had planted not just one but two miracles in her womb.

"Statistically, yes," the doctor answered. "There is additional strain, but your wife is a smart woman, she's in great shape, she has no bad habits that might put this pregnancy at risk, and the only reason she was sent here was because the primary care physician suspected twins because of the high HCG levels. Being a first-time mother in her late thirties, with twins, just means we're going to monitor her more carefully. But Mr. Wilmot," she leaned forward and held Matt's gaze like a standoff at an Irish bar, "we are looking at a perfectly healthy woman, in a perfectly healthy circumstance, with no expectation of problems. Do I make myself clear?"

Matt didn't waver, but he probably didn't dare because the doctor's cool gaze said he better not. "Yes."

"Good." She smiled at Elle. "I can't tell if they're boys or girls, and if you want to find out, the next ultrasound will be more indicative. We don't need to pester these two anymore than we already have, and judging from the measurements, I'd say you're at approximately eighteen weeks. That puts these babies due around the third week of May."

Spring.

In the thick of a cold, windswept December, it was hard to imagine that two tiny lives would join them in five months.

Another tear slipped down Elle's cheek, accompanied by a stab of gut-wrenching fear.

Twins. Two babies. Three boys. What was she thinking? Could she do this?

Matt's face swam in front of her. He smiled, the first smile she'd seen in days, and he looked right into her eyes and said, "It will be fine. I promise."

Her heart stutter-stepped. She'd heard those words before. They'd been meaningless then.

They were meaningless now.

But she drew a deep breath, because no matter what, God was by her side, when men proved unreliable. "I know it will," she whispered.

But not because of Matt or his empty words.

Because God had blessed her beyond all imagination, and she wasn't going to do anything to mess this up.

chapter twenty-seven

"I have a Christmas present announcement." Matt stood at the head of their celebratory table on Christmas Eve and waited until everyone looked his way. Amos wriggled, as if expecting Santa to come sliding down the chimney while Matt spoke. Randy and Todd exchanged secret looks, then giggled. They'd shared the news with them earlier in the day, and Matt had sworn them to secrecy but was kind of amazed they'd held it in once family arrived.

So far, so good.

He reached out and took Elle's hand and squeezed lightly.

She didn't squeeze back.

If he was a Robert Frost poem, he'd have miles to go before he could rest easy, because he'd messed up royally this time. He raised a glass high with his other hand. "To my beautiful wife."

Everyone smiled, happy because it was their first Christmas together and it was sweet of Matt to acknowledge that, and then he winked down to Elle and faced the gathered family again. "Who has made me the happiest man in the world. It seems Elle and I are expecting."

Everyone cheered—and why wouldn't they?—which meant he truly was the only jerk in the room.

Aggie threw her hands into the air. "I've suspected this for weeks, afraid to believe." She raised her wine glass and tipped it in Elle's direction. "From a beneficent God, much wonders come! To my new grandchild. May he or she be as beautiful as the mother who carries him."

"Them."

Aggie's brow pinched together as she stared at Matt. "*Them?*"

"*Really?*" Kate grabbed Elle, excited.

Even Aggie was caught by surprise this time. "Twins!"

"Yes!" Todd and Randy high-fived each other. "We get to have two babies!"

"Oh, Elle, this is the best Christmas present ever!" Kate hugged Elle tight. "I'm stunned."

"Me, too." Elle smiled into her sister's eyes. "But happy, Kate. So happy." Her words gut-punched Matt, because what right did he have to dampen her joy? Why couldn't he jump on the bandwagon of antici-pation like everyone else?

He shoved those thoughts aside, because regardless of his concerns, his goal was to do everything he could to keep Elle happy and healthy. If he focused on that…

He'd do OK. He hoped.

"Matt, you've got to be delighted!" Matt's mother hugged him, then Elle. "So much joy, so much change. This is the Christmas I've prayed for."

"When are you due?" Mary Lou asked, and when Elle told her, she grabbed Aggie's hand, two grandmothers, on a mission. "We must plan showers. And a nursery. And I can come and help over the winter, Elle." She swung around and held Elle's gaze. "Let me help with the boys and housework while you work. I have time, Daniel is healthy, and it will make the winter pass quickly if I'm busy getting ready for these babies."

"When will we know if they're boys or girls?" Kate asked.

"When they're delivered," Elle told her. "I want to be surprised."

"I think you already were," Jeff said as he took his turn for a hug. "This is great news, Elle. These babies will be blessed."

"Us, too." Elle smiled up at him.

"Shouldn't I finish the toast before we make housekeeping plans?" Matt nudged his mother, and she laughed.

"Yes, of course!" Mary Lou blushed and laughed. "To Elle and our new grandchildren." Mary Lou hugged her again. "To life."

* * *

"It was fun to tell everybody about the babies." Randy hopped into bed and pulled the blanket up tight, but Elle knew he'd kick it off again in the first hour of sleep.

"It was exciting, seeing all their happy faces." Elle tucked him in, said prayers with him, then kissed his forehead.

"Do I have to share a room with them? Because I know they're little, but they smell sometimes."

Matt laughed from the door. "True on all counts, and no. We'll figure out the nursery stuff."

"They could have the room downstairs," Todd suggested. Then he brightened up. "Wait, I'm the oldest. I could have the room downstairs, and the babies can have my room."

"I'm big enough for a room downstairs, too," declared Randy.

"There's only one, and I'm the oldest."

"Then Dad can build us another one, because I'm almost as old as you!"

"Then—"

"Are you two seriously arguing over this with Santa about to arrive?"

Their mouths clamped shut simultaneously. "No." Todd shook his head and backed toward his room as if just realizing the severity of the bad timing.

"I like my room just fine," said Randy, and he sent Elle and Matt an Oscar-worthy smile. "Good night! Merry Christmas!"

"Good night, honey." Elle kissed him again and moved to the door. "Sleep well."

"I don't think I'm going to sleep at all," Randy whispered to her. "But I don't want Amos to know. Aiden Butler said there was no such thing as Santa, so I'm going to watch for Santa's sleigh outside my window." He pulled out Matt's pocket camera. "I'm going to take his picture and show it to Aiden when we get back to school. That'll keep him quiet."

"That should do it." Elle smiled and shut the door.

"Wanna bet he's asleep in ten minutes?"

Matt propped one hand on the doorframe next to her, and his smile said more than words.

He was trying to reclaim what they'd had together. Elle recognized that.

But she was done with risks. Totally over them. No one had the right to hurt her or belittle her or demean her.

Not ever again, so she sidestepped around him and moved into Todd's room to tuck him in.

She could be normal—well, mostly normal—in front of the boys. She loved them, and their happiness meant everything to her.

But Matt's reaction had brought back a lesson learned in childhood and again in her marriage to Alex. Actions speak louder than words, and Matt's actions had cast a shadow of anger over her.

"I'm so excited about Christmas," Todd whispered as she tucked him in. "It's like my best Christmas ever, Mom!"

His tender proclamation melted her heart. "We haven't even had it yet, goofy."

"But we will." Todd smiled up at her, so different from the shy, timid, retiring child she'd met eight months before. "And it will be really cool."

Matt slipped his arm around her waist. The feel of him next to her. His hand at her waist. The smile in his eyes first at Todd, then her...

Self-preservation made her steel herself against all of it.

"It will be, Todd." Matt bent over and kissed him. "Maybe you and I can sketch out some nursery plans for Mom. Whaddya think?"

"I think great!" Todd snuggled down beneath his quilt, and come morning, he'd still be tucked deep into the covers. One always hot, the other easily chilled. And Amos, snug in a neck-to-toe blanket sleeper because he slept like a rototiller, arms and legs churning all the while.

"Come on."

Matt tugged her forward once Todd's door was closed. "We've got to wait them out until we're sure they're asleep, but I've got an idea of how to pass the time."

She stopped cold, because the last thing on her mind was—

"I figure if we get the kitchen cleaned up while they're dozing off, we have a head start on tomorrow." Matt turned, her hand still in his, and read the look on her face.

"The kitchen. Oh. Of course." She started forward again, embarrassed by her assumptions, but Matt wrapped their joined hands around her middle when she got closer.

"I will do whatever it takes to re-earn your love, Elle."

She gazed into his eyes, saw the sincerity there, but knew he didn't get it and maybe never would. "It's not about love, Matt. It's never been about love. I think I started loving you the day you sat on that Bobcat and didn't go ballistic over a wet seat."

He touched a hand to her face, one big, strong, beautiful hand.

"It's about trust."

His wince said her words hurt.

Well, join the club.

"We're different."

He inclined his head slightly. "I kind of like that about us, honey."

She didn't smile because nothing about this was funny to her. "You grew up pretty. You've always been good-looking, successful, and well-received. For whatever reason, my life never panned out that way. There was always this yawning emptiness, maybe of my own fault. I felt like I had to constantly prove myself to others. I never blended."

"What's wrong with being a standout?" He had the nerve to look honestly confused. "What's wrong with being amazingly talented and smart and athletic?"

Put like that it did make her sound somewhat neurotic. Was she?

Maybe. A little. And hormonal and on the edge of tears almost daily. "Because I would have just liked the chance to be beautiful," she whispered. "To not notice the differences, every day. To not have people raise their eyebrows at me."

"Elle…"

She unwound her hand and stepped back. "You made promises, Matt. In the moonlight and at the altar. And at the first sign of things not going your way, you broke them. You broke the ones you made to

God and me. And I had my share of broken promises when my father walked out of our lives, and when my husband betrayed me in front of the world." She took the handrail and started down the steps. "I have no intention of ever going through that again, so maybe it's better if we rethink the rules."

"Elle, I'm sorry." He followed her down the stairs and caught her hand before she stalked off into the kitchen. "Maybe you're right."

That made her want to cry, too, because she didn't want to be right. She wanted to be beautiful and beloved and have garden walks lined with roses that never, ever, ever needed spraying. She sighed inside, ruing the hot, emotional mess she'd become.

"You need to see this from my perspective."

Umm. No, she didn't.

"When we talked about this last summer, I didn't think having a baby was a real possibility. We were both sure it wasn't, so I never mentally prepared myself for the diagnosis. In my head, that was all a done deal."

"And then it wasn't."

"But that wasn't your fault," he went on. "And I was a jerk for making you feel that way. So here's my Christmas present to you, wife." He looped his arms around her. "I am going to spend the next five months earning back your love." He kissed one cheek. "Your trust." He kissed the other cheek, even more tenderly. "And your affection." He looked deep into her eyes. "Because once these babies are here, I'm probably going to get tired and somewhat stupid because that's the effect babies have, but I will spend these next months showing you how crazy-nice I am, so when I act tired and stupid after days of no sleep, you'll forgive me."

"So you're basically trying to bank forgiveness?"

He nodded happily, as if glad that she got it. "Yes. Because I'm a man, honey, and no one on the planet's going to believe I won't act stupid again. But just so you know?" He leaned in and kissed her, even though she didn't want him too, well…*kind of* didn't want him to but enjoyed the kiss, nonetheless. "Even when I'm stupid, I never stop loving you."

He laid his right hand over the small curve of her tummy. "You two are my witnesses. Daddy promises to be as nice as he can, as often as he can, under whatever circumstances prevail."

She wished he wasn't so charming.

She wished he wasn't so good at making her laugh, because she had a reason to be upset and mistrustful. Didn't she?

"I'll load the dishwasher." He bumped his forehead gently against hers. "If you can bring those last dishes around, we can get this done and unload presents from the spare closet."

A simple enough request. "OK." They worked in an easier quiet, and when the kitchen was done, Matt checked on the boys. "Sound asleep."

"Good." She started for the spare room, but Matt beat her to it.

"You go over by the tree. I'll bring things out, and you can arrange them. OK?"

It was nearly ten thirty, so his offer sounded just fine. "Yes."

Working together, it didn't take long. When they'd finished, the glow of the fire in the wood stove, window candles, sparkling tree, and gifts gave the room an old-time Christmas air.

"It's beautiful." Sentiment choked her again, but Elle utterly refused to cry. These sweeps of raw emotion were beyond ridiculous. Somehow, someway, she'd gain control over them. "A room meant for Christmas and children and lights."

"And next year two little crawlers, bent on destruction at every turn," Matt teased. "Twinkle lights, bows, wrapping paper, tiny toys…"

He was right. This wasn't a typical first pregnancy, not with three older brothers. These babies would need someone to run constant interference just to keep them out of harm's way. "If we can get through the first few years without them going for a joyride on big equipment, I'll be happy."

"Good." He switched off the lights, and his next words came quietly through the soft shadows of night. "Because I want you happy, Elle."

Mixed feelings grabbed hold of her. The temptation to turn to Matt was strong, but self-protection proved stronger. Maybe he meant it. Or maybe he just meant it *now*, when things were going all right, and that was a huge difference in Elle's world. She curled up on her side of their big, four-poster bed and prayed herself to sleep.

chapter twenty-eight

Focus on Elle.

He had to, Matt realized in early January when the doctor advised her to give up her work for the duration of the pregnancy. "We don't know enough about the toxicity of the fumes to fetuses, and if you can step aside from your work for a few months, that's probably best."

"Of course," Elle told her, but when they got home, she looked around the snow-covered house and yard as if seeing them for the first time. "I've never not worked."

Matt moved closer, not sure what to say.

She splayed her hands as if wondering what to do with them.

"It's not that long, is it? Four months out of a lifetime?"

She looked at him then, and it wasn't worry he saw in her gaze. It was fear. "It's not that." She laid her hands across her rapidly growing abdomen. "And it's not them. I'd do anything for them. It's not knowing if it will all still be there when I get back to it."

"The potter's shed?"

She made a face, a grimace. "Not there." She touched her head, her heart. "Here. What if there's nothing left when I take that seat in the spring? What if it's all just—gone?"

"Well, that's not about to happen," he told her, and something about his matter-of-fact tone seemed to help. "Wanna learn how to drive a plow? Because I'd be glad to teach you."

"I'm not beyond saying yes, because what on earth am I going to do for the next four months?"

"Grow our babies." He leaned in and kissed her gently. "That's a pretty big project right there, Elle." She didn't disagree, but she avoided looking outside, too, as if seeing the big, broad shed bothered her.

Matt understood more than she knew. The thought of his family business in jeopardy had kept him on edge. He'd shoved the concern aside because he needed to focus on Elle and the boys first, but steady snowfall kept him driving plows for long hours, which meant he was sleeping more than he was focusing. Watching Elle, reading the regret in her profile, he knew he had to do something to help her pass the time. But what?

He called Aggie from the cab of the plow and set up a time to meet. She walked into the local café the next morning, sat down beside him, and wasted no time. "What's wrong with Elle?"

"Nothing physical," Matt reassured her. "But the doctor said it's inadvisable for her to work in the shed while she's pregnant, which means four solid months of nothing to do."

"Oh." Aggie's wince said she understood his concern.

"You know Elle better than anyone. Four months of inactivity might make her crazy and possibly homicidal. She's already insanely emotional."

"Hormones."

"Yes, well, she's doubting her sanity one minute, and climbing the walls the next, then delightedly happy every time she sees an ad for baby things. I'd like to come up with an alternative plan if we can. I wracked my brain and came up with nothing, so I've come begging your help. Amos is in preschool, the boys are gone all day, and even a big old farmhouse can only be cleaned so often."

"I never expected her to get pregnant, so I never thought of her giving up work." Aggie gripped her coffee mug, thinking. "The chemicals, the dust, the fumes from the kiln. Even with protective gear, no one knows what long-term exposure can do to developing babies."

Dotty Murray, the town historian, moved their way from the next table. "What about quilting, Aggie?"

Aggie looked from her to Matt, thoughtful.

"Elle's an artist," Dotty continued, "and there's no old-world artistry more beautiful than a quilt. And not one thing dangerous about a needle and a thread."

"My sister has a frame she's not using," Aggie mused. "If we set it up in the living room, folks could even help do the quilting once it's pieced."

"Maybe a Memory Quilt," Dotty added, "with squares made by family. And with the faster cutting and piecing methods, she could do quilts for any room in the house. If she's a mind to, that is."

"What do we need to have?" Matt asked, because if these women were willing to help him keep Elle busy for the remainder of her pregnancy, he'd do whatever was needed to get the plans underway.

"Material, of course."

"And a sewing machine."

"Threads. Notions. Binding."

"A rotary cutter and quilting rulers."

"A cutting mat."

Dotty saw his face and laughed. "Come over to Eloise's with me. I'll get you set up."

Matt hesitated, not because he was reluctant, but would Elle welcome this idea coming from him?

Possibly not. "Listen, I love this idea, but if a guy walks in with all this stuff because he's trying to keep his wife busy, she might take it the wrong way."

Dotty grabbed his arm in a show of support. "Matt, you're right. I remember being well along with my John. I was let go from my job because back then some companies thought it was bad form to keep a woman on if she was in delicate circumstances." Her eye-roll showed the insensibility of that. "My husband thought he was being helpful by giving me all kinds of little projects to do. Now Thomas was a good man, and he wanted to help, but all I wanted was my job back. And the money that went along with it would have been a great help to a new family. So his projects to keep the little woman busy weren't exactly welcome, if you get my drift."

Matt got it, all right.

"What if you and I do it, Dotty?" Aggie asked. "We can gather the stuff, and stop over there tomorrow morning. What do you think, Matt?"

"If I were a praying man, I'd say you two are an answer to prayer," he told them.

Dotty kept her hand on his arm, but in a gentler fashion. "Any father of five who's *not* a praying man, should be," she told him. "No matter how strong or smart we are, before there was any condensed matter, before there was any light or darkness or big bang, something existed. Because we come from that something, into the here." She reached up and patted his cheek. "Praying gets us through, Matt. It's a help. And now, let's you and I head over to the store, spend a bunch of your money, and Aggie and I will pay Elle a visit tomorrow morning."

"Perfect. Thank you."

"Don't thank us yet," Dotty warned. "Elle might not look like Aggie, but they've got similar temperaments. Let's see if we can sugarcoat this just enough to make her try it, because if stubborn had a look?" Dotty sent a fond look to her friend. "It would be Aggie and Elle."

* * *

No work.

No throwing, no firing, no painting, no fumes—

How many times could you scrub a bathroom and not need to kill someone? Elle wasn't sure, but she figured she was going to find out soon…and then the doorbell rang.

She washed her hands, pulled off the apron, and moved to the door. "Mom! And Dotty, come in! This is such a nice surprise!"

It was a great surprise, but if she went too overboard with her mother, Aggie would know something was up, and she didn't want her mother worrying just because Elle felt like she might explode if she couldn't find something to do that didn't include a dust rag or a television.

"Well now, your mom and I were talking yesterday," Dotty confessed as she peeled off her jacket and hung it on the row of hooks inside the kitchen door. "And we got it into our heads that you might be interested in doing some kind of heritage work for these babies."

"Heritage work?" Elle pulled out a chair and sat down. "What do you mean, Dotty?"

"Well, I know you're busy," Aggie began, but Elle stopped her with a hand up.

"I'm not busy. I'm totally unbusy until these babies are born. Dr. Gartley and I agreed that I shouldn't be working in the shed until after delivery. So I can design, but no hands-on work."

"Elle, really?" Aggie reached out, looking surprised. "Then this is absolutely perfect timing, Dotty!"

"It seems like it could be," Dotty admitted. "Elle, I know you love to work with your hands, and it's going to be so busy once the babies are born. Aggie and I were thinking of piecing a quilt for each one. Something that would be uniquely theirs."

"A quilt?" Elle sat back, surprised, but then she smiled because she loved the idea of unique quilts for her babies. *Her babies.* The reality of God's grace still sent chills down her spine. "A heritage quilt."

"Yes!" Dotty slapped her hand on the table. "Now, your mother has a bunch of your old dresses and shirts. If we were to take pieces from that and then fill in with material from the store, we could come up with a lovely blanket for each baby."

"But what if they're boys?" Elle looked from one woman to the other as her mother bustled about the kitchen making tea. "We can't be too fluffy or flowery for little boys."

"True. So we could use neutral colors in between. Yellows and greens. Coral."

Elle loved coral and salmon and peach. As Dotty flipped open a book of quilt designs, Elle began to envision her own design, only with fabric instead of clay. "Can we do a scenic quilt?"

Dotty made a face. "I don't know what that is."

"If I create a scene for the middle, can we then create a design for piecing around the edges, to frame the center?"

"A panel quilt! Elle, that sounds marvelous." Dotty grinned excitement as Aggie poured tea. "An Elle Drake original! How perfect!"

It sounded perfect. It sounded like something special. Designing and creating the centered picture, then framing it with balanced shapes and sizes.

"What will I need?" Elle started to reach for a pad of paper to make a list, but Aggie stopped her with her hand.

"I think we've got everything you need in my car. Except for the center design. That, we'll leave up to you."

"You came prepared?"

"It pays to be prepared," Dotty declared, standing. "And you know your mother, Elle. When she gets an idea, she's all over it."

True, but how did her mother know she'd jump at this idea?

No matter. Just the thought of not being stymied for four months made the shortened days of winter a whole lot brighter. "Let's figure out a place to get set up."

"Perfect!"

* * *

Matt pretended innocence when he stopped home for lunch. "We having a party?" He hooked his coat, kicked off his boots, then put chilled hands on Elle's neck.

"Matt, you're freezing." She pulled away, but he saw more laughter in her eyes and less friction, so that was already a huge improvement.

"Which is why it's especially nice to have a wife to warm me up," he teased. "What's going on and who took over the living room?"

"We did." Dotty admitted freely. "We got this idea, and then Elle transposed it into a complete project."

"Like that's a surprise." Matt's coffee finished brewing. He picked up the mug and smiled over the rim as he took the first sip. "She's not only innovative with projects, she finishes them."

"Somewhat driven and hardworking, like someone else I know, perhaps?" Aggie murmured the words, and the truth in them surprised Matt.

He and Elle were a lot alike in that manner. Driven and focused, the eye on the ball, all the time. Funny, he'd never seen that before.

He moved over behind Elle and whistled softly against her cheek. Her very soft, pretty, pale cheek. "What are you designing? Because that's charming."

"You think?" She leaned back to look up at him, and he couldn't help himself—she looked so sweet and wondering and round and beautiful. He kissed her, just long enough to let her know she was still married.

The kiss left her wide-eyed and brought a hint of color to those ivory cheeks. "What's it for?" he whispered, because a soft voice just seemed right. So right.

"A quilt."

He played dumb and wished it was harder to do. "A quilt for what?"

"For the babies, actually."

He smiled and reached out a finger to the sketch. "Really? You can do this, Elle?"

She frowned.

"Transfer this," he indicated the pencil sketch on the easel, "to fabric?"

She shrugged as if anyone could do it. Matt knew better. "It's all about medium."

He had no clue what she was talking about, and his expression must have shown that.

"The kind of art, the substance, the matter. Normally I work with clay and bisque and oils and solvents. Here, my medium will be fabric and threads and Beatrix Potter."

A light bulb went off in his rusty brain. "My mom read those books to me when I was little."

"Timeless, right?" She smiled, and it was like her old smile, warm and full. "And I think it's all right for baby boys or girls, don't you, Matt?"

"It's perfect, Elle." He wanted to say more, so much more, to tell her he was glad to be included, that he wanted everything to be all right… but they had an audience. "One thing."

"Hmm?" She leaned forward to shade in a small spot, then looked back up at him.

"Can we put a Daddy Bunny in the picture?"

Her lips parted. She held his gaze as if reading what he longed to say, and then she nodded. "I think that's a lovely idea."

He stood beside her and watched her fluidly sketch in a father-styled bunny, sitting in an over-stuffed chair, but then she went further and put three little boy bunnies, clamoring around the chair in tiny overalls.

His coffee grew cold.

He didn't care.

Aggie and Dotty fussed over styling and cutting remnants on the opposite side of the room.

He barely heard them.

Before his eyes, Elle created a sketch of them. Their lives, their family, even to the little picture of "Goodnight Moon" hanging on Amos's bedroom wall.

A family joined together, with Elle holding two tiny, baby bunnies.

"I want to be holding a baby," he told her.

She sighed, rolled her eyes at him, but smiled and inserted a tiny bunny into his lap, then erased one of the babies from her lap.

"Now it's perfect."

"Not quite." She reached over and sketched in a dog sitting by the fireplace, watching over everyone.

Matt took the hint. "You want a dog."

"Everyone should have a dog," she told him without looking up. "Didn't you have a dog while you were growing up?"

They'd had several, in fact. "A dog can be a lot of work."

She scanned the picture of five little bunnies, then Matt. "Tell me about it."

He smiled because there was no other choice. "Before or after the babies?"

"After. When life settles down."

Aggie's snort indicated her opinion on life ever settling down.

Elle leaned back and stretched, then stood. "I think I'll sketch the other one standing. Leaning like that doesn't work anymore."

"Here." Matt put the palm of his hand against her back and moved it in long, slow circles. "Does that help?"

She sighed softly. "Yes. It's wonderful."

"Good."

She spotted his still-full coffee cup sitting on the table. "Your coffee's cold."

He shrugged as if cold coffee was of little consequence, gazed into her eyes, and said softly, "I was busy watching my wife."

* * *

Her heart rhythm spiked.

His words, so sweet. His touch, tender and kind. So much good about this man, the man she'd married with no real intention of falling in love.

But she had, she realized, and that's why his rejection stung so deep.

Forgiveness is of God. Seventy times seven, Elle. You know the Word, you understand the command. Get with the program here.

She understood all right, but she also believed in self-protection. She'd learned the hard way that guarding her emotions wasn't only a good thing, it was a basic necessity of life. "Well, thank you." She kept her words simple and polite as she moved away from his side. "I'll be glad to make you another."

Long seconds followed her retreat. He watched her, silent. A tiny muscle in the side of his jaw flinched, just once. "No need." He took the cup and walked toward the kitchen. "I'll just warm this one up and get back to work."

"Did you want lunch, Matt?" Aggie asked, but Elle didn't miss her look of assessment, wondering what was going on.

"I'm good, thanks. Continue on, ladies. I'll be back later." He warmed the mug in the microwave while he pulled his heavy jacket over his shoulders, but then he walked out the door, forgetting the coffee.

"You forgot your coffee, Matt!" Dotty called the reminder, but Elle crossed the kitchen and retrieved his mug.

"I'll run it out to him."

"Such love!" Dotty grinned and didn't know how far off the mark she was.

"Matt." Elle pushed open the back porch door and held the mug high for him to see, but Matt didn't look at the mug.

He looked at her, and even through the lightly falling snow, she read the pain in his eyes.

He didn't come get the mug.

He held her gaze, looking sad, so sad, and then he quietly put the truck in gear and backed around.

Two hearts held hostage by anger and fear.

That's what she saw in his eyes, and it was the same thing she saw reflected in her bedroom mirror.

Christ forgave those who betrayed him, who sentenced him, who crucified him. Why was it so hard to forgive her husband's moment of anger?

Maybe because it wasn't a moment. It was days. Long, cold, lonely days, that reminded her of her father, of Alex, of painful times she'd tried to push aside.

Had she ignored his hurt? His feelings?

Her joy had pushed her to blindside him with the announcement, not realizing how deep his fear went. She got it now.

She set the mug down on the porch and softly shut the door. He'd hurt her feelings, yes. But his expression said she was hurting his the same way, and what kind of wife did that?

The vindictive kind.

She rejoined the ladies inside, determined to somehow make this better. She'd let a lot of suns go down on her anger, so much that it was starting to become a habit, a habit she needed to break. But how?

Trust your husband with your whole heart and your whole soul.

Easy words. Tough to do. But she'd try, because for two smart, well-educated people, they were acting awfully stupid.

chapter twenty-nine

"Wow. You're getting big." Randy stared at Elle from across the kitchen, eyes wide. "I didn't realize how big people get when they're going to have a baby. Like they're going to explode!"

"Randy." Matt put his hands on Randy's shoulders. "While I'm sure Mom loves hearing your perceptions, you might want to go finish your homework before she does something rash."

"What's rash?"

"In this case, it could be murder. Go. Now."

"OK, but do you remember we've got the book fair tonight? At school?"

He didn't remember that, and Elle's grimace indicated she'd forgotten, too. "Six thirty?" Matt asked.

Randy nodded.

"Elle, can you go? I've got the town planning board meeting tonight."

"I'm supposed to do a virtual conference call with Hyland Manor at six fifteen to schedule the fall and Christmas releases. It's going to be thirty minutes, at least. Randy, how long does the book fair last?"

He frowned at her, then Matt. "Never mind. I don't have to go. I don't even like stupid books anyway. I just wanted to do something with my dad."

Matt bristled. "I've taken you to soccer practice twice every week since September and religion classes once a week. It's not like you're a forgotten child, Randy. But I'm on the schedule with the construction firm for the Crandall Heights subdivision. I have to be there to answer questions. It's my job."

"James's dad goes to everything, and he's got a job. And his mom comes and helps in school every week sorting things for the teacher."

"While sorting things sounds like lots of fun, it's hard to do when both parents work, Randy. But Dad and I have been able to help with field trips, haven't we?"

He nodded reluctantly.

"So at least our jobs are flexible enough to do that. A lot of parents don't have that option."

"You went when Todd's class had the book fair last week."

Guilt hit Matt. He'd taken Todd so they could have some one-on-one time. Now he was ruing that decision. If he'd taken both boys to pick out books, this argument wouldn't be taking place.

"Never mind." Randy hunched his shoulders and marched up the stairs, despondent.

Matt watched him go.

"Can Jason cover you tonight?"

He shook his head. "He's not familiar with the layout. He's working on the plans for finishing Wessington. Dad's got that bad cold and gave it to my mom, so they're both off the list for tonight. What about your conference? Can it be put off? And why is it scheduled at night?"

"Timing, just like yours," she answered. "We're accommodating the West Coast office. This launch has been in the works since September, but now we have to nail everything down so contracts can be signed. It's an everyone-on-board deal."

"Well, we have to find someone."

"Do we?"

Her question irritated him. "You think we don't?"

She stirred a pot of red sauce and turned it down to stay warm until the pasta was cooked. "There are always things in life to miss, aren't there? Missing a book fair isn't exactly a tragedy. Why not see if he'd like to make a special trip to the mall after soccer on Thursday, and he can use his money at the bookstore there?"

It wasn't a bad idea, and as Randy made a show of trudging back through the kitchen, Matt offered him the alternative.

Randy shook his head, eyes down, his lower lip thrust out, clearly unhappy.

"You've got to be reasonable, Randy." Matt bent to his level. "Schedules get messed up sometimes, but I'd be glad to take you book shopping on Thursday. I think it's a great compromise, and I'm sorry about tonight."

A tear snaked its way down Randy's cheek. He brushed it away with a quick dash of his hand as he stormed off to the family room. "I don't care about stupid old books anyhow. I don't even like to read most of the time!"

"Darned if you do, darned if you don't." Elle folded her arms over her middle, looking torn.

"And I hate giving in to his moods," Matt said. "Every time I think he's doing better, we get a night like this, and I feel like I've taken two steps back."

"Kate."

Matt looked back at her as he realized what she meant. "She'll be going with Jenny."

"If you can drop him off at her place—"

"Gladly."

"I'll check it out." A quick phone call later, the deal was struck. Matt called Randy out to the kitchen. "Hey, we've got this all worked out. I'm going to drop you by Aunt Kate's house on the way to my meeting, and she'll take you and Jenny to the book fair. OK?"

"You'd do that for me?" Randy gazed up at Matt like he was some kind of hero, an amazingly quick turnaround, even for Randy. "Thanks, Dad!"

"Elle arranged it, actually."

"Oh." Randy turned, pretending to be polite. "Thank you."

"Glad to do it." Her brisk tone said it was no big deal. "We'll have to eat quickly so you guys can leave on time. Randy, can you put the plates on the table?"

"It's not my night."

"No." Elle stirred the rigatoni. "But you're going to miss clearing tonight, so we'll do a role reversal. You set; Todd can clear."

"I don't know why I have to do girl's work all the time," he grumbled, but he accepted the plates from Matt and put them on the table grudgingly. "My dad never used to do this stuff when my mom was around."

Everything paused.

Matt stared at him, then Elle, then Randy again. "Look, Randy, that's not true. I helped when I could."

Randy rolled his eyes.

"And you were just a little guy. You can't possibly remember—"

* * *

Big mistake.

Like watching a bound-to-happen accident, Elle saw the emotional collision coming and could do nothing to stop it.

"I remember everything!" Eyes wide, Randy's face dared Matt to argue. "I remember so much stuff, and my mom was always there, she always came to everything, she never made other people do things for us because she loved us so much. Why'd she have to go and die, anyway? Because nothing is ever right again when people die!" He raced up the stairs, crying angry tears.

Matt seemed flabbergasted. He looked at Elle, then the stairs. "What just happened?"

"You hit a nerve."

"That's not exactly unusual with Randy."

"I know. It's just a really sensitive nerve with him."

"Listen, Elle." Matt came closer, and he looked kind of beat up. "I know things are messed up right now, I know you're mad at me, Randy's mad at me, and there are going to be three people on that planning board tonight who are mad at me because they didn't want this subdivision to go through and they lost by a one-vote margin in November. I'd miss this meeting if I could, but I can't. And I don't want to give in to Randy's temper, but—"

"He went for the jugular."

"With perfect aim," Matt admitted. "Can you possibly cancel your conference and take him? I know it's a lot to ask."

It wasn't a lot, not really. Not when the stark pain in Randy's eyes reminded her so much of her own youth. Wishing her father back, praying for his return. He'd left purposely, turning his back on his wife and kids, and draining the bank accounts before he did.

Carrie hadn't chosen to leave her precious family. She had no choice in the matter. Neither did Randy, a little boy who desperately wished he could remember his mother, and couldn't. "I'll go make a call."

Matt grabbed hold of her arm before she picked up the phone. He gathered her into a hug, a hug that felt so good she didn't want it to end. "Thank you."

She kept her head there against the curve of his shoulder and his neck, just long enough to relish his strength, his scent. How could she not appreciate such a good, hardworking, dedicated man? "You're welcome."

She made the call, crunched a few feelings, drew a resigned sigh, and rescheduled for earlier in the day when family time wouldn't be an issue, but she got it done.

The look on Randy's face when she slipped into her coat and grabbed her car keys made it all worthwhile.

Even if he was a brat.

"You're taking me to Aunt Kate's?"

"I'm taking you to the book fair."

"But?" He met her gaze. She raised one brow and waited. "You're supposed to have a meeting thing."

"I canceled it."

He gulped and looked a little guilty. Elle was OK with that. "For me?"

"Yup."

He bit his lower lip, then reached out to take her hand, a rare moment of solidarity in Randy-world. "Thank you."

She couldn't help but love this kid, despite his antics, his drama, his more petulant nature. She gave his hand a squeeze as Kate breezed in the door. "Kate, I'll be back with the kids when we're done at the fair. Thanks for stepping in over here."

"Glad to do it. Take my car," Kate told her. "It's already warm, and I'm going to check progress on this quilt idea I've heard way too much about already."

"Thanks, Aunt Kate!" Randy flashed her a smile as he pulled Elle toward the door. "See you later!"

"I'll be here."

He hopped into the back seat with Jenny, and they chattered all the way to the school. Not to her, but to each other, which made Elle wonder how badly her presence was really needed. But if it gave Randy comfort to have his stepmom along, that was a good thing.

"You've got your money?"

He nodded and patted his pocket. "Can I shop alone?"

"Yes, but we're shopping for books, remember?" She pointed out the huge array of wall posters as they entered the display-filled cafeteria. "Not posters. Books."

"Got it!"

A little boy raced their way. "Randy!"

"Jake!" They moved off together, smiling and happy. Jenny went the other way, and Elle wandered the various exhibitions, keeping a quiet eye on both of them. And when they had finished up at the volunteer-staffed checkout counter, Randy's teacher pulled her aside.

"You must be so proud of Randy," she whispered.

"When we're not ready to kill him," Elle whispered back.

The young teacher laughed. "Well, there's that," she agreed. "He's a smart aleck, and that gets him more than the occasional caution. But what he did tonight, for Jake. That was precious."

"What did he do?" Did Elle look as confused as she felt? "I don't understand."

"He used half his money to buy books for Jake, but didn't tell Jake he was doing it, and then he had me give Jake the bag and tell him they were a present from a friend."

Selfless love, not seeking grandeur.

Emotion swept Elle, not like that was any surprise lately. "He did that?"

The teacher nodded. "Shhh. I'm not supposed to tell, but I wanted to make sure you knew. He was so excited about coming here tonight. He told me today he was doing a big surprise tonight, so he must have planned the whole thing."

Of course he did. He was smart as a whip. And while Todd's sensitivities were easy to see, Randy hid his beneath a blanket of bravado.

Like you did, her conscience reminded her. *Pretending things were all right, and setting goals so that eventually they would be.*

"Thank you for telling me."

The teacher smiled. "Those are the moments teachers love to share with parents. The things that make good memories."

She wanted Randy to feast on good memories, but tonight's outburst made her realize how deep his wounds went.

Peace begins at home. Peace begins with a smile.

Simple thoughts of great truths.

Once the kids were in school the next morning, she e-mailed Gloria D'Amico and asked for a meeting. She spent the day working on the quilt design, deciding what to piece and what to paint, and when she finally got a reply to her e-mail midafternoon, she breathed a sigh.

"Tomorrow, three fifteen, my chambers."

Gloria wasn't cutting Elle slack. She wasn't meeting her halfway. She was staging the meet on her turf, her rules.

That was all right, because Elle wasn't meeting with Gloria to argue or berate. She was meeting with her to ask her help on a very special project. The worst the older woman could say was no.

She arranged for her mother to get the boys off the bus the next day, and Matt was picking up Amos. She parked in the Civic Center lot, went through security, and took the elevator up to the second floor of the Department of Justice. Small, worn signs indicated the various courtrooms. She followed the signs until she found Gloria's name on a door. A young woman directed her to a seat. Elle sat down and waited.

Five minutes passed. Then ten. Fifteen. And when she'd been cooling her heels for over twenty minutes, the glass-topped door finally opened. "The judge can see you now."

Look at the emotion behind the action. Art is better if we let the emotion guide us.

Words from an art institute professor, years before. Good advice for art and life. Elle walked calmly into Gloria's office and took a seat.

Gloria strode in through another door, looking like she wished she was anywhere else.

"Thank you for seeing me."

Gloria sat, folded her hands, and leaned forward from her side of the desk. "You said it was about the kids, and it's important. That was your ticket in the door. If you misrepresented your purpose in any way, that will be your ticket back to the hallway. State your business."

Elle withdrew a picture of Randy holding a box. She handed the photograph over to Gloria. "Jason had this photo at his house. All of Matt's photos of the kids were destroyed in the fire, except for a handful that were in the basement room."

"And you're telling me this because?"

"Randy was three when your daughter died."

The judge's eyes narrowed. "I know how old he was, and I vividly recall every single, stupid second of that horribly wretched day. Thanks so much for the reminder."

"And Todd was four and a half." Elle went on as if Gloria wasn't on the attack. She folded her hands together to keep them still, because the woman's dead-on stare was enough to make anyone nervous. "Todd remembers Carrie. He was old enough to bank a lot of things that have been reinforced with pictures and videos over the years."

Gloria glared, silent.

"Randy was too young, but he wants to remember his mother. He creates scenarios in his head, things he thinks they might have done. Places they might have gone. It's as if he's building a history because he doesn't remember the one that existed."

Elle reached over and tapped the box in the picture. "Randy kept this box in his room, tucked away, out of sight. It had a few special toys inside, a stash of candy, and a picture of his mother."

Pain twisted Gloria's features. "Matt has other pictures. Give one of those to Randy."

"I tried that, of course." Elle splayed her hands as if that solution was a given. "We bought him a similar box. Matt went online and bought the same toys he'd had before. We did everything we could to make it a reasonable facsimile, but it's not the same. Not to Randy."

"Get to the point."

Elle leaned forward. "I'd like you to spend some time with Randy. Talking to him, talking about Carrie, feeding his imagination. The fact that Todd has actual memories and Randy doesn't makes him feel disconnected. He loves his mother, he remembers the emotion of having a mother, but when he reaches for those actual moments, he draws a blank."

"You want me to come talk to him?" Disbelief caricatured Gloria's features. "I've been denigrated, ostracized, and left out of the loop for a long time, young lady. Matt hasn't wanted me or Al around those boys for years while he diddled their lives away. And here you are, in my daughter's place, asking me in as if that's going to solve anything. It won't." Gloria's fingers clenched the edge of her desk. "Because it won't bring my daughter back."

"Nothing will," Elle answered softly. "But those boys are your daughter, here on earth. Her lifeblood, her spirit, her children. And they need you. They need that connection to her through you, and you and your husband are the only people who can provide that. For Randy, especially, but it would be good for all the boys."

"What is it you expect? What is your bottom line with this request, because I'm already uncomfortable just contemplating it."

Elle shrugged. "Hang out with him, take him places, whatever you'd like to do. You're his grandmother, Mrs. D'Amico. You're his most direct connection with his mother, and while Randy pretends to be a hard-nosed kid, he's actually a little boy who really wishes he had his mother back."

Gloria's lips thinned as she appraised Elle. "Did Matt send you?"

"He did not."

"Does he know you're here?"

Elle hated to admit this, but had little choice. "No."

"Why did you come here, Mrs. Wilmot? What did you hope to gain? You must know that seeing you there, very pregnant, makes me angrier than any woman should ever be. I lost my daughter as she tried to give Matt another child. Seeing that you're in the same condition so quickly after your marriage doesn't exactly ingratiate the situation to me. I hope you're intelligent enough to comprehend that."

"Perspective's a funny thing, isn't it?"

Gloria pulled back a little. "How's that?"

"We can complain that roses have thorns, or rejoice because thorn bushes have roses," she said softly. "Abraham Lincoln."

"I know who said it!" Gloria snapped. "What I don't see is a vestige of relevancy."

"You and I are family." Gloria sent a pointed look to the digital clock, and Elle decided not to wait until she was asked to leave. "We are connected by these children. And when family's in trouble, they should look out for one another."

"You are not my family." Gloria didn't bother standing. She sat right there and clipped each word out. "I've watched as my former son-in-law has done everything in his power to thwart my relationship with my grandsons. He's shirked, shrugged off, and shunned every effort we made to be a constant in their lives, and now his new wife is sitting here playing nice, asking for help. I'm pretty sure this falls under the heading of too little, too late."

Lord, grant me patience, tolerance, and warmth. Lord, grant me patience, tolerance, and warmth. Lord—

"You and Randy have something in common, Your Honor. Your love for Carrie binds you together. It's up to you, of course." Elle stood. She couldn't button her jacket, so she thrust her hands into her pockets. "And I believe when you have time to think about this, you'll see what I mean, because there is no 'too little, too late' in terms of a child's well-being."

She walked out, half-expecting the judge to wing something at her head.

She didn't.

Elle didn't look back to read her expression. She'd issued the offer, an invitation that might make Matt angry, but she knew what it was like to wish and hope and pray a parent would show up. To imagine that parent with you, watching a performance, seeing a game, having a catch in the backyard. Even just to take you for ice cream like all the other parents did.

She'd deal with Matt. He'd understand or he wouldn't, but doing what was right for Randy took precedence, no matter what the consequences, because a little boy's heart and soul were too precious to take for granted.

chapter thirty

"You did what?" Matt didn't just look angry. He looked downright furious. "You went to see Gloria without my permission?"

"Permission?" Elle let the disbelief in her tone question his choice of words.

"Without telling me, I mean."

"I did, because it was necessary. You've been sparring with the woman for nearly five years. For the boys' sake, it's time for everyone to lay down their arms and come to the peace talks." She adjusted the stretch of the central quilt panel as she talked. Too tight and it would crinkle. Too loose and the painted and stitched lines would pucker. She frowned, testing the tension with her pointer finger.

"Stop poking that material and talk to me."

"Not poking, testing, and no. Not in that tone of voice. I did what was necessary, Matt. No more, no less. And I'll do it again if she stays distant, because discord in a family isn't good. Trust me, I know."

"You think I want to fight with Gloria? Argue with her? Deal with her?"

Good tension. She carefully tightened the thumb screws to keep it right there, then sat back and raised her gaze. "You and the D'Amicos are like that movie about the groundhog reporter. You wake up each day to the reality that Carrie's gone, but you can't move beyond your guilt and anger to connect the dots of your lives, so you're stuck there. Somehow, none of you have moved through the steps of acceptance with each other. So maybe, if Gloria and Al spend some time with the boys, with Randy in particular, the boys can feel that connection with their mother, Matt. A connection that was broken all too soon. And then maybe you can all move on."

"You think I don't know that?"

She sat silent, watching him.

"You think I don't understand that in a perfect world, we'd all go on together, laughing over good times, sharing memories, a stinkin' Hallmark commercial?

"It's not that easy, Elle." He paced the room, a model of frenetic energy. "We all lost something that day. Something precious, something good. But my reality was filled with three little boys who needed me for everything." He stopped pacing, splayed his hands, palms down, and frowned. "There was no time for anything. No sleeping, because I had a newborn who had his nights and days mixed up. The boys were preschoolers, filled with energy, always into something. There were schedules to meet, work to be done, and preschool and day-care costs were backbreakers. I had to use some of Carrie's insurance money to get by and hated that I had to do that."

"Why would you hate yourself for using money purposely?"

"It should be for college, or trips, or Disney World, shouldn't it? For something big and grand and marvelous."

"To offset their loss."

"Yes!" He ran his hand along the base of his neck. "Instead, I used nearly twenty thousand those first two years for day care, to stay afloat."

"And doing that allowed you to bid on six-figure contracts that put the company at record highs." She stood and lessened the distance between them. "You made a trade, Matt. And it was a good one. Why beat yourself up over it?"

"You don't get it." He faced her, and he didn't look mean or angry, he looked…lost and confused. "There's no way you can get it, Elle, so you should have left it alone. It wasn't your place to interfere."

"And yet, I did." It was late, they were both tired, and she refused to argue with him. "And I hope she takes me up on the offer."

She left him there, stewing, and went upstairs. She might be uncertain about some things, but she was fairly clear on one: unchecked anger wasn't in anyone's best interests, including her husband's, but she wasn't blind to the risks, either.

She saw the look on Matt's face when he talked about Carrie. He'd loved her, and the depth of loss engraved itself in his gaze. Bringing this to the fore meant comparisons, old wife to new.

Carrie had been a beautiful young woman. Small, curvy, vibrant, and warm.

Elle was different. So different. And yet he seemed to genuinely care for her, when she wasn't making him spitting mad.

She winced.

She'd gone to Gloria purposely, without telling Matt, convinced she was doing the right thing. Was it justified if it hurt the man she'd pledged her life to?

The pain in his face made her second-guess her decision, but it was done now. And in God's hands. And in the end, if it helped Randy adjust to his loss in a healthier manner, it would be worth the cost.

She only hoped Matt would come to see it that way.

* * *

He was being micromanaged by his wife, and it was driving Matt stark raving mad, even if she was correct…and Matt wasn't stupid enough to be blind to that possibility.

Right now he wished that overnight snowplowing didn't give him quite so much time to think as he maneuvered the monster-sized machine around the snow-filled, vacant municipal parking lot. But it did.

He didn't want to fight with Elle.

He didn't want two generations of good decisions compromised by one badly timed decision his father made nearly two years before and the looming payment that came with it.

He didn't want Gloria sticking her nose in where it didn't belong. He'd dealt with that for years. No more.

He didn't want Elle interfering with the past. It was over. Done. Why couldn't she just let it go?

He growled, turned on a country radio station, and moved snow with a vengeance.

Elle's ringtone interrupted him two hours later, and he had to take a breath to keep from barking at her. Clearly she'd pushed an old button by extending an olive branch to Gloria. Worse, she knew it. Double worse, he should be man enough to get over it.

He wasn't.

He hauled in a breath and picked up the call. "What's up?"

"I know you'll need to sleep today, but we have a meeting at the church about Amos's baptism at the Easter Vigil."

"When?"

"Six thirty."

Another meeting. Another night gone.

"I figured we could drop Randy off at soccer practice and then pick him up after the meeting."

"We both have to be there?"

"Yes." He wasn't sure if that was the priest's edict or his wife's, but either way, there would be no relaxing with ESPN or the NBA tonight. "I'll catch a nap when I get home, but if I fall asleep tonight, nudge me awake, OK?"

"Bud Wilson, the sheriff's deputy, will be there, too. His wife is preparing for confirmation. I'll borrow his Taser."

"Funny."

She laughed, and it should have made him mad. It didn't. It felt good to have her tease him, to meet him on equal ground. As long as she let the past lay in the past.

She wouldn't, which meant he'd be dealing with Gloria again, and that was about the last thing he wanted to do as Elle entered the last months of her surprise pregnancy.

Gloria plus pregnancy incited too many memories.

And fears, his conscience prodded. *Stop pretending you're not worried and deal with it.*

That was just it. He didn't want to deal with it.

He hung up the phone and completed the strip mall lot just as morning commuters were pulling into the drive-thru lanes at the coffee shop.

He parked the rig, got into his very cold truck, and drove home. He got there just in time for Randy and Todd to hug him good-bye and for Amos to spill his chocolate milk in his hurry to reach his father.

"Don't miss that bus, boys." Elle pointed to the driveway, and the older boys made it to the road just in time.

"And you're a mess, my friend." She smooched Amos's cheek, made him laugh, then tossed him a dishcloth. "Clean that up and throw the dirty cloth into the laundry basket, OK?"

"OK!" Matt watched as Amos cleaned up the mess and took care of the cloth. And when Elle handed him a wet paper towel, the little guy washed the sticky spot off the floor, threw the towel away, and washed his hands.

A year ago, none of that would have happened.

His boys would have missed the bus, Amos would have been having a ripping fit over a little spilled milk, and he would have been scrambling nightly to find someone to sleep at the house whenever snow was predicted.

The difference was like night and day and stood before him wearing an oversized shirt…

His shirt.

And maternity pants.

He loved her. Despite their differences, despite her independent nature, or maybe because of it…he loved her.

She made a difference, and she did it with a purpose and an objective.

"What are you looking at?" She caught him staring and made a face. "I know I'm a wreck. I haven't even had time to run a comb through my hair or grab a shower or—"

He stopped her with a kiss and knew he should be doing more of that, because kissing his wife made everything better. Why was he stupid stubborn and forgot that?

He kissed her long and slow and stopped when he didn't want to, but Amos was calling for help with his book bag. He leaned his forehead to hers and gently breathed in and out. In and out.

"What was that for?" she whispered.

Was she as shaken as he was?

He hoped so. "Because. Just because."

He felt her cheeks move when she smiled. "Best reason ever."

It was. He started to step back when the landline rang. Gloria's name flashed in the display.

Elle called for Amos to get his jacket and picked up the phone. "Hello, Gloria."

She nodded at whatever Carrie's mother was saying, then said, "Randy's got soccer practice tonight, so that's bad, but he's free tomorrow night and Saturday afternoon. Were you thinking to take just Randy, or Randy and Todd? All three?" She glanced at Matt, surprised, and what could he do?

"You're the one who gets to deal with the repercussions," he told her when she hung up. "Every time she took them last year, it was a battleground when they returned. Questions with no answers. Sullen looks, like it was my fault they didn't have a mother. And since when is she acknowledging Amos's presence in the world? Because not once has she ever included that little boy in anything. Oh, she did it carefully, always saying she wasn't up to managing little ones, that he was a handful, that he didn't listen."

"Which part of any of that was untrue, Matt?"

There was no talking with her. Not when he was this tired and Gloria was breathing down their necks like a power-hungry, flame-throwing medieval dragon. "You'll see."

She could have just walked out, ignoring his tantrum.

She didn't. She crossed the short span of space between them, cradled his cheeks in her hands, and kissed him gently. "Go to bed. You're exhausted, and if I haven't thanked you enough for working so hard for this family, let me do it now." She pulled back a little. "You're a good man, Matthew Wilmot. Thank you for that."

"Yeah, yeah."

She smiled down at Amos. "Great job getting ready all by yourself, partner!" She high-fived him and took his hand.

"Love you, Dad!" Amos waved with five-year-old excitement as Matt held the outer door open for Elle. "And I love you too, Mom!"

He called Elle "mom."

Elle turned at the door and met Matt's gaze.

Brilliantly happy.

Excitement and joy brightened her face, all because a little boy called her mom.

She kept things simple.

Why couldn't he?

She'd been handed a raw deal at the hands of a man who should know better. The entire nation had witnessed his affair and disregard for Elle. It had left her wounded, but she didn't stay down for the count, whereas he nursed those battle scars like they were fresh wounds.

Sleep now. Reason later.

But even after six hours of refreshing sleep, Matt woke up pretty sure he was just a jerk by nature.

chapter thirty-one

Todd slumped into the ladder-back chair on Saturday morning. "Do we have to go?"

The firm click of an upstairs door indicated Matt was leaving her on her own to handle Gloria. "Yes."

"She's grumpy," said Randy, and he made a foul face. "She acts like she's never happy to be around us."

"I'm going to label that a 'severe exaggeration on the part of the children'," Elle replied. "She's your grandmother. Give her a chance to enjoy the role." She handed Randy a basket of laundry. "Run this up to your room. Quick now. She's here."

"Aaarrrggghhh!" He groaned as he walked the square basket of clothing upstairs taking the slowest steps ever.

Elle didn't wait for Gloria to get to the door. She crossed the porch and pushed the storm door open. "Come in, Gloria. That sun feels good, doesn't it? A welcome change."

"Weather being a safe topic of conversation," Gloria noted. She wasn't friendly, but she didn't sound as snide as she had earlier that week. Elle marked that an improvement. "Todd. Hello."

"Hello." He muttered the word, chin down.

"Do you need to borrow a car seat for Amos?"

"I have a booster."

"Perfect." Elle crossed the room. "Randy, Grandma's here."

No reply. And no footsteps on the stairs either.

"Randy."

Todd slunk lower in the chair, and Elle hadn't thought that possible.

Amos came out of the bathroom with his pants undone. "Mom! I need help."

Gloria had been surveying the kitchen. Amos's words stopped her perusal. Elle wasn't sure if she was going to go ballistic, walk out, or handle the moment with grace.

The kitchen clock ticked into the emptiness, a chronic reminder of time passing by.

"Grandma!" Amos saved the moment as he realized she was there. He raced across the kitchen, loose pants and all, and launched himself into his surprised grandmother's arms. "I haven't seen you in forever and ever!" Delight poured out in his words, in his smile. "Look how big I am!" He stopped hugging her, climbed down, and stepped back, waiting. "I'm going to school with Todd and Randy next year, and I'm gonna be a big brother, and I'm gonna get—" He frowned and tapped one finger to his mouth, thinking. He turned toward Elle. "I forgot."

"Baptized."

"Yes!" He fist-pumped the air like he saw his older brothers do. "And I have to be good in church for a very long time." His face dulled, but then brightened. "But then I get ice cream."

Gloria's expression changed with each announcement, and by the time Amos got to the ice cream part, her eyes had softened. "That should be fun, Amos. And very special." She raised her gaze to Elle. "I received our invitation. Thank you."

"You're most welcome. And in May, Todd and Randy are both making their First Communion. Another invitation will be forthcoming, if we let Randy live, that is. Randy Wilmot." She called him again as she moved closer to the stairs and looked up. He stood at the top, arms locked, gaze stubborn. "You might look like your uncle, but you act just like your father," she told him, and none too quietly. "Get down here and hit the road, kid. I've got work to do."

His deliberate and loud steps thunked on each stair, until he finally trudged into the kitchen.

"Jackets."

Their reluctant movements were silent rudeness, but Elle ignored it. The boys and Gloria needed to work things out in their own way and their own time.

"Is Grandpa coming?" Todd asked as he yanked up his zipper.

"He can't." Gloria made a face of regret. "He's got that nasty cold that's going around, and he's pretty uncomfortable right now, but he's coming to Amos's baptism."

"I miss Grandpa.

"I know. He misses you, too. Next time, OK?"

"Sure. Where are we going?"

"The museum?" Randy asked, and he didn't sound excited.

"The science center?" Todd's question was more polite.

"The opera thing?" Randy dramatized his face, voice, and body to make sure everyone in a three-county area knew he didn't want to go to the opera ever again.

"Well, I considered all of those," Gloria told them. "And I was seriously considering the opera for the sheer beauty of it."

The two older boys shuddered and groaned.

"But then I decided we'd spend a couple of hours at Kidland."

"Kidland? For real? Like with the climbing walls and the bounce houses?"

"And the cool obstacle course?"

"And the pit of despair?"

"That's the one."

"I love Kidland!" Randy moved to the door. "Let's go."

"Come on, Amos. Hurry up and get your jacket on."

"Todd." Elle tipped his chin up slightly. "Really?"

He made a face. "Sorry. Hey, Amos. Want help?"

"I can do it." Gloria had helped him with the tight snap on his pants, but Amos was determined to zip his own jacket, and when he did it, he grinned at his grandmother. "See? I did it all by myself!"

"You're a big boy, Amos."

He gripped her hand, proud, and Elle was pretty sure he gripped part of her heart, too, because when Gloria looked back at her, her eyes looked damp. "Is five o'clock OK?"

"Five's great. Do you want to stay for supper? We're doing subs. You're most welcome."

Gloria looked almost tempted, then refused. "Not this time. Al's fairly miserable with this cold, and I promised him chicken soup. But," she met Elle's gaze, "perhaps another night?"

"Sounds good. Have fun, guys."

Randy and Todd charged out the door. "We will!"

"Bye!"

Matt appeared once they'd all piled in the car. "She's really taking them to Kidland?"

Elle cringed. "Yes. On a Saturday afternoon."

"Should we offer to help? We should, shouldn't we?" He said that, but looked kind of pleased that Gloria might be getting in over her head for a change.

"Do you think she has a clue what she's in for?" Kidland was a great place, but on cold, wet Saturday afternoons, it was besieged with kids of all ages, and prime time for birthday parties. Basically, the indoor amusement center was a zoo of feverish activity.

"Maybe her sister is meeting her." Matt gazed toward town. "I almost feel sorry for her."

"You could always stop by and offer your help in an hour or so." Elle set up her quilting project. "Dotty and Mom are coming over to work on the quilts."

"They just pulled in." Matt eyed the clock. "I'll check in an hour. If I just show up, she'll think I don't trust her. If I call or text her and offer help, maybe that's less intrusive."

"Grown-ups complicate things."

"Life complicates things," Matt shot back. "Sometimes the grown-ups are innocent bystanders. I'm going to seal that family room trim while the boys are gone. I'll open the windows, but if the smell is too much for you, let me know, OK?"

"Yes. Hey."

He turned.

"Gloria and Al are coming to Amos's baptism."

She couldn't tell if he was pleased or chagrined, but then he shrugged.

"She'll be glad it's getting done."

Elle and Gloria were in full agreement on that. "Me, too."

* * *

Matt waved to Dotty and Aggie as they came through the back door.

A part of him wanted to let Gloria face the afternoon on her own, survival of the fittest. He figured that might begin payback for her heavy-handed behaviors in the past few years. But…

She was coming to Amos's baptism.

She was taking the boys to a kid-friendly environment.

She was actually thinking of them, their ages, their needs. She was accepting Elle's olive branch and putting in an effort to end the standoff. The least he could do was meet her halfway.

He texted her about forty-five minutes later. "Kidland is crazy busy on Saturdays. Need help? I can be there in five."

Two minutes later, his phone buzzed. "We're fine."

"OK," he texted back and went back to work sealing the oak moldings trimming the ceiling. Another text buzzed as he finished the third wall.

"Are you still available?"

"Yes."

"Help!" And then she inserted an emoticon, a crazy face, blinking.

He laughed and realized that was the first time he'd laughed with Gloria since Carrie died. He grabbed his jacket from the hook and jangled his keys to get Elle's attention. "Gloria needs backup."

Elle didn't try to hide her pleased expression. "I'm glad."

He shrugged like it was no big deal as he noted the older women's work. "This is coming right along." Dotty and Aggie had pieced the outer frame of the quilt. The quaint look complemented the middle piece Elle had designed. "You've matched the feel of Elle's panel."

"Beautiful pictures deserve beautiful frames," Dotty reasoned as she smoothed puckers with an iron. "And to have the honor of working with an artist of Elle's magnitude is a wonderful thing."

"Dotty." Elle looked uncomfortable with the attention.

"It's a fact," Dotty insisted. "The work of your hands, the kindnesses you show, the peace you bring to others, making covering for beds. You're a Proverbs thirty-one woman, the kind others look up to."

"More sewing, less talking. You're embarrassing Elle." But Aggie smiled as she said it, and Dotty grinned.

Proverbs 31. They'd used that at their wedding, and it had meant nothing that day, but today, watching Elle form a blanket for their babies, seeing her hand at work in so many ways, he saw the verse come alive.

So some old guy wrote some pretty words thousands of years ago. Poets are a dime a dozen.

Maybe they were, but these words fit well. Valuing his wife…

He hadn't valued Carrie enough. He saw that once she was gone, because she'd done everything effortlessly. She made caring for children, babies, their home, and their schedules look easy.

It wasn't easy. It was hard, like quick steps to a dance kind of hard. He'd learned a valuable lesson. Just because a thing looked easy, didn't make it so.

He pulled up to the Kidland parking lot and had to park at the farthest end. By the time he got inside and found Gloria, more cars had pulled up, dropping unaccompanied kids off.

Mayhem. Madness. Fun. And when he stepped inside the sprawling play area, there was Gloria, in the thick of it. She spotted him and looked downright nervous, but strode his way. "I've lost them."

"All three?" Losing three at once was a pretty remarkable feat. He might have smirked, except she looked absolutely miserable. "Yes. All of them. What if—?"

Matt patted her shoulder. "Consider the odds. What are the chances that any crazed kidnapper is lurking in this madhouse, trying to kidnap one shrieking, wailing kid out of a few hundred?"

"There is sense in what you say," she admitted. "I had no idea it would be this busy."

"I'll go this way." Matt hooked a thumb to the left. "I'll text you when I spot a familiar face, OK?"

"Yes. I'll do the same over here. The older boys are fine, I know, but Amos…" Her voice trailed.

"Is probably having the time of his life."

And when he spotted Amos in a bounce castle a few minutes later, the little boy was jumping, nonstop. He saw Matt, waved like crazy, then tumbled into two other kids…and came out laughing. "That was so fun!"

Matt had texted Gloria when he found the boy. When Amos let go of him, he spotted his grandmother threading her way through pockets of kids between a maze-like network of ginormous attractions. "Grandma!" He yelled across the aisle, scrambled down, and raced her way. "Thank you, thank you, thank you for bringing me here! This is the most fun I've ever had in my whole life!"

Adorable. Sweet. Loving. Amos had none of the guile and all of the sweetness of youth, a kindly, caring child, and when Gloria bent low and gathered him into her arms, a slap of understanding made Matt choke up.

Gloria hadn't shied away from Amos because he was naughty. She hadn't avoided him because his birth caused Carrie's death.

She'd kept her distance because Amos was so much like his mother. Gentle, kindly, giving, endearing. Carrie's nature, alive in the son she never saw, never knew, never held, never fed.

A soft, cool breeze touched his right cheek, like a breath of fresh air. He turned, puzzled.

The breeze came again, almost as if Carrie were there with him, watching her son and her mother make amends.

Ridiculous, of course. He wasn't a believer. The whole idea of everlasting life had been debunked by science repeatedly.

And yet, the thought of Carrie being at peace, with God—

Was it possible? Even if it wasn't probable in his thick head, was it actually possible?

Gloria believed. She was mad as heck, but she believed. Elle believed. His mother believed.

Was he skeptical because he'd examined the concept and found it lacking, or was he skeptical because his father's nonchalant attitude had rubbed off on his boys, and Matt had never bothered looking deeper?

The latter, he realized.

He hung out with Gloria until their time stamps expired. When they all got outside, she turned right, toward her car, with the boys still in tow so she could take them for ice cream.

Matt turned left. "See you guys later."

"Matt."

He turned back when Gloria called his name.

She glanced down at the boys, then back at him. "Thank you."

"We survived Kidland on a Saturday. That's one for the record books." He reached out a fist and bumped knuckles with her. "You did just fine, Grandma."

She gripped Amos's hand and almost smiled. "So did you."

* * *

He stopped at the roadside mailboxes when he got back home. He grabbed theirs first, then walked the hundred feet to the business mailbox.

And there it was.

The final reminder of the upcoming payment due, a payment that greatly exceeded the late-winter funds in Wilmot Excavating's accounts. He thought his heart would stop.

It didn't, but it didn't feel all that happy and healthy either.

You're being stupid. And you've been acting stupid. What did Elle say about promises, that you shouldn't make them if you can't keep them? You promised her love and honor. You promised to cherish her. She's not the kind of woman that wants to be sheltered and protected. Don't you get that?

He got it, but he also didn't want Elle to think she needed to bail them out of a sticky situation. He'd already shaken her trust. If he came to her with this, would she understand the timing or figure she'd been set up from the beginning?

He stared at the reminder.

He didn't want to move. He didn't dare go into the house and face Elle and Aggie and Dotty and all of their sweet plans.

And how would his father handle this? Was he healthy enough to face this without another heart episode? Daniel knew the score, because half of the outstanding payments hadn't come in as yet and probably wouldn't until after April first, typical start-up time for area banks.

Thwarted by a month.

It made no sense, and yet it was perfectly understandable. Banks understood construction and followed rules. Companies abided by those rules. This year those customs hung the Wilmots out to dry.

He swallowed hard, and instead of moving the car behind the gracious, sprawling farmhouse like he'd usually do, he drove up the business driveway. He let himself into the office, turned on a light, and opened his laptop.

There had to be a way to do this, but there wasn't. No matter how he rearranged accounts, they were a half-million short. No one except Elle had a cool five hundred thousand hanging around that he knew of, unless they drained his father's retirement account and paid a hundred thousand in penalties for early withdrawal.

Movement in the driveway drew his attention. Aggie and Dotty were leaving. They looked happy. Elle looked happy as she leaned out the back door and waved.

Life out of balance, but not theirs. They were happy to embrace the simple things of life. It was he who was out of balance, off-kilter.

Could he go to her? Better yet, should he?

Father Murphy had talked about humility the previous week. Matt had listened, kind of, between Amos's too-loud whispers and Randy's occasional, noisy sighs. He couldn't ascribe the verse or even remember it completely, because he'd sat there feeling humbled already, waiting for the boom to fall, with no clear answer in sight. And today it did.

But as the ladies pulled out, he saw something else, something that made him sit up straight and tall.

Elle had grabbed a jacket, a big one. One of his barn coats, the kind he wore in the dead of night and the depths of cold. She'd pulled on big boots and crossed the yard to the chicken house, lugging a bucket of feed and one of water.

Humble yourself.

The beautiful words were there, right there, before him. His wife, his beautiful, artistic, gifted wife, was lugging food and water to the hens just because they needed it.

The gift to be simple.

He watched her disappear into the henhouse and reappear a short while later, undisturbed by the menial task.

Contentment.

He was a moron, clearly.

He'd spent months worrying, fussing, and fuming, and not trusting.

She'd called him on it before Christmas, when he turned his back on her and those tiny glimmers of life within. She'd called him on it again, when she went to Gloria and asked for help.

A humble heart.

With all the accolades and awards and money her work brought in, Elle had the sweetest, humblest heart he knew. She'd never think poorly of him. She loved him.

He left the office, crossed the yard, and went through the back door. She was back in the kitchen, and she looked up when he came in.

She smiled.

He hadn't exactly made things easy. He'd hurt her feelings, he'd been a jerk too often, and he'd left her out of the equation because his pride got in the way of his brain.

No more. He shucked off his jacket and his boots, crossed the kitchen, and handed her the bank notice. "Elle? I need your help."

She looked at the notice, winged a brow, and whistled softly. "Tell me this isn't what's had you riled up for months."

He winced because what could he say? "Dad took out this loan, assuming it would be business as usual to bank the funds to pay it back. Record rains last year said otherwise, and then Dad's heart went bad." He took a deep breath. "No one else knows about this. I found out about it when Dad was in the hospital, and I've been working to chip away at it, month after month."

"That's why you took on all those extra jobs. Why you never took a breath all summer, all fall." She took a seat at the table and faced him.

He sat down beside her. "Yes. I've gotten all but the last five hundred thousand in the account, and if I need to, I can drain Dad's retirement, but he's too young, and they'll hit him with a twenty percent penalty."

"Twenty percent?" Her eyes went wide. "Over my dead body." She looked horrified, but not by the thought of a half-million dollars. It was the idea of handing over a hundred grand because they were short on cash. "Matt, you know I have money. Why—" She stopped and looked sad. Really sad. "You thought I'd take it the wrong way, didn't you?"

"I'd lost your trust once, Elle." He shrugged. "I couldn't bear to have you disappointed in me again. But then today I realized that being quiet about it, and a jerk, meant I wasn't trusting you again. And that was just plain wrong."

"You came to me for help."

He nodded. "To my wife. Yes."

She hugged him.

She reached right out and hugged him, and the sweetness of that embrace made him feel better. Taller. Stronger.

A knock at the door interrupted them. Matt stood to answer it, but before he could, his father walked in. He took a seat, pulled out his wallet, and handed Matt a check.

Matt shook his head instantly. "Dad, we don't have to do this. It would be silly to pay all that money in penalties. Elle's going to front us the money, and we'll pay it back when the spring checks come through."

"No need." Dan tapped the check on the table. "I came to apologize, Matt. I put you in a rough spot, and your mother's fit to be tied now that she knows about it."

"You told Mom?"

"She got the mail and found the notice yesterday, which put me right where I belonged, in the hot seat. This wasn't your doing, and I let you shoulder too much. I came to apologize and let you know we've got the funds. No help needed, and it's not from my retirement account."

"Then where?" Matt stared at him, confused.

"I took a little lesson in humility and went to each of our customers and explained the situation. Seven of them were able to write me checks for at least seventy-five percent of what they owed, and that put us where we needed to be."

"You went to people?" Matt couldn't take his eyes off his father. "You actually went to people and asked for help?"

"Shoulda done it months ago. I'm a stubborn fool sometimes, and while I appreciate Elle's offer to help, I'd say she's already done her share for this family. And then some." Daniel reached over and patted Elle's hand. "But if that's chocolate cake I smell, I'd love a cup of coffee and a nice big slice. I've been on a diet for so many months and fretting over money, that it just feels plain good to put both behind me for a day."

He'd gone to their customers and asked for help.

Matt had come to his wife and asked for help. Could the Wilmot men finally be getting a clue? He was pretty sure that might be the case when his father leaned back in his chair. "And your mother reminded me that if Jason expects to enjoy the perks of being a partner in a family business, he needs to take his share of the responsibility. So I stopped off there before I came over here."

"And how did that go?" Matt was almost afraid to ask, because Jason didn't take criticism or advice easily.

"We'll see." Daniel offered him a candid look. "It might take some getting used to for him, but a flat wheel never gains speed. If we're in this together, we all need to pull together, and that's all there is to it."

"I'm glad, Dan." Elle had crossed the dining area and cut a generous slab of cake. "I don't know if it's something in the air or good old-fashioned prayer, but we've pulled a hat trick today."

"Eh?"

"You went to get help, Matt told me what was going on, and Gloria survived Kidland." She reached out and bumped knuckles with Matt's father and grinned. "We crushed it."

chapter thirty-two

Matt was pretty sure he must have set some kind of record since spring started a few weeks before. He'd been in church seven times. No, wait.

Make that eight.

Sunday Masses, Easter Vigil, and Amos's baptism, which had been crazy long and filled with incense and music. He had kept waiting for one of the boys to go into meltdown. They hadn't, so he hadn't been able to even use them as an excuse to sneak out for a few minutes.

Then First Communion. Reconciliation. All during the all-important kickoff of construction season.

How was a body supposed to get work done with this flux of constant interruptions? Moderation was key in most things. Didn't the church get the memo? And Dr. Gartley said the babies could come any time now, and since she'd made that announcement, he hadn't slept a wink, due to thinking too much.

But he pretended to sleep and faked being strong, when every ounce of him lived in half fear and mild jubilation at the thought of delivering two babies.

He knew the statistics.

He strode by the church on his way to a meeting with the mayor, thinking hard and wishing he didn't have to think at all.

Death in childbirth was rare, and that was good for the ninety-nine-point-nine percent. But it sure sucked pond water if you were in that remaining percentile.

"Matt!"

Father Murphy called his name from across the street. He turned and waited as the pastor jaywalked to reach him.

"You got an in with the county sheriff, Father, or do you just like to tempt fate?"

"I married him and his wife," Father Murphy admitted. "He cuts me a little slack. On the good days, that is, marriage being a tad difficult now and again."

"And a priest knows this how?"

Father Murphy laughed. "Twenty-two hundred families in this parish, Matt. I get to hear both sides, in confession and on the street."

"The inside scoop."

"Exactly." They were passing in front of the parish center. Matt pointed out the low spot beyond the side door leading down to the creek. "Does that ever dry up?"

Father grimaced. "Midsummer in a dry year. The creek banks to the left right there, and it leaves a pocket. Every time we get a spring rain, that section floods. It's a pricey fix, I'm told."

It could be, Matt knew, because conservation rules meant he couldn't just drop a truck load of sandy loam in there and grade it off.

"But that's not why I caught up with you," the priest continued. "We've got two openings coming up on the parish council. I was wondering if you'd let me put your name on the ballot for one of them."

Matt stopped. "You realize I'm not Catholic, right?"

"Well, no one's perfect," the priest joked.

Matt laughed, then sobered. "I have to believe that someplace in those twenty-two hundred families are two Catholic candidates, don't you think?"

"A great many," Father declared. "But first, your family is an integral part of this parish, and I'm smart enough to recognize that." He ticked off a second finger. "Second, you're a knowledgeable, successful businessman who looks at the big picture. Third, this is a three-year term that doesn't start until October, so the babies will be nearly five months old."

"Almost ready to vote," Matt agreed, laughing, and when the priest raised a brow, Matt paused. "Father, I'm honored that you'd think of this, and I really loved seeing Amos get baptized and having the boys make their First Communion. We've made my wife and my mother-in-law and even my mother very happy, and she's not Catholic, either. But this." He stared up at the church, the clean rose-toned brick rising tall and strong, flanked by two open-work bell towers. "It isn't me, Father. I come because my family comes, because it means a lot to my wife, and because people think it means a lot to my boys."

"You disagree."

"Well." Matt scrubbed his hand to the back of his neck, uncomfortable to be arguing faith with a priest. "Let's just say I'm smart enough to be skeptical."

"Your wife isn't smart?"

"Don't get me in trouble, Father." Matt nudged the priest's arm. "That's not what I meant."

"I think it is. Oh, not that Elle isn't smart, we all know the truth in that—she's brilliant and talented—but you think that having a simple faith in something unseen, unheard, marks the person as simplistic."

"Doesn't it?"

"No!" The priest laughed and grabbed his arm. "The exact opposite is true. Accepting the simplicity of faith actually strengthens our resolve to be better people. Better fathers, mothers, workers, leaders. But there, I didn't mean to browbeat you, and I respect your decision. But just so you know, we have a new class of initiation beginning in September. If you decide you'd like to join in, I'd be honored to sponsor you."

The priest's offer touched Matt. He hadn't argued his point or shoved documents on him; he'd calmly nudged a door open and then left it that way.

"I've got to do confessions." Father went up the steps faster than many a younger man, as if still excited about his work, his job, his office within the church, and Matt didn't know many people who felt that way about their jobs anymore. "See you Sunday."

chapter thirty-three

"Call Matt. Now. Please."

Aggie took one look at Elle's face and sent the text that interrupted Matt's meeting with the mayor.

"It's time," she said when she answered his call.

"Now?"

"Now."

"Are you home? How's Elle? Can I talk to her?"

"We're going to meet you at the hospital. Then you can talk to her."

"I can talk," Elle insisted. "You trained me up right, remember? This is normal, part of the process. Oh..." She stopped talking as she grabbed the back of a chair, trying to breathe slowly, in and out. In and out. And when the next pain hit, she was ready to go toe-to-toe with that Lamaze instructor who said the first pangs were often mild.

The boys were visiting Gloria and Al. She called Gloria from the car's Bluetooth. "Gloria, can you and Al hang on to the boys for us? I'm in labor."

Gloria drew in a sharp breath. The breath made Aggie frown, but then Gloria exhaled. "Yes, of course. I think we'll bring them back to your house so they're around their stuff, their things. Is that all right?"

"It's fine. And can you have Todd check for eggs? I never got out there today."

"Eggs, yes. Elle, I—" Gloria's voice choked. "I'm praying for you. For these babies."

Elle had thought this would be hard, but it was harder still because her delivery rechurned old waters. Losing Carrie had been a mile-stone bend in the road for a lot of people. "Thank you. And bless you for taking care of these boys. I'm not sure which of us will be more challenged."

But when she disconnected the phone and got broadsided by the next contraction, she was pretty sure caring for three boneheaded but cute boys was a piece of cake comparatively.

Panic rose as they neared the hospital.

She forced it down, but after all her brave words and enforced preparation, she felt one hundred percent unprepared.

"Remember Sarah, Hannah, and Ruth, so many who have gone before you. Your grandmother had babies like it was another day in the fields, a woman born to bear children. You're like her, Elle, in so many ways. You'll be fine. I promise."

Elle breathed deep as her mother steered the car toward the ER entrance. "I know. It's not me so much. It's thinking about the last time Matt and his family went through this. It keeps going round and round in my head.

"I know it's foolish to think about it, but I can't get past what happened then. Matt hasn't slept in days, and he's pretending to be strong, and I have no way to help him. This will be hard for him."

Aggie rolled the car to a stop, got out, and came around to grab a wheelchair. "Hard for him?" she scolded. "Men are ridiculous creatures, which is why they're not the ones having children." She bent low and looked her daughter in the eye. "You focus on your faith and giving birth. This isn't about anything that happened before. This is about the birth of your two new children, Elinora. You keep that in mind through all of it—that we're going to finally get to meet these babies! Dotty will be thrilled, and she can't wait to use those quilts! So much joy, so much strength you bring!"

Another contraction began to mount.

Aggie pushed the wheelchair through the automatic doors. "We now begin a new adventure, Elle. Let's do this."

Matt strode in right behind them. He bent, kissed Elle, and smiled into her eyes, but Elle read the fear behind the excitement.

He was just as scared as she was, maybe more, which meant she needed to calm down.

"Come to me, all you that are weary and are carrying heavy burdens..."

A beloved verse, Jesus speaking to lift the hearts and souls of the crowds.

Perfect for today.

She clung to the words as labor progressed and Matt's worry grew. She held tight to them as the pains overshadowed everything else.

She thought she walked toward labor informed.

Wrong!

She thought reading about this natural process would prepare her for what was to come, but as the pains progressed, she was pretty sure there were no words to prepare her for the reality, but still she clung to those words... *"Come to me, all you that are weary..."*

She refused medication to ease the pain. She wanted to be fully invested in this delivery. She wanted—

"Elle, you're doing great." Dr. Gartley's words penetrated. Elle nodded, pretty sure this wasn't great but *was* a necessary means to an end. "Your water's broken on baby number one, and I think we're going to be ready to push soon."

She had no words through the whirlwind of pain and pressure, so she nodded again. She might have said OK; she might have said nothing at all. She really had no idea. The doctor left, and when a sweet nurse hurried into the room to reposition her repeatedly, Elle thought it was all part of the norm.

Her mother had stepped out of the room. When she came back in, she bent to offer words of encouragement as the nurse shifted Elle a third time.

Looking concerned, the nurse helped Elle to a fourth position, glancing back and forth to the monitor beside Elle as new, stronger contractions hit. And as the nurse frowned and tried to reposition yet another time, Dr. Gartley flew into the room. "Too many decels, get her flat!"

"What?"

Fear. Elle heard fear in Matt's single word. She couldn't see him through the flurry of movements, and he seemed so very far away as the doctor and nurse fussed.

The nurse hit the switch, and the bed lowered as the doctor checked Elle. "I've got cord."

Elle couldn't see the nurse's expression, but she saw her mother's. And then Matt's. Both gray and pasty, which meant something was wrong, grievously wrong.

"Come to me, all you that are weary..."

"Attempting retraction."

Matt's face, so pale, so scared, so taut, staring at the doctor as if her edict spelled his future. Matt with no faith to cling to, no strength in belief, no God to stand on.

"No retraction, we're go!"

Figures streamed into the room. A flurry of hands and heads moved around Elle, a discordant dream as the contractions mounted.

Wheels. Motion. Movement. Noise as the bed sides locked up, into place. All done in a cyclonic dance. Clipped voices, orders, assents.

"Come to me, all you that are weary and are carrying heavy burdens..."

Matt's face, gone now. Her mother, too. She wanted to reach out and tell him it was all right, that no matter what happened, God was with her. With their babies. That she'd be with him, always, but there was no time for words. Dr. Gartley leaned over her. A mask covered her face, but she spoke loud and clear. "I know what you told me, Elle."

Elle blinked, understanding.

"No matter what happens, that the babies come first." She held Elle's gaze, held it tight. "But I'm promising you right now, everybody's coming out of this just fine. Stay tough, OK?"

"My strength is in the Lord..." Elle didn't realize she'd whispered the words out loud until Dr. Gartley nodded and smiled before she faded from view. "That's the ticket, honey."

chapter thirty-four

This can't be happening.

Five minutes ago Matt had been standing by his wife's side, knowing she'd be delivering the first baby soon, and now—

Fear stabbed. Hard, strong, unrelenting, heart-piercing fear.

A nurse hurried into the room. "Doctor sent me here to talk with you." She looked at Matt and Aggie. "We had a cord prolapse—the cord had slipped down and was being delivered before the baby. That meant that with every contraction, the cord was being compressed, cutting off the baby's oxygen."

Matt's heart froze at the thought of his child at risk, and he with no way of helping. He hated being powerless. He loathed loss of control. How could this be happening? How could—?

"The doctor kept pressure off the cord; they're doing an emergency C-section right now, and as scary as this seems, we do this kind of thing all the time."

All the time, she said, like it was nothing.

Matt knew better. He knew what could go wrong; he'd lived it.

He stared at the nurse, stared hard. "I don't know how this happened."

"Matt." Aggie touched his arm, and she looked more worried about him than about her daughter. What was the matter with people? Didn't they get it? Didn't they understand the seriousness of all this? It was life and death, for God's sake!

For God's sake...

His brain spun out of control, a whirlwind of images and emotion.

Elle, with her calm, unruffled personality.

Elle, creating beautiful pictures of faith, hope, and love.

Elle, beloved by so many, her images of God's grace displayed all over the world.

The Nativity sets she had the boys put out. Christmas in every room, she said.

The courage she showed in times of darkness and fear.

Her grace with Gloria, paving a path of righteousness. Dotty called her a Proverbs 31 woman, and Matt had shrugged it off, but in this kaleidoscopic moment, he saw the truth unfold.

Faith gave his wife courage.

Faith gave her strength. It offered her patience, warmth, and redemption, gifts she shared freely with his children, with all those around her.

He wanted that peace. He yearned for the cup overflowing. The words of the priest at the Easter Vigil, casting out evil and embracing forgiveness and redemption.

"For God sent forth his only begotten son..."

Sacrificial love.

Phrases jumbled in his head, phrases that had been just words in a book for so long, but now...

Oh, now!

They became ardent prayers, in his mind, in his heart.

Aggie seized his hand, and not any casual, light grip either. A firm, tight, hammer-hold, and she began to pray. "Our Father, who art in heaven, hallowed be thy name..."

"Thy kingdom come. Thy will be done." He joined with her, determined. He'd been a jerk at times, an egotistical, I-need-no-one jerk, but he was wrong. So wrong. He wanted his wife's strength. Gloria's passion. His mother's patience. He wanted to be the best man he could possibly be.

He turned to the nurse, and he said the words quickly before fear could grab hold again and silence him. "My wife is a strong woman." He held her gaze, hard and tight. "But more than anything, if there is a choice to be made in that room, she would want those babies saved. She would sacrifice anything to give those babies life." At this moment, facing the nurse, he knew Elle was right, and a man who loves his wife loves unselfishly. No matter how hard it is.

The nurse's eyes went damp, and she reached out and gripped his hand. "I'll pass that along right now."

She didn't offer false assurance. She didn't brush off his words or his fears. She took his words and his instructions and left the room quickly.

Our Father...

He prayed the two words, unceasing, knowing God would hear. He had to hear.

Aggie was crying.

He shrugged an arm around her and tugged her close, still muttering. *"Our Father, Our Father, Our Father..."*

"Mr. Wilmot?"

A nurse stepped into the labor room carrying a baby. Another nurse followed. "Would you like to meet your daughters?"

Girls.

Two girls.

Two perfect, absolutely beautiful baby girls peeked up at him. Tiny people. Brand new souls. He blinked, amazed at the sight of such perfection, such bounty. And then he drew his gaze up, strong and direct. "How is my wife?"

"Doing well!" The second nurse handed her baby to Aggie, while Matt accepted the first little girl. "She'll be in recovery for a bit. Then we'll bring her over to her room. She's one strong woman."

She was, and Matt hadn't appreciated the core of that strength. Now he did.

Father Murphy stepped into the room, smiling broadly, eyes wide. "Such blessings abound! Congratulations, Matt! It looks like I didn't have to wait until Sunday to see you after all!"

"It appears that way." Matt grinned at him, at life, at circumstance. "Girls, Father. Two girls."

"God has his ways of evening things out."

Matt would have scoffed at the casual remark hours ago. Not now. "He does indeed."

"I won't stay. I was downstairs visiting Mrs. Cady, and I heard the chimes ring twice, which meant twins were born!"

The hospital played the opening chords of Brahm's lullaby each time a baby was born. They'd played it twice for the girls, but Matt hadn't heard a thing. He'd been too busy praying. "And here they are."

"And Elle? How is our Elle?"

"Fine, they say." Aggie took her eyes off her new granddaughter long enough to respond. "I can't wait to see her."

"Tell her I'll be by soon. We'll plan their baptism."

"And we won't be waiting years either, Father," Matt promised. Nearly five years of shrugging things off. What was the matter with him?

The priest smiled acknowledgment. "Good to hear."

"In fact..."

Father Murphy paused. "Yes?"

"What you mentioned earlier?"

"About the council?"

"The classes, actually."

The smile that deepened the priest's laugh lines brightened the room. "I remember."

"Put my name in."

"As soon as I'm back at the rectory so you can't rethink the decision," the priest teased. "Georgia will be in touch. And while I know life is going to be busy," he aimed a look at the two girls as the nurses reclaimed them to whisk them to the nursery, "I'd still like you to think about the other, too, Matt. No pressure. But we could use more committed young fathers like yourself."

Matt thought back a year, how hard everything had seemed. The boys, Gloria, church, his father's health scare, and work.

"Do not let not your hearts be troubled." Father backed up a step to make room for the baby beds. "Christ's words of comfort to the disciples. Good words to live by."

They were.

Matt and Aggie gathered Elle's things and moved them to the room she'd been assigned across the wing. He made phone calls to the boys and his parents while Aggie called Kate, all the while waiting for his wife to be rolled into the room.

And when they brought her in, looking drowsy, happy, and worn, Matt's heart wanted to sing for joy. They'd probably ask him to leave if he did that, so he toned things down. But just a little, because he'd never been so happy to see anyone in his life.

* * *

Joy.

Pure, simple joy on Matt's face drifted through Elle's veil of sleepiness. She tried to fight her way out of it, but couldn't quite make it.

No matter.

His look and his voice eased her heart, her mind. She slept. And when she finally woke hours later, Matt was sound asleep in the nearby recliner, snoring lightly.

"Hey, Mom." A nurse leaned over her. "I know you got a quick glimpse earlier, but someone wants to meet you." She brought the head of Elle's bed higher, then reached into the rolling baby bed. "This is baby girl number one."

"A ridiculous title," Elle cooed as the nurse laid the baby in her arms. "Katerina, hello, my precious. Welcome to the planet, darling girl."

"Pretty name," the nurse whispered with a side look toward Matt.

"For my sister, her godmother," Elle told her. "Where is the other baby? Is she all right?"

"Sleeping soundly, and just fine. Do we have a name to put on her crib?"

"Emma."

Matt's voice drew their attention. He yawned, stretched, grinned, stood up, and moved to Elle's other side. "You are amazing."

"I'm mostly exhausted, and a little woozy, but thank you."

He bent closer, so close she could probably count the late-night whiskers on his chin, but who wanted to do that when he was so busy kissing her? "We did it."

"We did."

"They're beautiful, Elle. Each one of them. Your mother is at the nursery, praying over Emma."

"But she's all right?"

"She's fine. It's a Grandma thing, she said."

"In that case, I won't worry, but I can't wait to meet her."

"I'll have them bring her down." The nurse hit a button and asked the nursery to deliver Emma to her mother's room. "You need to see her, and she needs to see you. Dad got to meet her earlier."

"So did Father Murphy."

"Really?" Elle smiled, then frowned. "Are you guys telling me everything? Why did you need to call a priest? Are they really fine?"

"Stop." Matt shushed her with another kiss. "They're fine, perfect and strong. And loud," he noted as Katie started fussing. "Father was here to visit Mrs. Cady after her surgery and heard the chimes. He wanted to offer his congratulations. That's all. Stop worrying. Women of faith aren't worriers. Did you miss that passage?"

"No, but it's good to hear all is well. I can't deny that surprise ending shook me up a little."

"Me, too."

She reached out and took his hand. "I hated that you went through that alone, Matt. It broke my heart to see that worry on your face."

"I wasn't alone. I had your mom. And God. We had a nice little chat, the three of us, although the convo might have been a bit awkward on my end. Lack of practice."

"God never cares about showmanship where human hearts are concerned." She squeezed his hand lightly. "He's after the sincerity factor. You know, the quiet man in the back of the temple. The widow with her meager coins. Thank you for praying with her. Oh, Matt." She tried to sit up a little, winced when she realized her incision wasn't happy with that idea, but then smiled as her mother and a nurse wheeled Emma into the room. "Emma!"

"She looks like you, Elle." Aggie lifted the baby and handed her into

Elle's other arm. "Katie is a mix, I think, but when they handed Emma into my arms, it was like holding you all over again."

"She could outgrow it," Elle teased but then looked down at her baby daughter. "She's beautiful, Mom. I mean, truly beautiful."

"Like her mother." Matt smiled into her eyes and kissed her again. "You get to know Emma. Your mom and I want to have a little time with Katie-girl." He reached over and took Katie from her. "And I'm taking a four-week leave from work to help with the babies."

"You're what?" Elle looked up quickly, certain she'd heard wrong.

"Matt, that's wonderful!" Aggie shot him a smile of approval.

"Jason and Dad can handle things for a month. And then I am hoping my mom could step in for a few weeks. But I'm taking time to help my wife and my kids. No matter what."

"Good planning," the nurse told him. "You guys are going to be crazy busy, and Elle's going to need recovery time. Are these your first children?"

"Three boys at home."

She shuddered. "Help or hindrance?"

Elle laughed softly as she unbundled Emma to count fingers and toes. "Both. Daily. We are abundantly blessed."

"Amen."

Aggie laid a hand on little Katie, then smiled at Elle. "Who would have thought this a year ago when so much turmoil surrounded us?"

"Not me." Matt gazed at his wife and babies, and Elle couldn't have imagined or drawn a more beautiful look of satisfaction on his face. "But I am absolutely overwhelmed and grateful to be living the reality now."

Elle planted kisses along Emma's sweet, soft cheek, her heart overflowing with dreams come true. "Me, too."

epilogue

"What a perfect idea, planning the girls' baptism the same day as the parish picnic." Aggie and Mary Lou tucked chairs into the shade of a broad-branched Norway maple edging the town park, then set a small table between them. "And a perfect day, although hotter than it needed to be. Matt, did you get lemonade for Elle?"

"I sure did." He set the drink next to her, kissed Katie, then Emma, his mother, even Aggie, and finally Elle. "Dad and I are taking the boys over to the games. I'll be back in a little bit, OK?"

"Yes."

He grazed a finger along her cheek, her jaw, and smiled and winked as people started moving her way. "Good luck. Aren't there rules about bringing babies out in public so soon?"

"None that I follow," she said softly. "Besides, between your mother and mine, no self-respecting germ would dare get near these girls."

"They're precious." He smiled down at them, then back at her. "Like their mother."

Precious.

Her heart lifted at his gaze, his words. He'd stayed home with her as promised, and while things were still somewhat frenetic around their house, he'd been by her side during the crazy, confusing post-op month. Looking back, Elle knew she couldn't have made it without his help, his love, and his support. She reached up a hand and brought his head down for a kiss. "I love you, Matt."

He smiled then, right into her eyes, and winked. "Tell me something I don't know, darlin'."

"Elle." Orrie Wimple moved close on Elle's far side to get a glimpse of Emma. "Oh, my gracious. What an absolutely beautiful baby."

"Aggie says she looks like Elle." Matt set his hand along the baby's bright rose bonnet, trimmed in some kind of puff-ball flower. "She certainly has her mother's taste in clothing."

"Eclectic," said Elle.

"Charming," said Orrie. She set a brightly wrapped package on the table. "For the girls, something I thought you could use. For when they're bigger, of course."

Elle wasn't sure what to say. Orrie had been barely nice to anyone, ever, and she wasn't the kind of shopkeeper who sent out welcome baskets or congratulatory cards. Most folks said if usury wasn't controlled by law, Orrie would be doing it now and never blink an eye.

"And I wanted to apologize," she added as Matt moved away. Her expression said this wasn't exactly an easy thing to do. "I wasn't always fair to you or to Matthew, and you called me out on it."

"Orrie, I—"

She shook her head and raised a hand. "I was harsh and prejudicial, and I talked too much, and there are reasons behind it, ones I won't get into, but when Gloria told me you went to her, I realized I was the person at fault for so many things. And that's not the way I want to be remembered, Elle, so if you could use these not just for the girls, but maybe as—" she faltered and made a face.

"A peace offering."

"Yes."

Aggie slipped the ribbon from the pretty box, opened it, and handed it to Elle. Inside were two lace veils, handmade and trimmed with bobbin lace. "These were mine and my sister's when we were young, and I thought maybe the girls could wear them for their First Communion. When they're bigger, of course."

"They're splendid, Orrie." Aggie fingered the lace on one while Mary Lou touched the other. "I didn't know you had a sister."

"A twin, actually."

Aggie started to say something, but Orrie stopped her with a look. "We fell out, long ago, not like that's any big surprise to people who know me. I moved away and never bothered going back or seeing anyone, always thinking there'd be a next year. And then there wasn't. But I had these from my mother, and I remember that day being so beautiful and so special, and I was hoping it would be that way for your girls, too."

"We'd be honored to use them, Orrie." Elle smiled up at her. "Thank you so much."

"I forgot how important family is," Orrie said quietly. "Seeing you with Matt and those boys. And Gloria," she added, "made me remember, Elle. I'm grateful for that."

"Mom, can I please get another soda? And get one for Jake?" Randy raced up alongside, kissed the babies, and hugged both his grandmothers. "Dad said I should ask you."

"Did you say hello to Mrs. Wimple?"

"Oh, sorry!" Randy turned a brilliant smile her way. "Hi, Mrs. Wimple. How are you?"

"Fine," she told him, beaming. "Just fine!" She looked down at Elle and smiled. "What a difference you've made!"

"Thank you again," Elle said at just about the same time Mrs. Kominski shrieked in mortal terror across the green when a harmless sage-toned garter snake managed to find its way out of the purse at her feet.

She didn't dare look at Randy. Keeping herself in the dark was probably best. As he and Jake raced off to get cups of soda, the commotion across the green quieted.

Matt appeared at her side just as Katie started to fuss a few minutes later. "I figured feeding time was coming right up." He gathered Katie into his arms and helped Elle stand with Emma. "Let's get you guys home and out of the heat. Mom said she'd bring the boys home later."

As they pushed the old-time buggy through the park, congratulations rang out from multiple directions. Matt waved and smiled but kept on moving, and by the time they got to the SUV, Katie was whimpering and Emma looked downright insulted to have to wait the ten-minute ride home for her next meal.

They pulled into the drive within seconds of total meltdown status, got the girls changed and fed, and then collapsed in a heap on the family room sofa while the babies napped.

"Perfect timing," Elle whispered to Matt as he gathered her in along his side.

"Mm-hmm." He kissed her hair, then her cheek. "About what you said in the park a little while ago?"

"About loving you?"

She felt the curve of the grin against her forehead. "Yup."

"True words, Matt."

His smile deepened, and he snuggled her in against his chest, spoon style, as the babies slept nearby. "Good. Are you as tired as I am?"

"More."

"Then," he kissed her hair one last time, "a nap sounds better than anything right now, doesn't it?"

She laughed softly. "I can't disagree. Does that make us old or just tired?"

"It makes us parents, Elle." He snuggled her even closer, making her feel absolutely, positively beloved, wrapped in her husband's arms. "Just parents."

ABOUT THE AUTHOR

Born into poverty, Ruth Logan Herne is the mother of six and grandmother to fourteen. She and her husband, Dave, live on a small farm
in upstate New York. She works full-time but carves a few hours each
day to write the kind of stories she likes to read, filled with poignancy,
warmth, and delightful characters. She is a 2011 Carol award finalist
from the American Christian Fiction Writers (ACFW).

WITHDRAWN